Kurds The Forgotten Nation

Dana Caban

ISBN: 978-1-7750459-0-8

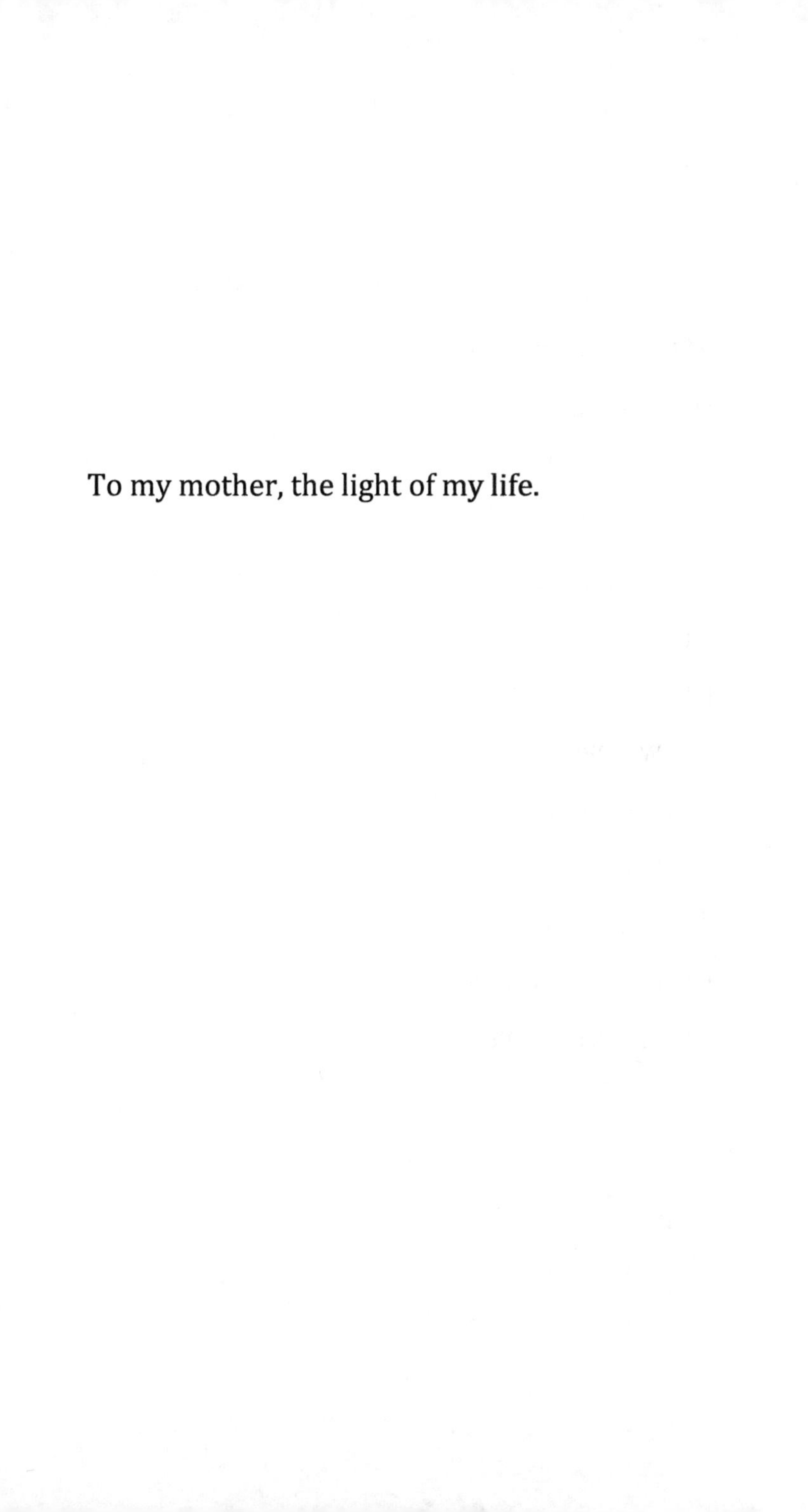

To my mother, the light of my life.

TABLE OF CONTENTS

THE BIRD'S NEST

Smko was only sixteen years old, when his father took his gravely sick mother to capital city Baghdad for treatment. Unfortunately, they never came back. They, and the other passengers died when their bus hit by another speedy bus on their way home.

Smko's father, a forty-years-old man, a successful textile merchant. He was slick in his business, greedy for wealth and cruel to everyone, nonetheless, his family also couldn't escape his cruelty. As young man, he would do anything to succeed, he would reach out to the most ruthless politician, listen to the advice of wealthy and powerful men in the city. Through his well-established connection with politicians, he could import goods from Istanbul, Cairo and Baghdad.

He had no real friends, he did not trust anyone and he lived for himself. He spent generously on himself, whereas, his family should ask for everything for household and the endless arguments, the shouting and asking for explanations, were always followed, when the mother or the son would ask for some extra money.

He had also few houses, which most of the time stood vacated, because he had evicted many tenants for late payment. He had no regard for sick, women and children, he would evict anyone regardless for their circumstances.

That fateful day, when Smko's parents died, stayed with him and haunted him for the rest of his life. He was happy in a very strange way for his father's death, and he was devastated by his mother's death. Only Smko knew his father's cruelty toward his mother and he always thought that his father's ill-treatment, was the cause of his mother's long illness. His father was a real monster with Smko's mother, every day, as soon as he returned home, he began insulting his wife, accusing her of doing everything wrong. The food was cold, a shirt was missing a button, his pants were not ironed well, these were few futile things that he got mad and beat his wife. He was never satisfied neither with his family nor with the world he was living in. he didn't just insult his wife; he constantly beat her, and if Smko tried to stop him, he was beaten too.

If it happened that if Smko need some extra money for school or to buy something for himself, he had to make up hundreds of reasons. He always felt ashamed among his friends, even though he was known for being a smart, good-hearted, kind and generous boy. His friends liked Smko for his good humor, but he never felt that way.

His father was always well-dressed in custom-made suits. He loved Western style of clothing instead of traditional Kurdish dress; he shaved every day, wore polished shoes, which his wife must do every morning, and traveled often, but to his family, he allotted just enough to survive.

Smko knew his father's cruelty, but the extent of such cruelty and his greed, he realized it at the funeral. Traditionally, almost every were in the world, when someone dies, the family, the neighbors and the friends of the deceased will gather at the funeral to pay their respect to the deceased, according their social status and religion. At the funeral, there were a handful of people, and among those few, there were more smiles and faces showing relief than the expressions one would expect at a funeral. Some whispered, "He will go directly to hell." someone else whispered, "His son will live like a king, if he does not turn to be like his father." At that moment, Smko understood that his father didn't have any friends, and it was his job to show them that he was different. He knew that his father never said a nice word to anyone and never greeted others with respect. All he had was his wealth and power, and he never used them to do any good. It was on the day of his father's funeral that he decided to build his own reputation, and he would do that by doing good to people for the sake of goodness and nothing else.

After three days, when the funeral finished, his auntie, his mother's sister, the only relative he had, took him home. His auntie and her husband, which they adored the boy and their home was the only sanctuary, in which Smko took refuge, when his father beat him, because he tried to stop his father's madness.

"Listen to me son, you know that your auntie and I have always treated you like our own son," said his uncle. "And we want you to feel that you are like a son to us. If you want, we would help you until you can stand on your own two feet, because I know you very well, and you have all potential to be a successful man. Be assured that we are not after your wealth. We never have been."

"I know Uncle," said Smko. "And I have always known that. I remember when my father was mad at me and my mother, I used to run away, and the only place I could think of, has always been here at your place. I remember how you and my auntie treated me, and I'll be more than happy if you if you help me."

Smko was still a young boy when the tragedy has fell upon him, but in a place like Kurdistan, manhood has no age. Any boy can be a man if the circumstances oblige him, and many boys had married in Smko's age. Boys aged six, seven, or eight years old were working to provide food for their families.

"If you stay here with us, we will do everything in our power to make everyone proud of you, son." his uncle said. "First I want you to quit school. I know it sound stupid, but it is the only way you can run your business. However, the young man Salih, who has been working for your father since he was seven years old, and he is the best man who can help you. I don't understand how he could take all the humiliations and pain your father gave him."

"Yes, he never complained about anything." Smko said.

"He is your age," his uncle continued. "Salih lost his father, and since then he has been his mother caregiver and provider. He will be a huge help. He knows all your father's customers, the prices, and the places. To be honest with you, most of your father's customers respected Salih and his opinions more than they did your father, even though Salih is only sixteen.

"That is one thing, and the other thing is this. The

boy I brought to help with the funeral service, Baram, is also an orphan. He is alone, working in the market, helping shopkeepers with their stocks and other thing. He too is a good boy, and you could bring him to replace Salih. You need Salih more inside the store."

Smko knew his auntie and uncle very well, even though he was only sixteen, but he knew that his uncle was a selfless man who was never after money or fame. Smko was happy to have them, and he knew that they do everything to help him to be a proud man in the future. Therefore, he listened carefully to their advice.

Smko also was aware that although he was young, but he could see at the marketplace boys working day and night to provide for their families and never had a chance to have any kind of education. He had seen Salih working hard to support his sick mother, and he saw many other boys around his father's store, waiting for any kind of work to be given to them, no matter how hard it may have been. Smko was ready to be a man. He now had plenty of money, but he did not need money to be a good man. On the other hand, money could help him to do many good things for others, like Salih. He wanted to build his reputation on compassion and love instead of greed and hatred.

The funeral ended after three days, and life went back to normal for everyone else, but for Smko, everything had changed. Nothing was the same. He had to change even more things, because as Smko recalled, his father's cruelty had gone beyond treating his own family poorly. It had also reached anyone who had contact with him, whether they were people he encountered in his business, his many tenants, or his neighbors. He treated everyone with cruelty. He was so cruel that if one of his neighbors was having a little financial difficulty and had come to him for help, he would suggest buying the neighbor's business from him instead of helping him. He had already bought two houses in that way, and in his cruel-nature, he had evicted the two tenants.

Now Smko had inherited a good fortune, he could have stayed at home and he didn't have to work his entire life; after all he was the only child. But instead he quit school, in spite his auntie's objection, and took care of his fortune.

Smko and his uncle went to the store directly after the funeral. They found Salih there. He had already opened the store, and he knew all the customers and where everything was. He was the one who took out big rolls of fabrics, put them on his cart, and push the cart by himself to its destination. Then he asked the customer to sign some papers, and if there was any money to be paid, he took it and came back to the store. He was the shopkeeper, the deliveryman, and the accountant. Salih greeted Smko and his uncle warmly and asked them if they wanted some of the tea he had already prepared. Smko greeted Salih and even shook his hand, which was an unusual gesture for Salih to receive. He hesitated at first, but then he too shook Smko's hand and said, "Welcome back, boss!"

"Please don't call me boss, and I would like to talk to you, Salih," Smko said.

"Right now?" Salih asked.

"Yes, bring three cups of tea and sit with us," said Smko. "It's early. We can talk while we are having our tea."

Salih brought three cups of fresh tea, pulled a chair up, and sat face to face with Smko. "Yes, boss?" What can I do for you?" Salih quietly said.

"First, you should learn not to call me boss," Smko chuckled. "And second, I'll be honest with you, I'm aware of my father's ill-treatment of you, and I'm also aware of your hard work." Smko sighed, then sipped some tea. "One thing you have to know is that I'm not my father, and I'll not be like him. On the contrary, I'll do everything to make things different. So, I'm asking you to forgive my father for what he has done to you, if you can and I'm asking you as your friend, not as your boss, to stay with me. Together we can change things. We may turn things around, but I can't do it by myself." Smko stopped suddenly when he noticed tears were running down Salih's cheeks.

Smko's uncle looked at Salih and put his arm around Salih's shoulders and patted him softly.

"It is okay to cry, my son," he said. "We have all suffered from the ill-treatment of your former boss, but now you have a friend to work with. Believe me, Smko is a fine young man, exactly like you, and I'm sure you two will be good companions. Smko needs a young man like you to rely on."

There was silence for a moment. Then Salih stretched his hand out to Smko. He said, "Let's shake hands as you said, like friends."

Smko was so touched by Salih's good-hearted personality that he squeezed Salih's hands.

"I hold nothing against your father. I have already forgiven him, and I'll stay with you. We will turn things around, my friend," Salih said.

"Do you remember the young man, Baram, who performed the service at the funeral, a young man about your age?" Smko asked.

"Yes, I do remember him. What, does he want to work here with us?" Salih asked. "I would be very happy if he wants to work with us. He is a fine boy, and he has no relatives here in the city."

"I already have sent for him; he'll come here tomorrow morning. If I'm not here, you will have to explain to him what he should do," Smko said. "And for one or two weeks, go with him so you can introduce him to our customers. Is that okay with you, Salih?"

"It is quite fine with me," Salih replied.

'If you don't need me for anything else, I have to go with my uncle now. He wants to introduce me to our neighbors in case I need help."

Smko stayed with his uncle and auntie until he turned seventeen. His auntie, a selfless woman who loved Smko, took care of her nephew, and she managed to find him a good girl before he turned seventeen. "A good woman is the secret to a man's success," she would say. "A woman will make a man concentrate more on his life, his business and his family."

One day when Smko came home to his auntie, he found that she had few visitors. His auntie asked him to come and say hello to them. He did what she asked him to do, and after the guests had left, his auntie asked what he thought about the young girl he saw. Smko was jumping for joy! "I'm going to marry her? What is her name? How old is she? Does she__"

"Take it easy, boy, take it easy," his auntie said. "Yes, she and her family agreed. That is why I arranged for the two of you to meet. Her name is Shereen. She is a distant relative, but good people, and if you like her as well, your uncle and I are ready to go and propose. And everything will be okay, son."

Three months after Smko met Shereen they got married. Smko had turned seventeen and she was sixteen. They moved back to his parents' house, after his auntie and few other women helped to clean the big house.

The day Smko saw his wife, he fell in love with her. She gave him peace and the sense of family and helping him to concentrate on his business.

His business was getting better day by day, and with his uncle's help, he began to understand it. He was getting much better at understanding and dealing with his customers, and his good reputation was setting roots in the marketplace and among his neighbors. Some thought his wealth was too much for a young man like him and that he would lose it within one or two years, but he proved them wrong. His charisma was his secret. His character, his generosity, and his humility earned him a respected place in 1930s Kurdish society.

His friend Salih, whom he called a friend, was very happy to work with Smko. Unlike his father, Smko was a more open-minded young man and could be asked for help without being interrogated for hours.

Six months after his wedding, Smko went to his uncle for advice, as he always did. "I want to do something good for Salih, the man my father treated so badly. I want to make up for the pain my father caused him," he told his uncle.

His uncle listened to him carefully and with

respect. “It is generous of you to think about the people who work for you, son,” his uncle said. “It is an honorable thing to appreciate others. What are you thinking of?”

“As you know, Salih is a poor man trying to take care of his sick mother alone, and they live in a single room of a house with two other families. We own the house next to mine, and it is empty, and I thought I could invite him to live there without having to pay the rent. With that, he might be able to get married and have a family of his own,” Smko quietly explained. “Otherwise he will never be able to marry. He is turning eighteen, after all. So, what do you think, Uncle?”

“First, everything you have is yours, so you may do what pleases you, son,” his uncle replied. “But in this case, I’m with you. You have my blessing, son, and maybe your auntie could help to find a good girl for him. After all, she is the expert in that matter.” He chuckled.

Within a few weeks, Salih moved to his new house with his mother. With the help of Smko's aunty, Salih had been able to find a good girl, and he married the girl.

Salih's wife, Roonak, was a very good woman from a very poor family. She didn’t have much education, but she was a very talented housewife. She was very handy. Embroidery was her passion, and she was a perfect cook; she was exactly what Salih needed to build a family and have peace of mind. He loved Roonak, respected her, and appreciated everything she did.

Salih, Baram and Smko were becoming more like friends than boss and workers. They loved to work with Smko, because, mostly for his appreciation and his kindness.

Baram was working hard, and he was making good money compared to what he was making before, but he always had a sadness in his eyes. Smko tried to talk to him many times. Maybe he could help him the way he helped Salih, and he asked him if he wanted to get married. Smko said he and his wife would help him to find a good woman, but Baram wasn't happy in the city of Slaymany, even though he was born and raised there. He had been abandoned when he was born, so he was put in the only orphanage in the city, which British opened. Baram had no one in the city other than Smko and Salih. But he knew he had some relatives in Qaladze, a small town few hours from Slaymany, and it was there he wanted to go.

Baram had worked for Smko for about two years. He was about to turn nineteen and wasn't married yet. He badly wanted to be married, but first he had to find some of his living relatives in Qaladze. Then he could get married.

One summer afternoon, the three friends were in the store, talking about life, when suddenly Baram asked Smko if he would let him to go to Qaladze for one or two weeks.

"You are my friend, Baram, and if that is what will make you happy, why not? Go, stay as long as you like, but do come back," Smko told him. "Who knows? You may find a good place." He was quiet for a moment. "Wait a minute, I have an idea,"

Salih and Baram looked at him with surprise and together said, "What idea?"

"You want to go to Qaladze, right?" Smko said.

"Yes, I do," Baram answered.

"Well, you know Qaladze is a small town and getting bigger quickly," Smko said. "It is very close to Iranian border. So, what if you had your own business there?"

"You mean to have my own business there?" Baram surprisingly asked. "But I don't have...."

"But did you listen to what I just said?" Smko replied. "We are friends! If I can help you to get on your feet, I'll do it. I'm not losing anything, so don't worry about money. Just go there, and while you are looking for your relatives, you can also look for a good place to open a business. Are we agreed?"

"Yes, we are," Baram said, and stretched his hand out to Smko. He took Baram's hand and asked Salih to put his hand on top of theirs. "Let's be friends forever,"

Smko said. "And let's not let money not anything else come between us. Let's build a big family together, and let's call it out family." The three of them vowed to remain friends forever, and from that day on they were inseparable.

The next morning Baram went to see where his destiny would take him, but after two weeks or so, he came back and one early morning, he appeared at the store. Smko was there alone. He greeted Baram warmly, saying, "Why are you here so soon?" I thought you would not come back until next month."

"Well, I too didn't think I'll be away only for few day, but I have some good news, Smko," Baram said and smiled. "First, I found some relatives who are still alive, and they are really good people. They were very happy to find out that we are related, although they are very distant relatives. But they are my relatives, and I'm happy to have them in my life. As far as business location, I have found a perfect place, big and very cheap. I paid half and the rest I have to pay when I go back."

"But you didn't have enough money to pay half. It must be very cheap!" Smko said.

"Yes, it is," Baram replied. "And one more thing."

"What?" Smko asked impatiently.

"I may marry soon, too!" he chuckled.

Smko stood up and hugged his friend. "I'm very happy for you, Baram. You see? The world is still a good place to live in!" Smko gently patted Baram's shoulder.

Baram stayed another three days, and then he left for Qaladze with as much stock as the truck could hold. This would fill his store, and Smko would supply him with more stocks anytime he needed it.

A year had now passed since Baram had left to go to his new town and new business. He had married, his wife was pregnant with their first child, and Baram was happiest man in the world. He used to say to his friends, "Why not? I was an orphan. I didn't have a place of my own, no job and no family. I was nobody! And today I'm Baram! I have a business, and most importantly I have my own family. All this thanks to one stranger who believed in me and wanted me to get a fresh start in life, who wanted me to be what I'm today, a man who became my friend when others didn't want to approach me because I smelled bad, a man who showed me that we can be everything we want. We are Kurds, we must help each other in time of need. We have to be like Jews; they are always united, and they are always there for each other."

Baram, Salih and Smko had laid the cornerstone of their lifelong friendship, which they hoped would last for the rest of their lives and the lives of their children.

Baram's textile business in Qaladze boomed. Within a few years, he was rich enough to buy a nice, big house with many rooms and a large garden. All this thanks to the grace of one stranger man, the one who became his longtime friend.

Smko's business was booming also. Now that Iraq was under British mandate, so they gave Smko permission to expand his business and import directly from England and its colonies at much lower prices. He had already bought two more stores and brought more people in.

Salih was his trustee. Whenever Smko was away on business trips, as he often was, it was Salih and his wife who took care of business and his family.

The two men became one family. Salih remained loyal to Smko, and they ran a good business together. They had everything and it was much more than most people could even dream about at that time and age. This was all thanks to Smko's work ethic, his gratitude for what he had, his generosity, and his ambition to be a better man.

In late cool afternoon in September 1939 Smko's first son, whom they named Sardar, was born. His wife, Shereen, was overwhelmed with joy. She was very much in love with her husband. She used to cry when her husband had to go on a trip.

Salih and his wife, had their first son, Sirwan, six months after Smko's son Sardar, was born, and the two families, had become one family, they were happy together. Salih's wife, Roonak, and Shereen were like sisters, and they were neighbors, and their husbands were like two brothers. They lived happily.

Smko had two more children, his first daughter, they named her Nazanin, and his second son, they named him Saman.

The community where Smko and Salih lived was growing. It was a good area, not very close to the center of the city, yet it had everything they need close by. The people were friendly, in large part because Smko and Salih had shown their neighbors the respect and care they deserved. In return, they too had become very compassionate with each other. It wasn't very crowded area, and at that time in Kurdistan, there wasn't a big difference between poor and rich. In any part of the community, one could find very poor and very rich families living side by side without any major conflicts. Many families wanted to build their home in that neighborhood where Smko and Salih lived.

Late one afternoon a well-dressed young man in his early twenties came into Smko's store, although he didn't seem to have come to do business. Smko greeted him warmly and offered him a seat. Salih brought them some refreshment, called Sherbet.

"How may I help you, my friend?" Smko respectfully asked. "You aren't textile customer, if I'm not mistaken."

"No, I'm not," said the man. "My name is Dawood and I work in the education department. I have some friends, who sent me to you for some advice." he took a sip of his Sherbet. "There is a piece of land, they told me it belonged to you. I wanted to build a home."

"I'm flattered Mr. Dawood," Smko said. "You are very welcome here. What can I do for you?"

"As a matter of fact, I'm here to ask about the piece of land you own that is close to your house," Dawood said. "I came here to ask you about the place you live. Is it a good area? Are the neighborhood friendly?" you know it's very important to have good neighbors, am I right?"

"Well, may I call you Dawood?" Smko asked.

"Yes, yes, please!" Dawood replied.

"Well, Dawood, let me be honest with you," Smko said with a smile. "You have chosen the best place in this town to build your home. I have lived there my entire life, and I'm telling you, it is the best. The neighbors are good. They are friendly and caring people. In fact, we are all like a big family, and we look forward to seeing you join us." He stretched his hand out to Dawood and shook it. "Take my advice and build your home," he said. "I guarantee you, you will never regret it, my friend."

"I'm sure we will be happy, but__" Dawood began. Smko interrupted him.

"Listen my friend, do not 'but' me," Smko chuckled. "If there is a problem, I guarantee you we will be able to solve it. And I want put a price on it. Pay what you can. I like you, and I want you to build your home close to ours. Take the money you would have spent on the land and use it to build your home. I'll give you good advice. Do you see that man over there? Smko pointed to one of his neighbor. "His son is a good architect, and I could ask him for advice if you like. Moreover, I could get you cement for very good price.

What else do you want?"

Dawood was stunned. His jaw dropped as he listened to the generous offers of this strange man. Now he understood what his friends had said about this man. He approached Smko and stretched out his hand to Smko, who grabbed it and squeezed it.

"Do you have a family of your own, or you build the house for your parents?" Smko asked.

"Yes, I'm married, and I have two children: my son, Kameran, and my daughter Salma," Dawood replied.

"Well, I have two sons, Sardar and Saman, and my angel daughter, Nazanin," Smko told him. "And Salih" he pointed to where Salih was busy with two customers "Lives next door to me. He is like a brother and best friend to me. He has only one son. I believe we can all live in harmony."

The two men sat and talked about many things. They spoke of family, children, school, and how to live in harmony and peace. After a long talk, Dawood stood up, excused himself, they shook hands again, he thanked Smko and left.

Four months later, the house Dawood had been dreaming to build, had finished, and he was ready to move in. As tradition required, the neighboring families invite the new comers to their homes and provide food. Shereen and Roonak were busy cooking for their own families, Dawood's family, and the men who helped Dawood's family to move in. when Smko and Salih came home around noon that day, they went directly to Dawood's new house. "It's beautiful," Smko said to Dawood. "It's well built and it didn't take long time either. And now let's go and eat, otherwise the ladies will get angry, and the last thing I want to do, is to make my wife angry."

Dawood's wife, Ezra, had already befriended Roonak and Shereen. Her boy Kameran, was two year old, and her daughter Salma was one. Dawood was a Jew. His family had lived in Slaymany for many generations, so many that no one remembered if it was ten or more generations.

Baram came to visit Smko and Salih as much as he could. They maintained the sense that they were one family, just as they planned. They didn't know what the future would hold for them, they would have to wait and see, but for now, all they have to do was live their lives in peace, love and harmony, and let their children grow up seeing their parents living as brothers and sisters, without judgment.

The three families built their bonds of friendship and became ever closer through the years. They hoped what they had started would last through the lives of their children and grandchildren. The three families were bound together as one, and they called their melded families the bird's nest.

Their children were growing up together. They had all started school; the three boys went to a boys' school, and the two girls went to a girls' school. They too had become inseparable.

Sardar was around twelve years old when he became aware of his feeling for Kameran's sister Salma. In the beginning, it was very painful for him. He even felt guilty, because tradition said that one wasn't supposed to fall in love with one's best friend's sister. Eventually, Sardar's own sister became aware of it, and then it was Salma herself who told Nazanin, Sardar's sister. For a while, it was Nazanin who carried love letters back and forth between the two.

Then Sardar found a way to write to Salma and give the note to her himself. He would write a letter to her, put it in a matchbox, and wait for opportunity to give it to her. Their love life continued in this way until they were sixteen.

Sardar was busy with school and his love life, so he wasn't aware that his sister had found her love in the same neighborhood. Nazanin had fallen for one of Sardar's best friends, Sirwan. The two young teenagers were madly in love and they didn't let anyone find out.

In a Muslim country love life for teenagers, like many other things, was absolutely a taboo. No one was allowed even to mention it. But the four lovers met frequently and talked without letting their families or the community know. They had the advantage of their families all being friends. Still, they were aware of the traditions, so there was no touching or kissing or anything like that.

Time passed. And as soon as the families had become aware of their children's love affair, Smko had talked to all of them and he advised them to allow the teenagers to get married and get over it. At eighteen, Sardar got married his lifelong love, Salma. Sirwan and Nazanin, too got married. Their parents thought it was for the best, instead of letting them continue to go around doing foolish things. A few months later, Kameran was married as well. His parents found him a beautiful girl from a good Muslim family who never had any objection to the mixed marriage.

Saman, Smko's second son, was not enthusiastic about his education. In fact, he hated school. He didn't want to go to school at all, but his father insisted the he should at least finish high school. Then he could do what he wanted to do. But when Saman got to a certain point, he quit for good and started working with his father. He did an excellent job, as if he were born to be businessman.

Smko managed to turn things around himself, although he was still tormented by an emotional roller coaster when it come to the memory of his father. Every time he heard the word father, it reminded him of those days when his father had beaten him for no apparent reason and of how he mistreated his mother. He did everything he could to make things right. He transformed his hatred into compassion and love for everyone, and he did much charity work, especially for the widows with children. Soon Smko became the man whom people turned to for advice or help. He never turned away anyone, either for money or for any advice. He was respected for his goodhearted character and his compassion.

QASSIM'S GOVERNMENT

On July 14, 1958, around three in the morning, Salma went into labor; the entire family woke up.

Smko's wife, Shereen, ran to the kitchen to boil water. She felt overjoyed as she got out towels and other necessities for the birth of a child.

Shereen asked Sardar to go and bring the midwife, who lived few blocks away from them, and then she ran back to Salma. After two hours of labor, at around five o'clock, the midwife wrapped the crying baby with a towel and gave it to the mother. "It's a boy," she told Salma.

Salma was overwhelmed when she saw her son. He was healthy and beautiful. She cried a few happy tears. Shereen took the boy and washed him. Then she wrapped him again and gave him back to Salma to feed him.

The baby boy was named Aram. He brought so much joy to Smko's family that the celebration party lasted two days. It didn't matter if a baby was a boy or girl. Either one brought the same joy to Smko.

On the same day as Aram's birth, around eight o'clock, the news of the assassination of the Iraqi king, king Faysal II, began to spread, to the entire country. Everywhere in the land, people celebrated. Iraq had been liberated from the tyranny of British colonist, or so most people thought.

The king was assassinated by an Iraqi Arab army colonel on July 14, 1958, and that was the end of monarchy in Iraq.

Iraq now became Republic of Iraq, and the new president, Karim Qassim, appealed to all Iraqi to unite and fight as one nation and one people against the British. The new government promised to change Iraq. He promised to take Iraq from the British and give it back its rightful owners, the people of Iraq.

Qassim, as all leaders, promised to unite Iraq and bring equality and justice, and prosperity. The Iraqi people listened, with hop and enthusiasm to the new president's promises and they revolted against the British. The Iraqi were united in their effort, from the Kurds in the north to the Arabs in the middle regions and the south.

Things appeared to be as Iraqi people wanted them, but soon events began to lead to something the Iraqis would regret the rest of their lives.

After Salma and Sardar had their first child, Aram, Kameran and his wife Nasreen, had their first son, too. They named him Awat. Sirwan and Nazanin had a son as well, who they named Shwan.

Shereen came out from the kitchen one afternoon on a hot day in July holding a tray full of freshly washed teacups. She found Smko waiting for her on one of the comfortable mattresses laid out on the floor of the veranda. He propped himself up on his elbow with a big pillow, waiting to have his tea before he went back to work. He had just awoken from his regular siesta.

"You're up already! Did you sleep?" Shereen asked.

"How can you sleep on a hot and humid day like this?"

"Well! It is all thanks to you!" Smko replied with a

smile. He lowered his voice. "You are my secret! Sleeping next to you makes me forget everything. You are my queen, and don't forget it!"

"What can I say, Smko?" she replied. "You wouldn't survive one day without me, admit it!"

"I admitted it to you the first night I saw you naked, Shereen," he said in a soft and passionate voice, a tone that said she was still the source of his joy, a tone that remained her that she was still an attractive woman whom he desired.

She sat on the mattress opposite him; then she took the tea kettle from the top of the samovar and poured fresh tea into a cup. She passed it to Smko.

"I smell fresh tea," Sardar said, coming into the veranda. He sat down next to his mother.

"Did you sleep, son?" his father asked him.

"Why shouldn't I?" Sardar asked.

"No, I just wondering," Smko replied, "because your mother couldn't sleep, but I slept like a baby!" "Don't tell the story, Smko, he knows it by heart," Shereen said.

"What story, Mom?" Sardar asked and looked at his father. "I don't know, let him tell it, I might learn something," he chuckled.

"Yeah, like father like son," Shereen said, she went

to Sardar and Salma's room to check on her grandson, Aram.

"I've talked to uncle Dawood about my education!" Sardar told his father. "He said that he'll send all our applications to the Ministry of Education__"

"What?' his father surprisingly asked, interrupting him. "Are you telling me that all three of you are going to the education institute?"

"Yes, Dad, we are!" Sardar answered.

"I'm so happy that you all chose to become teachers. All those years, you went together to school," Smko said as he rose and hugged his son, "so now three of you will start next September. That's good, and I'm very happy for you, son.

"You know my opinion about teachers and education," Smko said. "I've told you again and again that our Kurdish society very much depends on how many good teachers we can produce. Son, don't forget that more than half of the society is still not considered to be a part of it. Our mothers and sisters, all women, are kept out of society. They are prisoners of man's interpretation of religion and their steadfast on the old tradition, in which women around the world have been the victims. Half of our society doesn't participate in building the future. They produce children, take care of their families and satisfy their men.

"So, if we allow our women to participate in the society-building-process, we will create a new kind of society, one that is fully functional. That is my dream, son. I put my trust into your hands to make these dreams come true, because the next generation's intellectualism and their views, and their treatment of women, are all on your shoulders."

"I know, Dad," Sardar replied, "and I can't promise you that we will change our society. But I'll promise you that I'll never let your dream vanish. I'll keep it alive, and I'll start with my own children."

Shereen came out holding Aram in her arms. "Look who is here," she said.

Aram was groggy, having just awakened, and he was sweaty as well. Shereen was happy to keep her grandson in her arms, and she went to the bathroom to give Aram a bath and change his sweaty clothes.

"I have to leave, son," Smko told his son. "I would like to talk to you later this evening when I come back, and you might tell Sirwan and Kameran to come too." Shereen came out of the bathroom, still holding Aram in her arms, and she approached Smko. "Here! kiss your grandson," she said.

Smko bent down and kissed the boy in Shereen's arms. "Good boy, Aram," he whispered in the boy's ear. He kissed Shereen and went out.

Shereen gave Aram to his mother, Salma, who had

just come out of her room. She took Aram into her arms, kissed him many times, and handed him to his father. "Do you want some tea, Sardar?" She asked.

"Yes, I do, and I'll also go to get some water for my son. he's thirsty, aren't you, Aram? He tickled his son and left.

Salma watched her husband holding her son, the most precious thing in her life, bigger than life itself. She loved Aram more than anything. She used to measure him every day just to see how many centimeters he had grown since the day before. She was sure she couldn't survive one day without Aram. Her husband teased her that Aram had taken his father's place, but she was still as much in love with him as she had been many years ago when she was just a girl.

Salma had completed some education, but soon she quit because she was pregnant with her first child. She always wanted to be a nurse, but nursing didn't have a good reputation; Sardar encouraged her to continue her education when Aram was a little older. He never asked her to stop dreaming. Sardar was like his father, encouraging women to participate fully in society, and fight for their rights.

The entire family was awake by now. As they sat comfortably in the veranda, Sirwan and Kameran stopped by. "I hope you have some tea left for me, aunty Shereen," Sirwan said.

"It's right here, Sirwan," Shereen replied.

Sirwan didn't sit down, Shereen poured a cup of tea and handed it to him. Shereen loved Sardar's two inseparable friends like her own children. After all, they had all grown up in Sardar's home as much as in their own, perhaps even more.

It was true they had had more meals at Sardar's home they had in their own. But they were all one big family, as Smko always told them, even though Kameran's and Sirwan's families were not as wealthy as Smko's.

Kameran took Aram from Salma and started making funny sounds that always make Aram giggle. Aram loved their game so much that if Kameran stopped, Aram would start crying. Kameran had to continue until the boy was tired. Then he would kiss him a hundred times and give him back to his mother.

The three family had always lived as one big family. That was what Smko had always wanted. He was always saying, "Let's show others that we are Kurds, and we are united."

Sardar came out of his room and said, "Let's go, guys." the three friends left.

They walked down the dusty, unpaved street. It wasn't hot, and there were many people out at this hour, because it was the best time for people to come out. When the weather wasn't too hot, the shop-keepers opened their stores. Sardar and his friends headed to their usual place, the biggest teahouse in the city.

They stepped inside to the smell of fresh tea and cigarette smoke. They air inside the teahouse was very smoky. When the windows and doors weren't opened, breathing became difficult, but people still came and sat there for hours. It was a miracle that the entire city didn't have lung cancer.

The place was full of people, but Kameran spotted a table with four chairs and said, "Hey, guys, there is a table over there!" He hurried to the table and the others followed. As they sat down, a young man brought their regular game, domino, and he asked them if they want tea or sherbet. They all decided for sherbet. They thanked him and they began their game, drinking sherbet and smoking cigarettes.

"Do you know, guys, that Barzani has returned to Bahdinan?" Sirwan said "I believe he has already revived the old KDP, or Kurdish Democratic Party, and he is planning to launch a new armed struggle against the first Iraqi Republic."

"Yeah," Sardar said, "and I think my father wanted to tell me something about that. He told me to if you wanted, you could be there too."

"I like the man and I'll support him one hundred percent," Kameran said, and hit one domino tile on the table. "And if there is an opportunity for me to join his men, I'll not hesitate one second."

"Because you are an idiot, Kameran," Sirwan said.

"Why am I an idiot?" Kameran asked. "I'm just more courageous than you guys!"

"Yeah, right, you are so brave, Kameran," Sardar said, teasing him. "I remember you didn't have the courage to talk to Nasreen before you were married. If it wasn't for Sirwan and me, you would never have talked to her."

"Okay, cut it out, geniuses!" Kameran replied with a smile. "But I like the man, that is all."

"Tell me what you know about him," Sirwan asked. "He is not Nasreen; you just went crazy for her the first time you saw her."

Sardar hit a tile on the table, "can we play, please?" he said. "We will talk about it later with my father."

They all agreed and continued their game until late evening. When they all headed home, Sardar reminded them to come over his place.

The three friends were inseparable, in spite their class differences, and even though they were more like brothers. They had their own opinions on politics, social issues, and religion. But they were all Kurds, and they had one thing in common; Kurdistan and the desire for Kurdish people to be free.

Kameran was a simple, hardcore, naive Kurdish patriot who always followed his heart, and that landed him in trouble most of the time. Sirwan and Sardar always had to rescue him.

Sardar and Sirwan, on the other hand, were more critical about things. They never did anything blindly; they were more pragmatic and rational. Sirwan was more inwardly directed. He was more secretive and quiet, not because he didn't trust his friends, but because it was his way of dealing with things.

Sardar was more open to things. He never had any secrets, and he was also very open with his emotions, although he was critical of politics, religion and social issues. But he always kept an open mind. He never considered himself to be the only one who was right when there were other opinions to be considered.

Smko's family had just finished their supper. Shereen and Salma were busy removing the dishes and taking the leftover food back to the kitchen. Sardar was helping them in the kitchen, while Smko was busy playing with his grandson. Sardar took the tray of tea accessories out to veranda, where the family usually had supper.

Saman came out. He was dressed up, and he had oiled his hair. It shone under the light. "I'll go out, Dad, if you don't mind," he said."

"Don't be late, son," Smko replied.

"Yes, Dad, I'll be back by ten," he said. He kissed Aram, his mother and left.

Sardar sat opposite his father and was about to pour tea for him, when the door opened and Kameran and Sirwan came in. "You are just in time," Smko chuckled.

"When were they ever not just in time, when it comes to eating or drinking?" Sardar asked his father. "They are like cats. They smell things from far away." Kameran and Sirwan laughed and seated themselves.

They had tea and talked about many issues, but the main issue hadn't yet been discussed. For that, Smko told his wife that he would go up to the rooftop with the three young men so they could have a private talk. Shereen nodded.

The rooftop in many parts of Kurdistan was formerly used as a sleeping place. People used to put fences made of bamboo trees around the edge of the rooftop. Then they would lay their bed there, and it was often the best sleep one could get on a hot summer night.

Smko asked Sardar to go up and open the beds so they could get some cool air, after having been in the sun the entire day. He asked Kameran and Sirwan to take some refreshment too.

The fresh air made Smko feel alive. That was the best feeling about the rooftop, and it was a secret the British never understood the entire time Iraq was under their control.

There were many other neighbors already out on their roofs. Smko greeted a few of them over the top of their chest-high fences, and they greeted him back. They chatted a bit, then disappeared behind their fences. Smko turned back to the boys and said, "It is nice evening!"

The boys nodded. "Would you like some sherbet, Dad?" Sardar asked.

"Yes," Smko replied, "And I would like to talk about something. It concerns not only me or you, but all Kurds! As you know___" he took a few sips and asked Kameran to light him a one of his cigarettes. Kameran took out his pack and shook out few cigarettes, offering them to all.

Smko took out one and lit it, and said, "Well, as I said, we all know that monarchy has ended, and we have the first republic in the history of Iraq." he paused and took another puff of his cigarette. "Yet we don't know much about this government. All we know is that the new president, Qassim, had pleaded to all Iraqis to stand against the British. We Iraqis have all done what every patriot does, but I don't know. I want you to tell me what you think."

Sardar hesitated for a moment, and then he looked at his father. "I'm not ignorant; I know enough history to judge what is right and what is wrong," he said. "I assure you that we will remember this conversation we are having in the future, when we see what the Arabs will do to us. First Iraq has an Arab Muslim gover-nment, and as we all know, Arabs don't like us, they have never acknowledged our existence, and they never will.

"Arabs believe that Arab lands belong to Arabs and anyone else who lives on their lands is their enemy. They have invaded the land with swords, they brought their book and forced people like Kurds, Armenians, Berbers, and many other nations to their new religion, and they tried to Arabize other nations, which they forced them to convert to their new religion.

"And the secret behind that was not allowing other nations to translate Quran to their native language; instead, they had to learn Arabic and memorize Quran, and that was the first step toward *Arabization* of many of these nations. It forced others to lose their languages, cultures, traditions and religions." Sardar paused.

"They have invaded and looted our lands in the most barbaric ways, all in the name of Islam," he continued. "We are not Arabs. We are not Muslims, and we will not be forced to be. I'll die a Kurd not a Muslim. It would be better for our nation to get rid of that damn religion and go back to our religion, Zoroastrianism, and our book."

Smko stretched his legs and put his elbow on the big pillow. He was listening carefully to the young men. Their hatred for Arabs and their religion reminded him of his own hatred for religion, especially Islam, the Muslim clergy, and what they have done to Kurdish people. How many times had Kurds been used by Muslims! The most recent time was the genocide of one and a half millions of innocent Armenians

"I agree with you, Sardar," Smko said, "and I think we all agree on that, but what are our options if the government starts attacking us? Do we have a duty to protect ourselves or not?"

"I think if a large-scale attack on Kurdistan is imminent, we have no choice but to defend our land and our people, no matter what." Kameran said."

Smko was waving the mosquitoes with his cigarette smoke. "But what about the other part of Kurdistan? He said. "Is there a chance for Kurds to reunite under one flag and fight for only one goal, Kurdistan?"

"I don't believe it is possible for all Kurds to unite," Sardar replied, "because it is true, we all are Kurds, and we have different dialects and live in different part of Kurdistan, but there is one bitter reality; most Kurd will not agree to be led under one political party and one political leader. For example, Kurds from Turkey will not agree to be under the control of an Iraqi Kurd. And Iranian Kurds would not want to be call KDP, they want to have their own political party, and so on. We have a problem, not only with our enemies, but we also have a serious problem within. We do not see it now, and you may think I'm crazy, but we will soon see the division among us, because in one important way, Kurds, are like any other nation. Someone will come up as a leader, as the savior of our nation, but time will prove that he is nothing but a self-serving, ignorant person with no interest in saving our nation."

His father was amazed at and scared of his son's opinions. He was silent for a while, and his thoughts wandering. Smko was thinking about a dark time that might appear like spring clouds that come in fast, bring much rain and devastation flood, and disappear as fast as it appeared. He was terrified to think his family might disappear; he couldn't bear the idea of it. He sighed and came back from his thoughts, when Sirwan offered him some sherbet. "That is a scary thought, my son," Smko said. "It is possible, and I've to admit, I've never thought that way, but we must know everything, every possibility, in case___" he was quiet, "there is something else I have to ask you while we all are here." he wiped his eyes with the back of his hand and asked for another cigarette.

"What is it, Uncle?" Sirwan quietly asked.

Smko took his pillow, rearranged it, took a deep puff and leaned back on the pillow. "Well, you probably you don't know about Barzani," he said. "Now that Iraq has been liberated from the British. The Russian government has allowed Barzani to return to Kurdistan after a long exile in Soviet Union. When he arrived in Bahdinan, where his family and relatives live, he immediately revived the KDP, and they armed themselves right away, ready to demand the new government the right of Kurdish people, and the autonomy of Kurdistan. If the government refuses, the KDP will left with no choice but to fight. Many hundreds of brave men are already armed with what little they have, but they are asking for Kurds to join the fight.

"Myself, I have already sent the KDP a letter stating my loyalty to Kurdistan and Barzani's leadership, and if it becomes necessary for me to join them, I'll not hesitate for one second. I'm telling you this because if at any time you feel it's the right time for all of you to join, you will have my support. You are all my sons, and it is an honorable cause. We will not fight for ourselves, but for our children and their children, to be free and live in peace."

The three friends listened and were amazed by Smko's speech and his courage. He has been honest and straightforward. But, they wanted to know more, they still had many unanswered questions.

"What about other Kurds from other parts of Kurdistan?" Sirwan asked. "Are they ready to join the armed struggle? Do they feel the same about Barzani? I don't think so. If they felt the same way, you would see the Kurdistan's mountains crowded with armed men. But that is the biggest problem we are facing. I don't believe the Kurds are ignorant. They know if they let anyone, a feudal and land owner, a religious man, the head of tribe, a man like Barzani, lead them, they will be enslaved in his grips forever.

"A man who never had a strategy, how he will lead the Kurdish people? He already has his written strategy, the Quran! And the Quran will lead us back to the dark-age. We are Zoroastrians, we don't need Islam and Quran. We don't need a man like Barzani to be our leader. We will end up doing the same mistakes as we did with the Republic of Mahabad. While the president of the Republic and his ministers were hanged, Barzani fled to Soviet Union. He didn't suffer as much as a scratch! If he was a Kurd and fighting for Kurdish people, why didn't he continue the fight? Why didn't he stay and die for Kurdistan? I can't follow a religious man who is more a Muslim than he is a Kurd. The best thing for Kurds to do is to reclaim their true identities as Kurds and get rid of Islam and Arabic traditions. It is written in Quran that the Quran came down in Arabic for Arabs, not for Kurds.

"If we follow Barzani and give him the right to be our leader, he will take us back to dark-age. We are giving that right to a man hardly anyone knows, and when things go very wrong, we will have no one to blame but ourselves. That is what I think."

"To tell you more," Sardar said, "I'm afraid that because most of our people are illiterate, and they have been used by religious men, as you mentioned earlier, it will be easier for them to follow someone like themselves. Most of our people are religious, god-fearing men and women who do believe that their god will lead them to a promised heaven. Those people will blindly follow Barzani without examining him or asking whether he wants liberate us as Kurds or as Muslims. I don't think that he will follow his roots as a Kurd. I think he would rather follow his religion. I may sound like communist, but I'm not, I'm just a poor Kurd like you who wants my people to be free from the hands of invaders. It doesn't matter if the invaders are Arabs, Persian, Turk, or an ignorant Kurd. I'll fight even Kurds if they try to monopolize Kurdistan."

"Then tell me what you will do if the government invades Kurdistan?" Smko asked them.

"I'll fight even though I don't know Barzani, because I can't allow myself to lean back and wait for Arab soldiers rape and kill my wife, my daughter and my mother, I'll fight with all my force. I'll defend my land, my family and my honor." Kameran said.

"I'll do the same and even more, but I would have to be sure Barzani is the man I could trust," said Sardar. "If

I'm ready to die for my country, I have to know if my leaders are ready to die too. Otherwise, I don't know."

"You are all right," Sirwan said. "We will all fight for the cause, but I don't want to be killed by Kurds. That is what scares me the most. I too will die for this land, but I'm not ready to fight with religious man like Barzani."

"I have to say little more about the subject, if you all allow me," Sardar said. "Let's imagine that the war already started. Do we fight to free Kurds only in Iraq? Or we will fight to free all Kurds?

"It is possible that you may know the answer, but I'll tell you what I think. I believe we are fighting the

Iraqi government to free Iraqi Kurds, even though we all know that the other Kurds who live in Turkey, Iran and Syria have lived under the same repression by their governments. Now, if Barzani truly believe in the unity of Kurdistan, he would join all Kurds and show them that we all fight for one cause. But he hasn't done that. He knows very well that he would not have the support of all Kurds."

Smko looked at his watch, "Wow, it's already ten o'clock," he said. "Thank you, my sons. I hope we all learned something tonight. Now if you'll excuse me, I have my wife waiting for me." he got up and slowly climbed down the ladder.

Sardar, Kameran and Sirwan sat there for a while

longer. They liked what Smko had discussed with them. And although they were not so old, Sardar and

Sirwan was nineteen and Kameran was twenty, Smko always treated each one of them the way they deserved to be treated, and the three young men felt more confident in themselves.

At the end of August, the three young men, as they hopped, received their letters of admission to the education institute. They would start in September. They were very happy that finally their dreams of becoming teachers were coming true. Even with the political unrest in Iraq, the three friends had decided to finish what they had dreamed about for so long.

The Iraqi government, was moving toward a police state, and life for all Iraqis had become more difficult. The economy was going from bad to worse, and the price of everything was skyrocketing. The military buildup in Kurdistan was obvious. The government was spending millions in Iraqi revenue, with Russian to build a strong army. The democracy most people dreamed about had become unlikely, and all political parties had been banned from the political arena. The communists were on the run. The Kurdish language was banned from all schools and the language of education had become Arabic. Half of Iraqi army was in Kurdish territory, which made the Kurdish people uncomfortable, especially the leader Barzani.

The rebel began their attacks on the military's small bases and border checkpoints, and that made the Iraqi army to lose its patience with the Kurds.

The Kurds were not the only one who had been targeted. The Jews suffered the worst. Jews had lived in Kurdistan for centuries without any problems, but now the Jews who chose to stay, after the creation of Israel, had to pay huge price. The government started accusing the Jews of being the Zionist agents. Many Jews had already been executed in Baghdad and many other would follow. The Jews had no other choice than to leave the home of their forefathers and go to Israel.

The most tragic aspect of all this, and the one that stayed with all Kurds, was that the Jews were forced to sell their homes and belongings on short notice. Those who considered themselves to be the friends and families of Jews often chose, with a broken heart and tears in their eyes, to buy their properties and belongings, thereby not allowing the government to sell it cheap. It was difficult for most people to watch Jews selling the home of their forefathers, and giving it up and selling it for almost nothing. The situation for most of the Jews who lived in the government-controlled territories was turning from bad to worse, but the Jews who lived among the Kurds were much better off. If they didn't hold a government job, they were safe. Many other Jews had already moved from Baghdad to the north.

Finally, the three friends finished their studies and were graduated. Kameran's father, Dawood, did everything he could to keep the three new teachers in the city of Slaymany, and he succeed, in part because he was working in the education department. Soon all three had found jobs in three different school. The would start in September.

Sardar and Salma had another child, a beautiful and healthy girl. Salma wanted to name her Bayan.

Kameran had another son, beside his son Awat; he named him Ako. And Sirwan to had another son, who he named him Diar.

Life to seemed to be going well for the three families; they didn't have any financial problems, especially as they all had jobs, they could support their own families and lift the burden from the shoulders of their parents.

The political situation in Iraq looked like it was heading nowhere. There was no freedom of press, nor free speech; in fact, all human rights were ignored at every level of the government. The prisons were full and the number of exiled Iraqi was increasing.

Attacks on Kurdish territories went beyond just an attack on Kurdish rebels, but also included the indiscriminate bombing of villages, and town and killing of many innocent people.

The situation was pushing more and more young

Kurdish men to join the rebels in the mountains, and many others both young and old were working as sleeper cells. They worked underground in the cities and towns, but what Kurdish people didn't know that this was just a beginning of the long and bloody battle between the Iraqi army equipped with the latest Russian jet fighters, modern tanks and other weapon and the Kurds that had no such weaponry. They also didn't know that lives were going to change forever. Joy, happiness, and prosperity would be replaced by pain, sorrow and destruction.

Smko was very worried about his family and the families of his friends. He wasn't sure if he would stay or if he would be asked to join the rebels. Therefore, he asked Salih and Dawood to come to his place and give him some advice.

It was late evening when Salih and Dawood along with their families, came to visit Smko. The women and the children sat separately to give the men the freedom to discuss their issues.

"I'm very worried about the situation, and I'm asking you both to give me your opinions on the subject," Smko told them.

"We do what is best for all of us, but our families come first. If we can't protect our families, I'm sure we can't protect anyone else," Dawood said.

"That is why I'm thinking to divide my wealth among you, my brothers," Smko said. "I would like to register one store in each of your name. In this way, we can save something if we are to lose our fortune. We wouldn't lose everything. Do you know what I'm saying?"

"Yes, but what is on your mind?" Salih said.

"Well, I have nothing to hide from you," Smko said, "but if something happened to me, or if the government takes over my business, we would have a little left if I put half of our fortune in your names. Am I right?"

"I think it is a good idea, even though I don't like it a bit," Dawood said. "I would rather die than to see Arabs take what I have worked for my entire life."

It was a long night, and they discussed many things, and finally they all agreed with Smko's plan.

As soon as Smko had time, he registered two of his stores Dawood's and Salih's names, and this way he secured the survival of the business for the families.

Life for people in Slaymany was going from bad to worse. The presence of army in the city made people uneasy. Women were now kept inside their homes. They were not as free as they were before, because they had become the target of insults, humiliation and harassment by armed soldiers. And there was no one to complain to.

THE JOURNEY

Early one morning in September of 1963, Smko's family awakened by a heavy banging on their door. It wasn't someone knocking; it was someone pounding and banging. Smko ran to open the door as the banging continued. Before he could reach it, the door was flung open by what Smko now saw was a group of fully-armed soldiers. Ten to fifteen Arab soldiers rushed inside, all speaking Arabic. Smko tried to talk to them in Arabic, but they didn't seem interested in that.

They ran to the rooms where his children and wife

were sleeping. Few soldiers pushed Smko outside, and then they found Sardar and Saman and grabbed them out of their rooms. They shouted in Arabic to get outside. They gathered the women and children and pushed them outside as well. They began to search the house and turned everything upside down. They mixed sugar, rice, tea, flour and dry beans together on the floor. They didn't stop there; they didn't leave a thing untouched. Tearing apart even mattresses and pillows with their bayonets. They brought down every shelf, they threw every drawer in the house.

Smko's blood was boiling, but when he saw his wife and the rest of his family coming out, he tried to control himself and wait to see what would happen.

The soldiers went house to house and took out every male aged fifteen and older. They had been given order to arrest every male over fifteen. The military trucks were full of men and boys. The soldiers drove their trucks loaded with people to the military base and the rest of them pushed the women and children back inside their homes. Anyone who tried to come out was beaten by angry soldiers. Some were shot dead in front of their home and women and girls were lamenting over the dead bodies of their beloved one.

The entire city was in morning and total shock; no one knew what was going on. There wasn't enough room for all prisoners, so they had converted the football stadium into a temporary prison and kept it guarded by heavy-armed soldiers, day and night.

After the arrest of almost every male, the government had declared curfew for the entire city. Anyone who came out would be shot.

Many families lost their loved ones, and many families were obliged to bury their dead in their own back yards.

The curfew took toll on people all over Kurdistan, but especially in Slaymany. The army enacted an embargo on the city, so food supplies were not coming in. there was no fuel or electricity, and people couldn't go out to work. It was the end of the happy days in Kurdistan.

The mass arrest of people and ruthless enforcemeant of the curfew, didn't do lessen the attacks on the government by the rebels, but in the contrary, the rebels increased their attacks and the support for the rebels among people has increased too, and that eventually, led the authorities to release most of the prisoners. Many people had been executed, some were sent to prison in the south and never heard from them again.

Smko, and the rest were released after few months and returned to their families, but they were changed forever. Nothing was the same now. They have lost the most precious thing, their freedom.

The day after Smko was released, he gathered the families and talked to them. "Our lives have changed and we have lost our freedom," he said. "We can't sit back and wait; we have to do our share. The Arabs invaders will stop at nothing. They came here to stay." he wiped the tears from his eyes. "Freedom isn't sold at the marketplace, and they will not give to us. So, we have to take it by force." He chocked as he talked. His wife put her arms around him, proving to him that he was right.

Sardar was quiet, his head was bowed on his knees. He didn't know what to say or do. He was worried about his family and he loved them too much to leave them. But he also loved his country too much not to fight for it. He raised his head and looked at his father. "I'll join the rebels, Dad," he said. "I can't let my children live like slaves under Arab occupation. I'll join the fight as soon as I can, maybe even tomorrow. Who else will join? If anyone else want to go, that would be good. Otherwise I'll go by myself. As long as you're here, Dad, I won't be worried."

"That is an honorable thing to do, son," Smko said.

Salma was quiet the entire time, but when he heard her husband talking about joining the rebels, a chill ran down her spine. "I__I don't know, what to say!" she said haltingly, and burst into tears. Shereen went to her and took the baby girl from her. Sardar approached her as well, and put his arms around her.

"I love you so much, Sardar, and I don't want you

to go!" she said. "But I love my children even more, and I don't want them to be slaves__" she wept.

Sardar was sobbing by now; he couldn't find any words better than his wife's. He just put his head on her shoulder and sobbed too.

The families talked the entire evening until late in the night, they looked at the situation from all aspect and decided what was best for them as one family.

The Iraqi army raided all the Kurdish territories. Soldiers were swarmed into villages, towns and cities, they had orders to arrest, kill and destroy everything they encounter along their way. The summary executions of innocent people became a daily routine for the soldiers.

People in Slaymany, Kirkuk, Arbil and many other Kurdish cites witnessed the barbaric killing of many innocent people. The bloodthirsty soldiers never turned away from killing men, women, children and even babies.

Sardar, Sirwan and Kameran discussed their own futures and that of their families. Sardar had already decided to join the rebels and had discussed the matter thoroughly with his father and his wife. Even they weren't happy about it, they felt they didn't have any other choice.

Kameran had also decide to join, and he too discussed it with his family. The only one left was Sirwan. He didn't want to join. For one thing, he didn't like Barzani, and he didn't want to support a man he didn't know, a man who didn't know where he stood on the Kurdish issue. Was he truly fighting for Kurdistan, or was it for his control of Kurdistan? He asked himself the same questions over and over, because he didn't want to do something that he would regret later. He needed more time; it wasn't an easy decision. His other consideration was that he thought he could be more useful here in Slaymany than in the mountains. They understood him completely, and they were happy in some ways that one of them wanted to stay to look after their families.

Once they decided to leave, Sirwan said he would find someone to take them to the closest town, where they would continue on foot. Smko decided they should go Chwarta, and from there, to Mawat.

Two days later, Sardar was ready for the journey. No one could tell where it ends, but Sardar was sure he must take it.

Sardar came to his room and found Salma sitting quietly, pale and totally devastated. She didn't know what to say or do. "I know how you feel my dear," Sardar quietly said and sat down next to her on their bed. He put his arms around her. "Don't worry. We will be okay."

She lifted her head, and Sardar could see she had tears in her eyes. "Let us come with you, Sardar," she whispered. "I don't want you die alone. If it's about our freedom, then don't we have a right to be part of it?"

"I don't want you to die," he said. "That is why I'm leaving to make it better for all of us. You stay here and raise the kids, at let them know we are Kurd and that we will be free one day."

She threw herself into his arms and burst into tears. Sardar held her tightly in his arms. "Sirwan decided not to go," Sardar said. "He had different opinion. He doesn't believe people are ready to take arms. He didn't want to go, and he realized he could do better here. I respect his decision. He is my brother and my friend. And it's good that he will be here. If anything happens, he will the man to take care of everything."

Slowly the family was waking up, and they were aware of what was awaiting them. They were about to let their beloved sons to go. They would help fight for the freedom of all Kurds.

Smko heard a knocking at the door and went to see who it was. He unlocked the door and there were Kameran and Sirwan. He greeted them and asked them to come in. "Is he ready?" Kameran asked.

"He will be ready in few minutes," Smko replied. "Come and have some breakfast."

"No, Thank you, Uncle. We have to leave as soon as possible," Sirwan said.

Sardar freed himself from his wife's arms with difficulty, took his few belongings, and left the room. When he came out and began to move toward the door, his father said, "Sardar, wait," Sardar stopped and turned. He watched his father go into his room and came back out with his prayer beads in his hands. "This is very helpful in time of stress, and it helps you to focus," he put it around Sardar's neck. It was beautiful prayer beads, a dark ocean green with Buddha's figure on each bead. "It was a gift from a British man," Smko said. He kissed Sardar and Kameran again and he went back to his room.

It was late October, and it was little chilly, but that wasn't going to be a problem. The weather wasn't going to stop the army or the rebels from fighting.

They got into an old Land Rover, which Sirwan had borrowed for the trip, and he drove away.

"Saying good-bye to people you love is the most difficult thing anyone ever has to do," Sardar said, he was sitting in the back seat of the Land Rover, while Sirwan drove and Kameran sat with him in the front seat.

There was total silence in the vehicle. The tension was so palpable that they finished two packs of cigarettes in two hours of driving. They were on a mission. Sirwan's mission was to make sure that his two friends arrive in Chwarta safe and sound.

Kameran and Sardar's mission was to reach, as soon as possible, the nearest Kurdish rebels group. Chwarta wasn't far from Slaymany, just few hours driving. And there were no problems getting there, but then the difficulties would start; they have to walk from there.

They were silent the entire way, but there wasn't any other reason than the separation from their families. Sirwan worried he was betraying his friends in some way, but Kameran and Sardar assured him that nothing would ever come between them.

Sirwan stayed with them in Chwarta at the home of one of Smko's friends, he knew through his business, and they talked the entire night through. Their mood brightened somewhat, and they were able to laugh and tell a few jokes. Kameran and Sardar teased Sirwan for long time. They were all happy that the tension had melted away. Tonight, they were boys again.

Next morning, Kameran and Sardar were ready to say good-bye to their friend. They embraced each other for a long time, and then Sirwan drove away.

Kameran and Sardar pulled their hood over their heads, took their few belongings and started up the road leading to the mountains.

It was almost November, in the northern part of Iraq, there are two or more months of snow fall, and it's very hard for people to cope with the cold without fuel. During the winter, the roads were muddy and impassable. Most people used animals as a means of transportation in the mountains.

They walked in the chilly morning through narrow mountain passes, over hills, and across rivers, had passed few villages. They grew tired; the cold weather forced them to slow down. It was late afternoon when they saw a village. And they approached it from the hill side they were descending, the village seemed very quiet, as if no one lived there. As they got closer, they saw an old man pulling two mules. He looked tired; probably he was on a long trip from one of the neighboring villages, or perhaps he was using his animals for transporting goods from the Iranian border. Goods were often traded between villagers from all sides of the Kurdistan's borders. This was and still is a vital source of support not only for the villagers themselves but for the rebels as well. The trade allows them to support themselves during harsh embargoes and other economic sanctions imposed on them by the Iraqi, Turkish, Iranian and Syrian governments.

The two young men greeted the old man with respect. He replied kindly, saying, "You have come from far away, if I'm not mistaken." He welcomed them warmly and they shook hands. "It's easy to recognize one's own people by the way they dress, their looks, their cleanliness and the way of speaking."

"Yes, we came from far away," Kameran replied. "In

fact, we came have come from Slaymany." Both Kameran and Sardar knew how to properly speak to villagers, because they have special way to greet each other. And Sardar and Kameran knew it, from the many trips they did to Kurdistan and had friends from far villages who came to study in the city.

"Well, I'm sure you don't know anyone here," the old man said.

"No, we don't know anyone," Sardar replied.

"Then wait five minutes, and I'll be back. I'm going to water these animals and you can come home with me."

Sardar and Kameran thanked him, and they asked him if he needed help, but the old man shook his head and left.

After few minutes, he came back and asked the two young men to follow him. "It's not far," he said. "We live behind those houses over there." Again, he welcomed them, and soon they were standing in front of a little house made of mud bricks. It had light blue frame windows, and there were many chickens were sunning around in front of the house. An old and a young woman were busy cooking in the veranda, and when they saw the two men approach, they stood up and welcomed them. Their host stepped inside and asked them to follow him. Inside three small children played and a young man was busy reviving the fire in the wood-burning oven, typical Kurdish village home.

The oven sat in the middle of the room and a metallic pipe ran up through the roof.

The young man stood up and greeted the two men, and respectfully asked them to sit, pointing to few mattresses on the floor, which covered with colorful carpets. "Get closer to the fire," the old man said. "You must be freezing!"

They sat in the warm room and had supper. Tea was served continuously. "Where are you headed?" the old man asked.

"Mawat," said Sardar.

"If you leave early in the morning, you will be there by the evening," the old man said.

Next morning when the two friends woke up, their host offered them breakfast. The old man asked his son to go with them and show them the right road to take. The two friends shook hands with the old man and thanked him and his family for their hospitality. The old man handed them a bundle and said, "Take this for the road. It is some boiled eggs, bread and onions." They thanked him again and followed the son.

The hospitality was one characteristic all the villagers were known for. Anyone who was passing by a village in Kurdistan, no matter what time of the year it was, would find the villagers frank, honest and hospitable. They would share their food, give you shelter, and guide you on your way as best they could.

The two friends were back on the road; they took two breaks to eat the food their host gave them that morning. By the evening they were close to the town of Mawat. They could see it below them as they descended a mountain. Mawat was a small town with two or three hundred houses, and mostly the inhabitant were mostly farmers. The two friends were excited to reach their destination. Slowly, on narrow, muddy roads, they came down from the mountain. By the time they arrived, their shoes were soaked, their clothes wet, and they were mud to their knees.

They entered the town and they noticed there were many armed men, "Peshmarga", both old and young. They had gathered in front of a house that looked like a mosque. They approached the gathering and greeted them. The men returned the greeting, but appeared to be very suspicious of these strangers who had come to town. One of the Peshmarga approached them and asked them what they were doing here in Mawat.

Kameran asked the man if he could tell them where they could find "kak Sddiq" Mr. Sddiq.

"Do you know him?" The man asked.

"Yes, we do," Sardar replied.

"Follow me, please," he said. "Kak Sddiq is in his office, but he has some guests. He will be finished in few minutes. Are you from Slaymany?"

"Yes, we are," Sardar said. "My name is Sardar." He stretched out his hand, and the other man shook it. "And this is my friend Kameran. We are both from Slaymany."

"I'm from Slaymany too," the armed man said. "I'm Khabat, and I left Slaymany almost three years ago. I have had no news about the city, I hope you have some good new to tell me. Those other guys are mostly from Slaymany."

"We're everywhere!" Sardar said and chuckled.

"Yes, we're Khabat replied.

The door of a small mud-brick house opened, and four armed men came out. Sddiq was a man in his forties. He was a simple man, a former officer in Iraqi army who didn't know much about politics but considered himself a patriot and devotee of the KDP. He was dressed with traditional Kurdish dress; unlike many other Peshmarga, he didn't wear turban. Now he is the commander of the Peshmarga in Mawat and its surrounding.

He shook hands with the men who just came out of the house, said good-bye to them, and turned to go back to his office. "Excuse me, kak Sddiq!" Khabat said. "These two men just arrived from Slaymany. They want to see you." he waved Kameran and Sardar closer.

Sddiq took few steps forward and looked at the

two young men. "I hope Smko didn't send you to fight___" he laughed and ran to them. He opened his arm and hugged them. Then he put his arms around them and went inside. "What are you doing here, sons?" He asked them to sit on few old chairs, and himself sat on a chair behind an old desk.

"Well, as you may know the situation in Slaymany is becoming unbearable for people." Sardar said. "And after the arrest of half the city, no one feels safe. We have all been arrested, even our fathers. My father advised us to leave the city, saying that we are better somewhere else. He asked us to join the revolution." he handed him a small envelope. "This is a letter from my father."

Smko and Sddiq had a long friendship, which goes back to their childhood. They had done a lot of good things together while Sddiq still was living in Slaymany.

The three men talked for a few hours. Then Sddiq showed them around. "Many Peshmargas have their families with them," he said, and they could see many children running around. He stopped. "Wait a minute, you are teachers, right!"

"Yes, we are," Kameran replied.

"Why do you ask?" Sardar asked.

"Well, we have two or three dozen children, and they aren't doing anything," he said. "Why don't you guys open a school and teach our kids. That is ten times better than killing the enemy."

"Khabat! Khabat!" Sddiq called the young man who had brought the two friends to him.

Khabat ran over, "Yes, kak Sddiq," he said.

"Listen, find a place for your friends for tonight. Tomorrow we're going to open a school for our kids," Sddiq said. Khabat took the two friends and showed them where they could stay.

Early the next morning, Sardar and Kameran woke up with other men. The commander of the group, kak Hawar, asked someone to get some bread and asked Kameran and Sardar to go and see kak Sddiq.

CITY UNDER SIEGE

Three months after the two friends left, Slaymany had become the city under siege. The military was everywhere, and life for ordinary people had become very difficult. No one ever knew what would come next.

The government had ordered the Jews to leave the country. If they would not leave willingly, they would be forced out. Many had already left for Israel, and many others were preparing to leave as soon as they could. It was heartbreaking; for centuries, the Jews had lived in Iraq, without any major conflicts with others, especially in northern, where Kurds lived as one nation with Jews, Christians, and many other religious and ethnic groups. They even intermarried, no one asked questions about one's religion. They considered themselves Kurds and they proudly defended Kurdistan.

One day, when Dawood came home, he went directly to see Smko. He appeared to be very angry. After he sat down, Smko asked him, "What is wrong, Dawood?"

"The bastards have fired me!" He said, bursting into tears.

"What?" Smko surprisingly asked.

"Yes, I'm fired, Smko," he replied, "from my longtime job. I'm a Jew, nothing but a Jew."

"Dawood, calm down, my friend," Smko said. He put his arms on Dawood's shoulders. "You are my brother, my friend, and the grandfather to my grandchildren. What do I care what other thinks? Don't ever forget that, I'll die to protect this family, and you are a part of this family."

Salma heard her father talking to Smko, so she came out. As she approached him, Dawood freed himself from Smko's arms and threw himself into his daughter's arms. "We will be okay, Dad," she said. "Don't worry, we still have you. We need you and your grandchildren need you, too." She kissed him and said,

“Sit down, I’ll bring you a cup of fresh tea. That will make you feel better.”

Dawood let Salma go and sat down with Smko. Already he was feeling better.

“It’s not a big deal, Dawood,” Smko chuckled. In fact, I’m happy they fired you! You don’t need them! Do something else. There is a store in your name, or, if you like, tomorrow you could buy a different store and do something else. Then the government will not bother you anymore.”

“You’re right, I don’t need them. I have my family and I’m not going to starve to death. As you said, I’ll do something else,” he said.

Within two weeks, Smko managed to buy a little store for Dawood. He filled it with vegetable and fruits. “This is very good for you, and no one will suspect you of being anything other than a vegetable vendor,” Smko said. “Nowadays, the only thing people will buy is food.”

Dawood was happy again. He made many new friends and found it didn’t take him long to learn the to run his business. Life had returned to normal, and for the moment, he was spared.

One day, after Dawood had been fired, Salih came to see Smko to talk. Shereen hear a knock on the door and went to open it. “Hi, Shereen, is Smko there?” he said.

"Yes, he is in the living room," she said and let him in.

Salih asked Smko if they could talk in private. Smko nodded and told Shereen to give them some privacy. She nodded and left the room. Smko lit a cigarette, "What is on your mind, Salih?" Smko asked.

"There is a good possibility that we have been watched," Salih said, "and I have a feeling that they will raid your business soon. If they find anything, one rifle or some ammunition, they will execute both of us on the spot. The government has too many agents and spies, and they pay good money to people to sell their souls. You don't know who you can trust anymore. it's as if the entire city is full of spies. There are too many ignorant and selfish men out there ready to do anything for a little money." He paused. "I think we have to stop what we're doing for a while and move somewhere else in Kurdistan. We have too many responsibilities, and our families can't afford to lose us."

Shereen tapped on the door and came in with a tea. She put down the tray, left the room and closed the door behind her.

Smko sipped his tea, then put down the cup. "Well, Salih, we've been together for a long time, and we know each other well," Smko said. "You know me; I can't leave just like that. As you know the revolution depend mostly on the people like you and me to donate money and help with whatever they need. We must continue to support the effort. If we all leave, who will help? On the other hand, as you said, we could do the same thing we're doing here somewhere else if we want to. So, tell me your plan."

Salih relaxed a little bit, "I think you could sell your business___" he began, but Smko interpreted him.

"Why don't you call it ours instead of mine. You know you and Dawood have always been a part of the family," Smko reminded him.

"We could start selling the business and move to Halabja. The government has little control on that city, and we could settle our families and live there forever. it's still Kurdistan, right?"

The two men talked a lot that afternoon, and Smko agreed to do what Salih had suggested to him. He sent Salih and his son Saman to Halabja to see what option they had.

Three days later, during the late afternoon, while Salih was still in Halabja, two military trucks full of armed soldiers, led by a military Russian-made jeep, stopped in the marketplace. The soldiers jumped out of the trucks and surrounded the place. Two officers got out of the jeep and headed inside the market, followed by six or seven armed soldiers. They were led by a Kurdish informant directly to Smko's store. One of the officer ordered the soldiers to pull Smko out of his store.

They rushed up to Smko, grabbed him by his rams and began beating him. The neighbors were shocked to see Smko beaten this way, in front of everyone. It insulted both Smko and the neighbors, but they were powerless against the armed soldiers. Two or three soldiers continued beating Smko, and the rest of them searched the store for guns and other things. Several soldiers turned the store upside down as other busied themselves beating Smko.

He didn't make a sound; he didn't scream or shout. The pain began to take over his mind, so he couldn't answer when an officer demanded that he tell them where he was hiding the weapons. Their questions were in vain; Smko didn't give them that satisfaction they wanted. He lost consciousness, and still they beat him. Then the officer asked the soldiers to stop. He approached Smko and said, "Wouldn't you rather die than talk, dirty Kurd?" but Smko wasn't answering. The soldiers took his half-dead body and threw him inside one of the trucks. The rest of the soldiers jumped inside the trucks and drove off through the narrow streets of the marketplace.

The officers inside the jeep weren't satisfied with how their mission had worked out, so they ordered the soldiers to drive to Smko's home.

No one knew why all these soldiers were coming to their neighborhood. The trucks stopped and the soldiers raided the house. They were told not to come out until they had found the weapons. Their informant had told them that Smko was hiding them somewhere. Shereen didn't have time to answer the banging on the door. The soldiers broke it down with two or three blows. They rushed inside with no regard for the women and children, pushing their way in, and began searching the house. After few hours, they still hadn't found anything. They had broken windows, doors, and plates, they tore apart boxes and threw things everywhere. Shereen and Salma and the children were pushed into a corner by two armed soldiers. They squeezed themselves together, so afraid they thought they would die, so afraid they couldn't cry, not even the small ones. The scene was terrifying. Finally, the soldiers gave up. They had turned the house upside down, but they hadn't found anything. They rushed out, jumped into their trucks and drove away, taking Smko with them. They didn't let the family know that he was lying on the floor of their trucks, half dead.

When they had left, Shereen stoop up and looked out the window to be sure the soldiers were gone. She grabbed the small girl and asked Salma to stop crying.

"It's not the time for crying. let's get things put back," Shereen commanded the family.

Smko's family had no idea what had happened to Smko. Shereen tried to encourage her children to be brave. Soon neighbors came over to help them clean up what was left.

Smko didn't come home that day, nor the next. Shereen began to realize he would never come back home. After three days of searching, the hospital contacted Smko's family. They said they should come and take his body home. Smko had died from his extensive head injuries the same day he had been beaten. The military had given his body to the hospital to inform the family after three days.

Dawood was paralyzed by the death of his longtime friend and protector, and as soon as he heard the news, he gathered people and gave them directions to prepare an honorable funeral for the man who had died because he was Kurd. Most people knew Smko, and they also knew that his older son was with the rebels, so to honor him they arranged a big funeral. Smko was buried in Slaymany close to his parents and grand-parents.

Now it was Dawood's duty to look after the big family Smko had built. First, he had to send someone to find Salih and Saman who still was in Halabja, to tell them not to come back to Slaymany yet. Next task was to make sure to take care of the business. But Smko's store had been confiscated by the army. They had emptied and looted it, taking whatever, they wanted, but Dawood wasn't worried, because Smko had left him with some of his savings, another portion with Salih, and yet another with Shereen. She had enough for a long time. Smko knew who to plan for the future. That was why he had always given his family enough for a year; in case something happened to him.

Salih and Saman stayed in Halabja two more weeks. Then his son Sirwan went after him to bring them back home. When they came back to Slaymany, the city looked like it was still under siege. Now Salih and Dawood wondered how they would tell Smko's son Sardar the heartbreaking news.

"I think it's better not to tell them," Sirwan said to his father and his uncle, "because I know Sardar and Kameran. They will come back when they learn this, and their lives will be in great danger. No one will be able to guarantee their safety.

"But we can't just leave them uninformed like this," Dawood said. "They will blame us for not telling them what happened."

"Don't you worry, Uncle Dawood, I'll take the responsibility for this," Sirwan replied. "Whether they come back or not, nothing is going to change. Uncle Smko is dead, and he will not come back anymore whatever we do." They all agreed not to let Sardar and Kameran know about Smko's death.

"Look what had happened to our lives," Salih said. "Life has become unbearable for all! The Iraqi government has placed severe economic sanctions on the Kurdish territories. We have electricity only few hours a day. Rationing our heating fuel was the most brutal punishment of all. You know this winter was one of the worst we've had. It was very cold, and heating fuel wasn't available for most people, except those who sold their souls."

"And don't forget supplies of medicines. Those were in shortage everywhere in Kurdistan as well," Sirwan said. "The slightest sickness might lead to death. Basic food supplies have been rationed, and other families only few coupons for food. It hasn't been enough. The rations they got by coupons for a month, wouldn't last a week."

"All these arrest of young men, without any obvious reasons, has been the most painful thing to see. Many families haven't seen their, husbands, and sons and fathers for months," Dawood said. "Those men were providers for their families, whether big or small, and now most of these families living in total destitution. There is no help coming to them. It's a great tragedy."

"And the humiliation the women and girls are facing from the bastard Muslim Arab soldiers are unbearable for most of people," Salih said.

The siege was pushing more and more young men to join the rebels in the mountains, contrary to the government's plan to force people to abandon Barzani and his rebels. They didn't realize that what they were doing was pushing more people to take up arms.

Salih, Dawood and Sirwan managed to convince

Saman, Smko's second son, to go back to the business. He was just about to lose his mind over his father's death. They thought it would help him if he did something. They thought that he shouldn't be sitting around grieving his father's death or thinking about how to revenge it. It would help to more to earn money for the family. They still had two other stores.

They stuck together, as Smko would have wanted them to. They were one real family, and they would remain as one family in good times and bad times.

THE REBELS

It was a beautiful day, despite the cold. Kameran and Sardar had had a good night sleep after their two-days trip to Mawat. They felt refreshed and were ready to take the task that had been assigned to them.

Sddiq was standing in the sun in front of his house. When he saw Sardar and Kameran, he approached them. "Did you sleep well last night?" he asked.

"Yes, thank you," they answered.

"Well, I have already asked some of the guys to empty a house for the school. it's the end of the town and is a good place. No one will bother you or your students." he then asked them to go with him to see the place. When they got close to the house, he pointed it out to them and said, "It is a big place; there is room for fifty kids if they sit on the floor. You'll have desks and chairs, whenever we can find them, and you will have your own place for living. You will be able to live here! So, what do you think about starting tomorrow morning?"

Kameran and Sardar loved teaching children, that is why they wanted to become teachers in the first place; after all, it's their profession. They gratefully accepted the offer.

The opportunity was a very good for a village like Mawat, and there were many children who wanted to learn. So why not! They shook Sddiq's hand, and promised him that he would not be disappointed.

The next day Kameran and Sardar left their new friends and headed for the school. It had been cleaned during the night. They brought two beds in and a wood-burning stove for heating and cooking. A few old rugs covered the room's floor.

The big windows brought a lot of light in and would make it easier for students to see their books. A medium-sized blackboard hung on the wall. Two boxes of papers, notebooks and pencils.

"It really has all it needs to call a school," Kameran said.

"Yes, it has, and now it's our school!" Sardar said.

At eight o'clock the next morning, the students began to arrive. Sardar and Kameran standing at the door, asked them to take off their shoes and take a place on the floor, until at last they had twenty-two students. "How are you children?" Kameran asked them.

"Very well, thank you, mammosta," the children chimed in one voice. Mammosta, means, Sir, or teacher in Kurdish,

"My name is Mammosta Kameran and this is Mammosta Sardar." Kameran said.

"Good morning Mammosta," they chimed again.

"We are going to teach you in this school from eight o'clock to noon every day except for Fridays," Kameran told them.

"We all have to keep our school clean, and you have to leave your shoes outside the classroom. Do you understand?" Sardar asked.

"Yes, Mammosta," they all answered together.

"We don't have books for today, but we will find books for all of you," Sardar said. "Today we are going to learn the alphabet. Mammosta Kameran will give you all paper and pencil, but you must leave them here when you go home."

At noon, the two teachers let the kids go home; they ran out of the school shouting, singing, full of joy. After the children left the school, both sat quietly on the floor. They looked at each other and laughed, they were happy, too. "It's hard to remember all their names," Kameran said.

"Did you noticed the little boy, Arras, who was sitting at the first row?" Sardar quietly asked.

"Yes, I did! He seemed like very smart boy."

"Yes, he did. He reminds me of my son Aram." They were quiet again. They, terribly missed their family, and they could not do anything about it but wait and help the children to learn something and they might make some changes in their society.

A few days later Sardar found out that the little boy Arras, his father was killed the previous year, leaving behind two small children. Arras became Sardar's favorite and best student.

The two friends had a good start in their new life as teachers in a small town of Mawat. They were happy doing something good for the community they lived in, and they did their best to educate the children. They were still considered rebels; it was just that instead of taking up arms, they were teaching. Their efforts were very much appreciated by the townspeople and the rebels alike.

People from cities and towns of Kurdistan began to collect book, notebooks, papers and other school materials and sent it to rebels wherever they were. The two teachers, finally got what they needed for their school. The provided them with books, papers and pencils. They even managed to get desk and chairs for all of them. They were respected for their valuable work.

One day when Sardar was sitting on the bench in front of the school, he noticed many rebels going and coming some distance away. They looked very disturbed. "Kameran! Kameran!" He shouted.

Kameran was busy preparing dinner inside, but when he heard Sardar calling him, he left the room and came out. "What is it, Sardar?"

"It looks like something going on over there, do you see all those Peshmarga over there?"

"Yes, I see, they are going somewhere," he said.

"I don't know," Sardar replied. He began going toward the crowd to see what was going on, when he saw Khabat coming up the street. He greeted Sardar, and asked him where he was going. I was going to see what is going on, Sardar answered.

"Let's go to the school," Khabat said. "I'll tell you."

Both men returned and went inside. Kameran greeted Khabat and asked him if he asked him if he wanted something to eat. He accepted and thanked him. They all sat down and Kameran served them.

"You don't know what is going on?" Khabat asked. "We were hoping you would tell us," Sardar said.

"Well, Ibrahim Ahmad and Jalal Talabani, along with their followers, have separated themselves form the KDP, and they have created their own political party," Khabat said.

"Who are these people?" Sardar asked

"Well, Talabani is Kurd for sure, he had joined the KDP in the early forties, he was the youngest and the most brilliant members. He advanced rapidly through the party ranks, but even from the very beginning he had found many faults in the party and its leader. He was known for his modern, socialistic and liberal ideas."

"I don't understand," Sardar said. "If he was so smart and brilliant, why then he didn't try to change the mindset of people and make them to realize the faults in party and its leader through the process of education and__"

"My friends!" Khabat interrupted him. "Talabani had never wanted a man like Barzani to lead the

Kurdish political struggle against our enemies. He thought of Barzani as a landowner, a feudal, religious, old-fashioned man who had no credibility to lead a nation."

"But why he followed Barzani, if he knew everything about him?" Kameran asked.

"I think, in the beginning, Talabani hadn't have any choice, but to follow KDP," Khabat replied. "However, because he was too young to ask for the leadership himself, and for another, he didn't have experience and charisma Barzani enjoyed. Ibrahim Ahmad and Talabani had had fundamental differences with Barzani going back some time, so it was clear that a separation was inevitable."

"This is a huge blow for the revolution," Sardar said, "because our enemies are busy day and night searching to find a weakness inside the revolution. When they have found a weakness, they will apply the strategy of divide and conquer. They will turn one against other, and they will use money and power to conquer anyone who is interested in either. We all have our weakness for money and power."

"This separation will do our enemy a grate favor." Kameran said. "How can we fight our enemy if we are divided? I'm sure this will lead to deeper conflicts."

"Where is Talabani now?" Sardar asked.

“He is believed to be in Hamadan, Iran, but I'm not sure,” Khabat replied.

“It’s clear, they are fighting for power, Kameran said.

“If I were you, I would choose my words very carefully, Mammosta Kameran,” Khabat said firmly.

Sardar was shocked to hear Khabat say this. So, they should choose their words carefully? Did they have to be careful about everything they say and whom they talk to? Why we should be careful?” he asked.

“Listen, you are good people, and you are my friends. I don’t want other people to hear bad thing about you, you know what I mean.” Khabat said. “Just be careful to whom you’re talking.” he stood up, thanked them for the dinner and left.

Sardar and Kameran were in shock! They couldn’t understand why they had no right to criticize other people. They remembered what their friends Sirwan had told them; these landowners didn’t like criticism, and they will kill anyone who get in their way.

It had become clear to them if they wanted to survive they did indeed need to be careful what they say and to whom they talk. Here they had thought the name Barzani was a god-like name to anyone who pronounced or heard it. Instead, they now found it might be considered as blasphemy.

They had found that Barzani, like Iraqi army, was spending huge amounts of money on collecting info-rmation on the Kurdish people. Anyone who was thought to be an enemy of the revolution, including Talabani followers, government agents and spies, would face kidnapping, torture and death.

Barzani, like Iraqi government had controlled Kurdistan with an iron fist. Freedom had long gone, there was no democracy and no criticism allowed. There had been neither freedom of media nor free speech among Kurdish people for some time, and no one dared to say anything against the Barzani tribe and their allies. Barzani himself was the captain of the ship, and he was free to sail it anywhere he pleased.

The two teachers suddenly felt isolated. They couldn't trust anyone they talked to, and they were afraid of being labeled as spies or traitors, especially since they lived among people who blindly supported Barzani and who were ready to die defending him.

The revolution was expanding in spite the split between Barzani and Talabani. The rebels assault on the Iraqi army's small compounds, police stations, and military checkpoints became more frequent. On the other hand, the Iraqi army had also increased its bombardments on all Kurdistan.

However, things were going well for the two teachers, and long as they could their mouths shut and refrain from criticizing anyone.

So, because they were inexperienced patriots and didn't want to get themselves in trouble, they kept themselves busy with the children.

One day, nearly three years later, the two teachers were busy doing some gardening behind their school, when Kameran heard an airplane. He imagined that all rebels in the town were running to their posts and take their positions. He stood up and listened carefully, and then he asked Sardar if he heard the noise too.

"Yes…but it must be very far away," Sardar said.

They waited but nothing happened this time. Then Kameran had an idea. "Sardar, come here," he said. "What will happen if there were an air raid? With all these kids, it will be catastrophe! I think we should dig a shelter for the kids. What do you think? you're still the smartest."

The two teachers looked around and found a place between the back wall and the hill that protected the school. It seemed the ideal place. They could make a somewhat larger room with very low roof. "We will ask Sddiq to help us with it," Sardar said. "We should be able to get this done, now that is the summer break."

The next day the digging had already started and all was going according their plan. They wanted the dug-out area to big enough for all children, and they wanted to put in as many sandbags as possible for protection. In a week, they had finished it. They exercised few times with the children, who laughed and thought it was fun. "This is the best idea anyone has thought of. Now we can save at least some of our children. Thank you, my friends," Sddiq said.

Three months after they had built the shelter, one day in late October, the children were busy in their classroom studying and singing, when suddenly they heard Russian-made MiG fighter jets. The two teachers rushed the children into the new shelter. They evacuated everyone from the school within minutes.

The rebels too, spread themselves out of harm's way. Many ran to the mountains, while others jumped to the anti-aircraft machine guns that had been installed to protect the rebels and the town.

The airplanes roared two-by-two over the town, dropping their payloads of bombs where they could find targets. The rebels fired back at them, and there was chaos everywhere. Women ran screaming, lost and terrified by the sound of exploding bombs.

The two teachers sat in the shelter with the children, doing their best to ease the fears of the kids. They were all crying. Some wanted their moms; others wanted to go home. Sardar's favorite student Arras was sitting tight up against him, holding onto his arm. The children were terrified, but then Kameran started to sing, and asked the children to sing too. Slowly the others followed, and that eased the tension.

For more than half an hour, the four planes dropped all the bombs they were carrying on the town and its surroundings. Then they left and there was silence. The two teachers were singing when Khabat came to the shelter. “Come out, it’s finished,” he said. He grabbed two kids and went out.

They came out slowly. All around them, they saw smoke, fires and people crying or looking for their children and relatives. Most of the children ran off to find their parents. It was a horrible scene to witness. Few people were killed and several seriously injured, but fortunately the children escaped unharmed.

Sardar barely noticed that Arras was still holding his hand, but when he became aware of the small shaky hand in his, Sardar looked down at the boy. Arras was looking up at Sardar. He appeared to be so scared, that he couldn’t cry. He remembered his own son Aram, took the frightened boy in his arms and went to find his mother. Sardar found the mother sitting on the doorstep, sobbing even though she wasn’t injured. The raid made her so confused she didn’t know what to do. When she saw Arras with Sardar, she burst into tears, as if she would never see her son again, and yet here he was, safe and sound.

Sardar put down the boy. Arras walked, then he ran as fast as he could, throwing himself into his mother's open arms, the best place, a fortified castle, for a terrified child. Sardar turned back and went to help the other wounded people. He thought many were dead, but fortunately, there were only two casualties and five injured.

"I now realize that we are dealing with an enemy that has no pity on women, children, or the elderly," Sardar said.

"Well, it's better to learn that now that later," Kameran said.

"It isn't only the Iraqi army we are fight with," Sardar said, sighing, "We are in a bigger game. We are dealing with superpower. We are in the middle of what they call it 'Cold War'."

"Iraq has signed deals with the Soviet, and they renew those deals every year. Through those arms deals, the Soviet Union supplies weapons to Iraq, although they know that Iraq is involved in a bloody civil war with Kurds. And Iraq is using those weapons against its own people.

"Although, Russian-exported-communism was quickly spreading, and as most people considered Russians to be a friend to repressed people, but in eyes of Russians Kurds weren't repressed people, just a disease for Iraqi regime. Iraq has allied itself with the Soviet-Union. America is helping Iran and Turkey; the Soviets are helping Syria and Iraq. and they are both doing everything they can to keep it that way.

"The Soviet wants Iraq to remain a Russian ally, and they have supplied Iraq with its modern weapons and its technology. As for America, on the one hand, they don't care much about what goes on inside Iraq, but on the other, they don't want to anger the Russians more than they have already with the missile crises."

"Don't you think one day one of the two super powers will help us? Will they be a player in the game?" Kameran asked.

"No," Sardar replied, "and let's not be ignorant. Neither Russians nor American have any idea what we want. They don't see that we are fighting for our freedom. They see a bunch of armed men killing each other for their own interests. I once read that one western leader, described the Kurds as a bunch of nomads, an uncivilized people in the mountains. We have no one to blame but ourselves." He sighed again. "I miss my family, and I want to see them, I can't take it anymore! It has been almost three years since we saw our families. it's unfair!"

"I miss my family too," Kameran said, "but we can't go back. it's too risky for us and for them too. We will just have to wait and see what will happen."

The two teachers spent their most of their time

helping the children do their work. They had also begun to help the rebels learn reading and writing as well; half of the men in the rebel forces were illiterate, so the two teachers had set up a night class for them. They had to consider the benefit of traveling to other villages and learning a little more about their country. They had seen for themselves what was going on in the life of poor villagers.

Qassim's government didn't last long, but he and his regime succeeded in leaving a legacy of hatred among the Iraqi people. It created a new ideology among majority Sunni Arabs, that Iraq is a Sunni Arab country and the minorities such as Kurds, Armenians, Assyrians, Turkmen, or Jews, had no right.

However, after the overthrown of the British-made-monarch, few other governments had come to power, but none of them were civilian, all of them were military generals, Sunni Muslims Arabs. The power struggle among different fraction of the Arab tribes led to the destruction of Iraq and division among people.

In February 1963 Qassim's regime was toppled by another Arab army general, this one even worse. It was the same military regime but a different leader. He continued the strategy to Arabize Kurdistan.

However, he didn't last long either, and 1966, he was ousted by his brother, another army general, who didn't come to change things and listen to the demand of Iraqi people, but to continue as his ancestors had, terrorizing all Iraqi people. He ruled Iraq with an iron fist, and finally he too was kicked off his throne, only to be replaced by another Arab Sunni Muslim military general. This period was the birth of the Ba'ath Party and the death of all hope Iraqi people had.

Ahmad Hassan Al-Baker was one of the founder of the Ba'ath party, which was and still is the most dangerous political party that has ever existed in Arab countries.

He and his followers believed in one Arab land, which stretched from Morocco in the west to Iraq in the east, one nation and one religion. Everyone else was considered of the enemies of the great Arab nation and had no place the great Arab land.

He brought Islamic fascist ideology from the dark age to modern time, forcing other to leave their religions, cultures, traditions and ethnicity to become Arabs. That was the ideology of the Ba'ath party.

Dawood invited Salih and his son Sirwan for supper. The three men were still totally broken by their loss. Smko had been their pillar when they need support, and now they had to support each other during difficult times.

"It appeared to me that the Iraqi people may have

preferred the monarchy and the British," Dawood said in a sarcastic tone. "Within a few years we have seen four army generals come and go. it's a sign that no one really cares about the Iraqi people. All of them were struggling for power to control the Iraqi wealth and through controlling the wealth, they could control the people, just as much as our Kurdish leaders were doing to Kurdish people. In fact, there is no difference between Kurdish leaders and Iraqi leaders."

"As we all know, the situation is going from bad to worse for all Iraqi, but especially for Kurds," Salih said. "The new government has passed a new law concerning the military service. It says that all male who are at least eighteen and not going to school, and who have not been exempted for any medical reason, have to do two years of compulsory service." he looked at his son Sirwan, with much worry in his eyes, because Sirwan and Saman were the two men who were ready to be called for service. "Be careful, my son."

"That is a big blow for many Kurds. No one wants to serve in an army that has killed thousands of innocent Kurds," Sirwan said.

"There are already many young men who have fled the territory controlled by the government and taken refuge within the rebel-controlled territories. That has caused an extraordinary increase in the numbers of Peshmarga," Salih told his son.

"I know what do you mean, Dad. I'll be careful, don't worry, and if there are any dangers, I'll leave."

"The pressure on the people is too much to bear," Dawood said. "People are praying for a miracle to happen, but there are no miracles for us." He chuckled. "Did you notice that half of the young men have already left the city? Mostly they have joined the rebels. Others have stayed in the villages with friends and relatives, far away from the government's reach, but that isn't long-term solution for most of people. People need revenue to support their families, and if they are hiding in the villages or anywhere else, they can't work. No work means no revenue."

The men were engaged in their usual conversation, about politics and the situation of their families, trying to find a way to protect Sirwan and Saman from having to join the army. Dawood and Salih knew many people in the government, so they paid to get temporary papers for Sirwan and Saman, but they must be very careful not to tell even their closest friends that they had done that.

Late in the afternoon one day in early 1966, Salih came running home to tell his son the good news. He realized it was the worst news anyone could tell a Kurd, but he was a father, and he didn't want to see his only son to be executed publicly.

Sirwan came out from his room and saw his father was out of breath. "What happened, Dad?" Sirwan asked his father.

"I was running," Salih said. "Let me catch my breath." he paused. "The miracle people were waiting for has finally happened, in the right time and right place."

"What miracle are you talking about, Dad?"

"Talabani has decided to leave the KDP forever and join the government against Barzani and his forces." Salih tried to explain the situation to his son.

Sirwan could not believe what he was hearing. His knees wouldn't hold him up anymore, and his legs involuntarily bent. He sat on the floor. "What a disaster!" he cried. "It's a tragedy, it's not a miracle, Dad! it's the end of our future!" he was almost sobbing.

His wife, Nazanin came out and sat next to him. She put her arms around him and said, "don't worry, Sirwan. It will be okay. Please don't worry." she tried to comfort him, but her effort was in vain.

In 1964 just few years after Talabani had joined Barzani to fight for independent Kurdistan, he and his followers, separated from the KDP and fled to Iran and resided in a city of Hamadan in the Iranian Kurdish territories. However, after few years, they knew they couldn't stay in Iran forever, and they were forced to leave Iran. So, as he was a lawyer, he knew how to deal with situation like the one he had found himself in, so he quietly approached the Iraqi government and begged for forgiveness and swore that he would be a good and loyal servant to Iraqi government.

Few weeks after intense negotiation, Talabani had returned into the arms of the Iraqi authority, he arrived in Slaymany with his followers. Talabani left Barzani and returned to Iraqi government. He has dropped his pants and knelt to swear that he will be loyal to the Iraqi government and its leader and will be the protector of the Arab nation.

As soon as he arrived in Slaymany, government had guaranteed amnesty for all his followers and they got permission to have their own party head-quarter in the city, and they were provided as much weaponry and other necessary things needed for him and his followers. They would have a salary and in return, Talabani and his armed forces would provide security and order to the city and prevent the Barzani's forces to attack the city.

Talabani was a lawyer by profession, and what lawyers do, is to win no matter whom they defend, criminal or innocent alike, it doesn't matter as long as they win. Talabani is not better than any other lawyer. He wants to win and it doesn't matter who loses.

The family, like many other families, gathered again to discuss the situation and try to find a way to deal with the new development. Sirwan still was angry and didn't know what to do. "Talabani like Barzani, doesn't care how many men and women sacrifice their lives for Kurdistan, or how many children will be without father or how young girls become widow." Sirwan said. "Neither Talabani nor Barzani are ever able to see a bigger picture. They can't see that they could fight together to victory, then let the people decide who is better, and through the process of democracy. They are fighting for the control of Kurdistan's resources."

"There are mixed feelings everywhere," Salih said. "The news was shocking for many and a great relief for the others. People are divided. Half of them love Talabani and the other half hate for what he has done."

"I believe that Talabani's differences with Barzani weren't ideological but personal," Saman said, and for the first time he gave his opinions on politics. "Talabani, as everyone knew, very much wanted the leadership of the Kurdish movement under his control, as much as the Iraqi leader killed one another just for the control of the leadership. He also thought that he was a better man than Barzani to lead the Kurdish movement. But his choice of how to fight the enemy, in that effort now is completely dangerous and unpatriotic. Everyone knew Barzani's intention from his long history of struggle for Kurdistan, but now Barzani is the hero, and Talabani is the traitor. Just look and see during few months of his reign in the city of Slaymany, Talabani has already earned the most shameful and humiliating title, "*Jash*", foal or young donkey. Others calling him '*Mam Jalal*' the pimp or "*Rewee*", the fox."

"But everyone knew Barzani's intentions weren't the freedom of Kurdistan, but the enslavement of Kurdish people into the darkness of religion and the landowners' grips," Sirwan said.

"That is not completely true, son," Salih replied. "If everyone knew Barzani's intentions, he would be alone in the mountains. But look, now there are many thousands of young men ready to die for him."

"You know Talabani's action will have many consequences for our nation," Dawood said. He paused. "One of them will be that it will create a vacuum. The young, energetic, and the intellectual people might lean toward Barzani rather than Talabani, but not because they see Barzani is better than Talabani. On the contrary, they are left with a difficult choice; they can choose a traitor who was ready to participate in the killing of innocent Kurds, or they can choose a man who decided to fight with only few men, who, with few rifles in the high mountains, began the fight and will continue. Most of people became aware of the conflict as a personal conflict started by Talabani, and it was he who left the KDP, and it was he who decided to join government forces to fight Barzani. Talabani has made people see that Barzani wasn't the traitor. No, he is still in the mountains and fighting."

In the beginning, things went well for Talabani and his followers, but after a year, it became clear, even to of his followers that things weren't going as they thought they would. Leaders that Talabani assigned to be responsible for the security and city's management, becoming more and more arrogant and irresponsible. Corruption took roots in their souls, and they were blinded by the flow of money and power. They were driving new vehicles and getting everything, they ever dreamed of without doing anything for poor people.

He had created a small army for himself from the most ruthless criminals and thugs in the city and its surrounding. They had nothing to do, except sitting in their few pick-up trucks, fully-armed, as if they were in the battlefield, and go around city. They were pretending to be the protectors of the poor. They didn't protect them, but they scared them, insulted them, but whenever they heard people calling them Jash, they wanted to crawl back under their rocks like cockroaches.

Soon they stopped pretending to be the protectors the Kurds. Instead, they began eliminating anyone who might be a member or a follower of the KDP. The kidnapping of innocent people, the tortures, and the imprisonment of suspected KDP followers were all getting scarier by the day.

Nonetheless, the attacks the Talabani forces and their basses in the city, by KDP's rebels were on the rise too. Every night there were one or two homes destroyed by the rebels' rockets. Their hunts for each other became daily routine. Brother-killing had started. Both sides forgot the enemy, the Iraqi government. Instead they were hunting each other.

In Slaymany, life under the Talabani's control was very difficult for people. They were worse off than they had been with the Iraqi army. Anyone who dared to criticize them would be eliminated within twenty-four hours, yet people wouldn't stop their sharp criticism. Among the sharpest critics was Sirwan. Anywhere he had the chance, he criticized them. He had become their number one enemy. Sirwan's father begged him to stop. "They will kill you someday," he used to tell his son.

Sirwan, Saman and many other young men had been spared from military service, and that was because of Talabani's betrayal, but that didn't make him lovable; on the contrary, most people had come to realization that he too was crazy as the entire Iraqi psychopathic government.

Sirwan had sacrificed his entire life to raise people's awareness about the two clans, Talabani and Barzani that fighting each other, pretending to be the liberators of the Kurdish people. He wrote in newspapers whenever he was allowed, he had given speeches and he criticized them at every opportunity he got. That angered Talabani and his followers, and they wanted him dead. They tried to buy him, but their effort was in vain, and they tried to silence him but they couldn't, he continued his fight against all of them. Sirwan was as ferocious as ever. The problem for Talabani was that Sirwan wasn't Barzani's follower, so Talabani couldn't accuse him of that. He was Talabani's enemy, but he was Barzani's enemy as well. He criticized them equally.

Salih Sirwan's father worked with Saman in the store, to help him and keep him busy as well.

One day in the afternoon, Sirwan went to the marketplace to see his father and wait for him until it was time to go home, as he often did, especially he didn't have job. "Where is Saman?" he asked his father.

"He went early to see some friends, and he asked me not to wait for him." Salih said.

Sirwan helped his father to put things back inside the store; they close it and headed home. It was already dark, and the two men walked slowly through the narrow streets. They arrived at their neighborhood and entered the street leading to their home. Around the corner of the home next to theirs, Sirwan sighted two men. They seemed to be just standing there talking. When Sirwan and his father reached their doorstep, one of the men greeted them and asked Sirwan, if his name was Sirwan.

Sirwan said yes, but he could say nothing else, for

the other man took out his gun and fired three shots into Sirwan's head. And then the other man fired three shots at Salih. Both fell. Sirwan was already dead, but Salih was still alive, so one of the men fired two more shots at Salih's head, and now he was dead too. The two men slowly, without hesitation or panic, walked away and disappeared into the darkness of the night.

The father and the son were gunned down by hateful men like traitor Talabani, Barzani and their followers, who wouldn't accept criticism from the people they were supposed to help and protect. Their shameful and heinous act resonated through-out the city. Sirwan and his father were not the only one who had been killed by Talabani's or Barzani's criminal clans. Talabani and Barzani were chasing all those who weren't agreed with their policies, and by now it became clear, for most people, that those who pretended to be leading Kurdish people to liberty, were nothing but a bunch of powerful criminals working under the cover of the Kurdish political parties. In fact, it became obvious that they were fighting for monopoly of Kurdistan rather than for the freedom of people. They continued committing their shameful and barbaric crimes against poor people, and there was no one to bring them to justice and hold them accountable, no one to make them pay for their crimes.

The funeral of the father and the son turned into a huge demonstration against Talabani and his followers.

Sirwan and his father weren't rich or famous people, but Sirwan was Talabani's enemy. Sirwan tried everything to tell people that neither Talabani nor Barzani was the right leader, and that they were both self-serving criminals. Every chance Sirwan had, he had criticized Talabani and Barzani, and he wanted people not to be fooled by their promises. Sirwan's ideas were influencing many young and old people. Talabani and Barzani both knew if they allow young people like Sirwan to turn his ideas into political ideology in Kurdistan, and if the young people were given the freedom to do so, they would take power and destroy the entire foundation of a society that was built on injustice and monopoly and was controlled by ignorant religious clergies. They would destroy a society that had been split into two clans of Talabani and Barzani, and they would build a society with openness toward democracy, equality, and freedom for all.

Nazanin, Sirwan's wife felt more dead than alive. First, she lost her father, Smko, and now she lost her husband and her father-in-law. She didn't know how she was going to take care of her two sons, Shwan and Diar. She was heartbroken, and she had become hysterical. Every time she heard a bang on the door or anything sounded like a gunshot, she ran outside to see if her sons were dead. She was terrified. Her mother, Shereen tried to console her daughter, even though she herself lost her own husband as well.

Dawood wasn't the same. He was getting old and

he was worried about his wife Ezra. She was sick and hadn't seen her son Kameran for many years.

Beside taking care of a small business, Saman now had the duty to watch his nephews, all of them. That included Sirwan's two sons, Kameran' two sons and his brother's children. He had to be a model for all of them. His nephews and his only niece all loved Uncle Saman, and he loved all of them. He couldn't live one day without them.

Saman was still living at home with his mother. He wasn't married; he was afraid to get married and have kids. He didn't want to have kids and lose them, or he wondered what would happen if he were to be killed.

Now his worries were greater than ever. He didn't know if he should inform his brother Sardar and his uncle Kameran about Sirwan and uncle Salih's death or he should wait until time solved the problem for him. He asked his mother about it, but she told her son not to tell them. "We don't know how they will react, so just leave it for now," she said, and that was Dawood's opinion, too, so he kept it for himself. But he was tormented by it. He wished they were her to take some of the burden off his shoulders, but he had to wait and see what the future would bring to him.

Life was changing for most of the people, as well as the endless war; the attacks on Talabani and his followers were intensified. In Slaymany, the kidnapping of Talabani followers became routine, and the brother-killing had just started. Things were getting bigger and bloodier. Consequently, life for many of Barzani's followers in Slaymany had become difficult and even dangerous. In cities, towns, and villages, people were divided in two groups, one was the sympathizers of Barzani clan and the other was the sympathizers of Talabani clan. Both clans constantly sought each other's followers to harass and insult. This terrible treatment of innocent people became unbearable. This is going to continue for generations to come, Saman thought for himself.

THE 1970 AGREEMENT

Sardar and Kameran had no idea what was going on in their city. They couldn't contact their families for their safety and the only new they were getting was from the KDP, which was propaganda for Barzani and his party. They never told the truth. There was only one side of every story, the KDP's side of it. They would report on the crimes committed by Talabani, but they never said anything about their atrocities.

"What will we do?" Kameran asked.

"Well, my friend, the conflict between the two Clans has reached a critical turning point that will change the history of Kurdish people and the political landscape in Iraq," Sardar said. "Brother-killing is now a reality, and we have to deal with it. It will never end. It has taken root in the minds of those who have lost their loved ones, those whose sons were killed by on clan or the other, and it will continue to the end of time. It will create a gap, a hateful gap, among the Kurdish people. Kurdish people are no longer Kurdish people, but have turned to Talabani clan and Barzani clan."

"I still don't understand their conflicts," he said.

"They are the leaders," Sardar chuckled,

"They want what is best for them! That is the bitter reality. Now the rebels have to fight on two fronts; there is the Iraqi army at one hand and, if they have time, the Talabani at the other."

the two teachers were doing what they thought best for the Kurdish people; teaching a generation of boys and girls to be more open to other ideas and living in peace meant to allow other to have their opinions and to be able to express them without fear of being killed. Yet, they have to be careful on how to convey their message.

"I'm very tired and I miss my family. I want to go home," Kameran said.

"What?" Sardar surprisingly asked. "Do you want to leave and go home? You will be killed before you reach home! It would be better of us to continue doing what we've been doing the last four years."

"I'm not a member of any party and I'll never be," Kameran said, "but I'll serve my people any way I can. I'm not afraid to be branded however people choose, because those innocent children will be my witn-esses. They will know if I have done right or wrong."

"That is exactly why you shouldn't go back," Sardar said, "because you are not one of them."

The two teachers became even more careful of what they said and did, although their relationship with the rebels and their leaders in Mawat were very good. They were respected and were highly appreciated by all, and they built those relation-ships through their good works. They were never asked what they were thinking and no one asked them to be more engaged in the revolution. No one asked them to be real rebels and take up arms.

Sardar's attention was focused on the boy Arras. He was eleven years old now, and he was always ahead of his class. He was a very bright kid, Sardar thought. Sardar loved his students, but Arras was special, because, probably the boy reminded him of his one son Aram, whom he hadn't seen in five years.

Besides teaching the children, the two teachers were doing a lot of research on Kurdish history to raise their awareness about the history of their people. They were reading anything they could get in the remote mountains of Kurdistan. Sddiq and Khabat were their suppliers. They were good friends to the two teachers; they truly believed what the two teachers were doing.

Three more years went by. Brother-killing had begun and had reached its peak. There was no peace in sight anywhere.

One day the two teachers invited Khabat and another man by the name Ali to join them for a meal. Ali came from Bahdinan; he was a messenger, directly from the headquarter of the KDP in Bahdinan where Barzani resided, for the commanders in Mawat. They had finished eating and were drinking tea. "What is the new up there?" Kameran asked Ali.

"Well, things are happening. The war probably will end soon, my friends," he said with a smile on his face. "How is that possible?" Sardar surprisingly asked.

"You may not have been aware of many things, the negotiations between the Iraqi government and Barzani," Ali said. "It is the Iraqi government that initiated the talk, and it has been going on for months now. They want to put an end to the war and make peace for all Iraq, but Barzani has refused to accept the Iraqi proposals. According to Barzani, the Iraqi government can't be trusted. All they wanted is to try to win some time, and then they will resume fighting again, or even worse."

"So, what else is new?" said Kameran. "Are our leaders going to accept the deal?"

"I don't know," said Ali, "but the talks between them are still going on, even as we speak."

Sardar said, "as we all know, Iraq has had four different governments since the removal of the monarchy, and none of them had any intention to deal peacefully with Kurdish people. We won't be expecting anything from this one, either."

"The two sides, according the sources, which many weren't aware of, have reached some sort of agreement for Kurdish autonomy in relation to the central government," Ali said. "The Kurds will govern their territories. Kurdish language, for the first time would be the official language in all Kurdistan. The only problem is that they couldn't reach agreement regarding the city of Kirkuk, the most oil-rich Kurdish city, but in any case, they want to give peace a chance. According the agreement, government will have four years to complete all the aspects of the agreement. Soon the president will announce the agreement and its contents, if every-thing goes as they have planned.

The two teachers said good-bye to their guests and came back to their room. Shocked, confused and happy in the same time. They didn't know what to believe, but at least they had hopes that they might see peace again and be reunited with their families.

The rumors of a peace deal with Iraqi government were getting louder and louder by day. The one evening, they heard shots fired very close to their school. At first, they were afraid to go out. The sound of rifle shot was getting louder and didn't show any sign of stopping. Then they began to heard singing. It was the Peshmarga and the villagers. At this, they looked out the window, and what they saw made their jaws drop.

They went outside to see villagers and rebels dancing hand in hand. Shots were fired into the air, and there was joy in the village. The two teachers didn't need to ask. They understood the reason.

They saw Khabat. "Join the dancing!" he said. "It's not every day we get autonomy!"

They joined the dancing and celebrated for hours. When they were tired, they sat, drank tea and smoked. The real news was announced by the president, Al-baker himself, and everyone was listing eagerly.

It was March 11, 1970, and the Iraqi president had declared autonomy for Kurdistan.

Two days later the two teachers packed their belongings and left their home, the school and their students.

Before they got to the Land-Rover, Sardar told Kameran he had to do one last thing.

He ran to Arras's home. There he found Arras with his mother, when he saw Sardar, he ran to him as if he were running to his own father. Sardar went to his knees and opened his arms, and Arras threw his tinny body into Sardar's arms. Arras was eleven years old now.

Sardar was overwhelmed by his emotions. He pulled the boy to his chest and sobbed. Arras's mother started sobbing as well, when she saw her son with a stranger who had become like a second father to her son.

"You are a big boy now, and you will need to take care of your mother and sister, Arras," Sardar said. "They will need you one day. But if you ever need me, you can always find me, and if you want to continue your studies, you can come to Slaymany and ask anyone where we are, they will tell you. Here is my address in Slaymany." Sardar tried not to cry, but he was too emotional; he wept quietly.

Sardar wiped his eyes, took out his prayer-beads and put it around Arras's neck. "My father gave this to me before I left home, and now I give it to you to keep. You have to change the cord from time to time."

Arras looked at his mother and she nodded. She couldn't speak, tears were running on her cheeks, she approached them, looking quietly at Sardar. Then without a word, Arras went to his mother. Glued himself to his mother and burst into treas. Sardar turned back toward the vehicle, still sobbing.

They got into the vehicle and drove away. After a while the sadness of leaving their school and friends in Mawat began to dissipate. Sardar and Kameran now felt overjoyed. It had been almost seven years since they had seen their families and friends, and they were very excited.

There was celebration in every village they passed through. It was spring, and the weather in Kurdistan is fabulous, every spring, everywhere you go, everything is green, the trees, the fields and the mountains.

It was the perfect time for celebration. There was dancing and singing on the road, and the villagers invited by-passers to join them. Armed men were everywhere, as if the entire Kurdish people were rebels.

They arrived at Slaymany at night. They were amazed to see their city again. There was dancing going on there, too. The bars, stores and cinemas were open. There were many people on the streets, but they wanted to reach home as quickly as they could.

They took a shortcut to get to their homes. When they arrived in their neighborhood, they found many people sitting in front of their houses under the streetlights. There were many children who seemed just like themselves when they were that age. They entered the street leading to their houses and they noticed that no one recognized them. They were surprised, but then they remembered they both had thick beards and mustaches. That must be why no one recognized them.

They came closer to their houses, overwhelmed with joy to be so close to seeing their families and friends. They had no idea what was waiting them in the shadow of all celebrations.

Sardar spotted his wife, Salma, sitting with Kameran's wife Nasreen and several other women. They were busy with the kids.

There were three or four kids playing under the streetlight, and Sardar could remember himself doing the same with his friends once, long ago. He suddenly realized one of the kids was his own son, Aram! Kameran saw him too, and said, "look how big he is!"

Sardar saw his son had grown and changed. He took a few steps toward Aram and knelt, sobbing. He opened his arms and called out, "come here, my son! it's me, your father, Sardar!"

The boy stood there without a word. Here was a skinny, long bearded man, and he wasn't sure what to do. But when Sardar asked him again to come to him, Aram slowly approached his father and hugged him. Sardar couldn't hold back any longer; he burst into tears, and he was crying so loudly that Salma heard it and turned to see her son in the arms of what looked like a stranger. She dropped what was holding and ran to her son. "Hey! Hey! Get away from my son!" she yelled.

Then Sardar looked up at Salma, letting his son go. He was kneeling, and now that Salma was before him, he cried even more. Then Salma realized this was the man she had fallen in love with long ago, it was her husband and the father of her two children! She went to Sardar, knelled down, and threw herself into his arms and they cried on each other's shoulders.

While Sardar and Salma were crying on each other's arms, Nasreen realized that Sardar had come home with her husband, Kameran. She stood up and began walking toward Kameran, but her emotions were so immense, she fainted and fell. Kameran ran toward her and other women also come to her aid. Kameran sat on the ground and cradled her head on his lap. He was crying, "please don't leave me now, I've just come back!" he was about to lose his mind. He shouted, "please! Someone help me!"

Sardar saw what was happening. He got up and ran toward Kameran. He bent down, lifted Nasreen into his arms and rushed inside the house. "Ge me some cold water!" He shouted. Someone got him the water, and he sprayed Nasreen's face with it. She opened her eyes, and when she saw Kameran standing there, she began to cry.

"She is alive!" Sardar cried out.

Kameran bent down and took Nasreen's arm and helped her to stand. She stood up and threw herself into Kameran's arms, and they both cried.

Sardar, still sitting on the floor, raised his head and saw his mother leaning against a wall alone, frozen and pale. She seemed she had aged a lot. Tears were running down her thin cheeks. Sardar stood up, wiped his eyes with his sleeve and slowly walked toward he. She was shivering, biting her lips in the fear of been reminded of her dead husband. He approached her, softly placing his head on her chest. He sobbed quietly as she softly patted his shoulders.

"Cry, my baby, cry," Shereen said. "I was afraid I would never see you again, son." She kissed his head. I love you, son, I love you very much."

The house was filed with neighbors and other families. There was no time for anything else but crying and comforting each other, but that didn't stop Sardar and Kameran from wondering where Smko, Salih and Sirwan were.

"Where is my father?" Sardar asked.

The room became dead silent. "Please, everyone, go out to the other rooms. Salma, Nasreen, please take the children and leave," Shereen said. Everyone left. Shereen remained with Sardar and Kameran. "What is wrong, Mom?" Sardar asked.

"Listen to me both of you," she said firmly. "Your father was killed long ago." Sardar and Kameran froze. "A year after you left, the army raided his store. He was arrested and beaten to death, and now it's the past. You have your families to think about, and you can cry as much as you like, but nothing is going to change." They remained silent and didn't utter a word for a while. Then Shereen thought it was time to tell them about Sirwan and Salih, too. "There is another thing you should know, and you should hear it from me rather from anyone else," She said.

"What, Mom? Sardar said. "Is there...can there be anything worse than this?"

"Three years ago, Sirwan and his father were killed by Talabani, too," she said, shocking them again. She stood up and left them alone to deal with their pain, grief and sorrow.

Kameran's parents had arrived, but Shereen didn't allow them to see their son yet. They understood, and they all sat quietly until the door opened and Kameran came out with his eyes all swollen and red. He greeted his parents. They understood their son's reaction to the news and they weren't expecting anything less than that. The joy of their sons' return had turned to everlasting sorrow and there was nothing to say. Sirwan wasn't there anymore! Who would they argue with? Who would share their experiences and with whom they plan their futures?

Sardar came out too and asked Kameran if he wanted to go with him to see her sister Nazanin and her kids, before they went to bed. Kameran stood up without a word and headed for the door, with Sardar following.

Nazanin and her two sons, Shwan and Diar, were still living in their home next to Sardar's with her mother-in-law, Sirwan's mother, who had become paralyzed on the day she had found out about the death of her husband and her only son. She couldn't talk and she was dying. The doctors had given her less than a year to live. She wasn't eating and she wasn't sleeping. The only thing she did was to stare at the door, as if she was waiting for her loved ones to come home. She insisted her bed be moved to face the door. Probably her hope was that someone would walk through the door someday, and it was the only thing that kept her alive. Neither Nazanin nor her grandsons wanted to deprive her of that last hope. They tried their best to make her as comfortable as possible and help her to her final journey.

Sardar knocked on the door and pushed it open. He found Nazanin's door unlocked as always, and he and Kameran entered. Nazanin was tending to her mother-in-law. She had just fed her, and it was time to clean her and prepare her for sleep___if she would able to sleep. The boys were talking loudly, and Nazanin said, "could you please talk quietly?"

She didn't get any response. Instead, she heard her

brother's voice. "How are you Naz?" he asked softly.

She turned and looked toward the kitchen door, and there she saw her brother, her confident, the uncle of her two orphaned sons, and the best friend of her beloved husband. She slowly rose, and put down the little towel she was cleaning her mother-in-law with.

Sardar was still standing there watching his sister. She waited for few more seconds, as if she was waiting to see her husband appears with Sardar as he had done so many times before. Then she walked toward him, biting her lips, trying to keep from crying, shaking as if she was sick. Tears ran down her cheeks as she approached he brother and suddenly she became hysterical. Sardar rushed to her and let her fall into his arms he tried to comfort her, but he was crying too. And he couldn't get a word out. He let his tears run, what could he do other than crying for his lost friend, for a brother he would never see again? The two were inconsolable.

"Those murderers, the traitor, Talabani Jash, the shameless cowards, killed my love and the father of my two innocent children," She said, still leaning on Sardar's shoulders.

Sardar saw Sirwan's mother move her arm, and with grate effort, she managed to pull one bony arm out from under the blanket. She moved one finger.

When Sardar saw her move, he left her sister and went to Sirwan's mother. He knelled down close to her bedside and took her small hand and kissed it. Sardar felt her trying to squeeze his hand. He raised his head and saw two tears falling down her cheeks. He bent down and kissed her eyes. "I love you, auntie, and I'm sorry, I'm really sorry," he said in low voice. He was sobbing. Kameran stayed in the other room with two boys, because he wanted to give Sardar and his sister some privacy. He talked to the boys instead, and then the boys asked his to go and see their mom.

Kameran entered the room. He found Sardar and Nazanin sitting close to the bed where her mother-in-law lay. When Nazanin, saw Kameran, she stood up and ran to him. Kameran opened his arms and took her into his arms. "I'm sorry Naz. It was my fault. I shouldn't let him stay alone here. I should have convinced him to go with us." Kameran sobbed, "If only he had come with us, none of this would have happened!"

"No, Kameran," Nazanin said. "Don't blame yourself." She was crying too. "If he hadn't been killed by the Talabani Jash, he would have been killed by Barzani. You know him, he was against all of them." She tried to convince Kameran. Then she said, "come sit with us, please."

There was a long and deafening silence in the room, until Sardar said, "how are the boys doing, Naz?"

"They are okay, I guess!" She said. "They are going to school, and during the summer they help their Uncle Saman in his store."

They sat there and talking to the boys and their mother. When suddenly Sirwan's mother sighed loudly and was then silent. Sardar, who was still sitting closest to the bed, but his hand on her forehead. He felt strange; he took her pulse, and there was none. He said, "She was gone long ago. But now she has died with dignity. And she got her wish to see her two other sons, as she considered us, she got to see us. Finally, now she has gone to her resting place. In some ways, she was probably dead a long time ago, but she has been clinging to the tiny hope to see us before she continued her journey."

There was no crying, just quiet peacefulness. Sardar said, "Auntie has gone," and he told Nazanin to take the children and tell the rest of the family. Nazanin took the children and left.

"She wanted to see us before dying," Kameran said.

"Yes, she was waiting for this moment," Sardar replied. "It's very strange to know that you are dead but can't let go yet, because you know there are things must still be done."

Dawood, his wife and Shereen came to see what they could do. Sardar told them to stay until he could go and bring people to prepare her for the funeral.

Next day, Kameran and Sardar came out from Sirwan's house, where they kept the body for the night. They held her coffin on their shoulders and were surprised to see so many people outside waiting to go to the cemetery with them to bury Sirwan's mother. Two other men were right behind them, ready to take over with the coffin when needed. They took her body to the cemetery where her son and husband were rested.

Kameran and Sardar weren't aware of how many people were following behind them until the two other men took the coffin from them. Then they looked back and saw the parade of people on that early morning, thousands of people who didn't go to their jobs, but instead come to pay their final respects to the mother whose son and husband were killed by Talabani.

Kameran and Sardar didn't have a chance to carry the coffin again, because so many other people wanted the honor of carrying the coffin of the mother who gave birth to that fine, brave man, Sirwan.

Sardar amazed by the scene. He now realized what their friend had meant to people and he hoped that one day all Kurds would reunite for the grater goal, Kurdistan.

Even though Sardar had now lost his father, Smko; his friend and brother-in-law, Sirwan and Sirwan's parents, he was still grateful for what he had. He was looking forward to better days ahead.

The celebration over Kurdistan autonomy went on for weeks all over Kurdistan. The two friends went to the cemetery, every Friday to visit their beloved ones, who died for an honorable cause. At the same time, both were reinstated at their school and began teaching once again.

The agreement between the Iraqi government and the Kurdish authorities was supposed to be the beginning of a new era in the history of Iraq. It was a golden chance for the authorities to do something for the poor Kurdish people.

Three months passed and Sardar was worried again. "I hope our leaders take advantage of the situation and try to rebuild our country," Sardar told Kameran one evening.

"Don't worry, my friend. Give it a little time to work." Kameran replied.

"Yeah, you're right," Sardar said, "we have to wait and see what will happen. However, I don't have a good feeling about anything. Do you know where the fox is?"

"Do you mean Talabani?"

"Who else?"

"Well, he is not a Kurd. He is a bastard. He loves Arabs and he always did. Some says, he has taken refuge in Syria. He has kissed his uncle's butt Assad so he could stay in Damascus, just like when Barzani took refuge in the Soviet Union. Others say he is in London." Kameran said.

"I hope he never comes back to Kurdistan," Sardar said. "At least he should have the dignity to die outside Kurdistan, after what he has done to the Kurdish people.

"One thing I don't understand," Sardar continued. "First he sold his soul and dignity to an Arab government. He fought Kurdish people and caused as much as pain and sorrow to the Kurdish people as the Iraqi army did. Then he fled with his tail between his legs to another Arab government, where Kurdish people aren't even considered Kurds, their existence has been denied. How can he stay in Damascus and see Kurdish brothers and sisters treated like animal by Syrian government? If he is not a bastard, then I don't know what he is.

"He did the most damage to our cause. His shameful and cowardly actions have changed the course of history! He is as guilty as the president of Iraq. He is a criminal and he ought to be brought to justice and be hanged publicly. That is what I think."

Two years after the agreement, life hadn't changed much for most of ordinary people.

Sardar was restless as ever. He never had a good feeling about the peace brought by the agreement. He didn't have much extra time on his hands, but when he did, he went to other places to see for himself the process of the agreement. He, especially wanted to see to what extent the two sides were committed to it. He was interested in what Kurdish authorities did, and he watched them closely. He hoped at least to see gradual and slow transformation of Kurdistan, but to his astonishment, he didn't see anything that could be viewed as a sign of progress. There was little rebuilding of destroyed or crumbling schools and hospitals and other important infrastructures and nonetheless, there was very little or no help for poor people. There was also no sign of reconciliation among the different political factions and bring together those families from both sides, who lost their loved ones and make peace between them. KDP, and especially its leaders still were holding on their old and corrupted ideas and never allowed anyone from all other political factions, even from young members of KDP to put their ideas on who to run a country. On the contrary, what he saw was alarming. First, from the government side, were the military buildup in Kurdish territories had become the priority for the government. Almost every city and towns suddenly had more and more Arab authorities and the military had built more compounds and checkpoints, both small and large, in the Kurdish cities and towns that were close to the Arab territories. Government had also signed more arm deals with the Russians.

Secondly, from the Kurdish side, the looting of Kurdistan by the corrupted leaders was more obvious than ever. Everyone, whether a major or a minor player, was busy buying lands, confiscating people's properties, especially if they weren't KDP's followers. The KDP was busy giving important government posts among themselves and their allies from other tribes. Poor people were totally ignored and land reform wasn't a subject under discussion, Barzani and his tribe's allies were getting richer and the poor farmers were ignored far more than they had been before. It seemed that no one had time for farmers, whom the entire revolution had been depended on during the many long years of armed struggle for Kurdistan. Sardar wasn't happy to see any of that, and he was sure that the next war was approaching when, he didn't know.

Sardar came home one day after visiting the city of Kirkuk, a disputed Kurdish city few hour drive from the capital city of Baghdad. He wanted to see Kameran and discuss his visit with him. After he went home and had some rest, he went to see him.

"I have been looking for you," Kameran said. "Where have you been?"

"I went to see some places and I came to see you." Sardar replied. "Are you having anyone for the evening."

"Yes, I told you about that three days ago. Did you forget? What is wrong with you? You seem tired." A knock on the door interpreted their conversation and Kameran went to the door. He opened it and greeted his friends and their families and let them in.

They all sat together and talked about families, business, kids and their schooling and many other things. After they ate, the men retreated to one room and left the kids and women to have their privacy.

Sardar was first to tell his friends about his many recent visits, researches and his discoveries in Kurdistan. He began by saying, "My friends, as you know me, I'm not as optimistic as many appear to be. In fact, Kameran and I were about to talk just before you came in. Our problem is that we are naive. We don't understand the trick that was played on us, and we don't really want to figure it out either.

"In the last few weeks, I have been in many places in Kurdistan, especially in Kirkuk. As you all know, that was one of the main points of contention in the agreement between Barzani and government. The city of Kirkuk now belongs to Kurdistan, but you should see what is going on there. Most of the Kurdish farmers were forced to leave. Their homes and land were confiscated. They had brought twice as many Arabs to Kirkuk as there were Kurds living there and has given them the land they have confiscated from the Kurdish farmers.

"The Arabs represent the majority in Kirkuk now, so we have already lost the city. The agreement for which we sacrificed thousands of innocent people is gone, and war will start soon, that is how I see it. He paused, lit a cigarette and continued. "Never believe that Barzani and his followers are better than Talabani. They were all aware of the removal of the Kurdish families from Kirkuk and their replacement by Arabs, but they didn't care. They have no time to think about poor Kurdish farmers. Barzani never worked alone, so he must satisfy the wolves that surrounded him. Their claws are stuck in Kurdistan, like vultures' claws on a carcass, they don't give it up easily. They feel they are the God-appointed guardians of Kurdistan and its people, but they also want their monopoly on Kurdistan to continue down the road to their sons, grandsons and so on."

The discussion became heated after they heard Sardar's opinions on the future of Kurdistan. One of the guests took out his cigarettes and offered one to everyone. They all took his offer, some lit theirs and others waited. "Maybe Kirkuk will bring us together and unite us," he said.

"I have thought about that too," Sardar replied, "But if the blood of thousands of innocent people didn't bring us together, I don't think one city will be able to do the job.

"Did any of you see or hear any of the KDP's leaders, or Barzani himself, speak recently? Did they attempt to reach out to tens of thousands of Talabani's followers, to tell them that, Talabani may not be here among us, but Kurdistan is still here and it belong to all Kurds. However, it's our obligation to participate in rebuilding our country, but we didn't hear such encouragement from our leaders, and you know why? Because, they don't care about people.

"The most important thing they should have done before anything else was to reach out to all Kurds despite their geographical differences and tell them that we've proved to our enemies that we're able to stand against our common enemies, and they should invite all Kurds to come and see for themselves what we have achieved. Then, I think, that all Kurds would have stood behind our leaders and die for Kurdistan.

"But they didn't show us anything for us, Kurds to be proud of, and that is, because they never believed in people." Sardar sighed and took a deep puff of his cigarette. Then he looked at his friends and blew the smoke into the air. "All KDP leaders see us as their enemies. It doesn't matter to them if you are Talabani's follower, independent, communist or just a simple proud Kurd, but if you aren't Barzani's follower, you are their enemy. It's as simple as that.

“If we stay alive, we will see what will happen to Kurdistan. The two clans, both Barzani and Talabani, have planted the most lethal poison in our nation’s soul: ‘brother-killing,’ the best weapon to control a nation. We have now become each other’s enemies, and this could continue forever.” Sardar noticed that tears were rolling down his cheeks. He raised his arms and wiped his cheeks with his sleeve.

“They have created confusion and a war among us,” he said, his voice rising, “and both this confusion and war have but one goal; to destroy Kurdistan and control of its wealth.

“I know one thing for sure, that what Talabani has done was a most intolerable crime. But imagine, if he had joined our struggle against our common enemies, whoever they might be. That alone would have sent a message to our brothers and sisters across Kurdistan that one day, together, we will have our country.

“Al Kurds never fought together, I mean all Kurds, from all over so-called ‘Grate Kurdistan’. Despite the artificial borders marked by our common enemies, we are always busy fighting each other. When will Kurds from Syria completely join ranks with Kurds in Iraq? When will Kurds from Turkey run to join their brothers and sister in Iran? Why we must smuggle food from Iran to Iraq, from Iraq to Turkey, and so forth? We have always fought alone!

“The sad thing is we always blame others for our

misery. We always complain that the world has forsaken us, but I think we have forsaken ourselves."

"But why we can't have one nation under one leader? After all, we are all Kurds," one asked.

"Well, I'll tell you why," Sardar replied. "First, if anyone else heard what I am about to say now, I'm sure I would be branded as divider or traitor. Listen carefully. The idea of the Grate Kurdistan is a confusing concept. It was conceived by Kurdish leader and religious clerics, people like Sheik Ahmad Barzani, Qazzi Mohammad, Sheik Mahmoud and Mustafa Barzani, along with that psychopath, Talabani. As you all remember, we have fought the Iraqi government alone. We didn't have thousands of Kurds from other parts of Kurdistan, but don't forget, there are more than twenty million Kurds! Imagine if we were united, as one nation, if we had tens of thousands of Iranian Kurds, tens of thousands from Turkey and tens of thousands from Syria, what a great force we would have. But we don't have that unity or the trust that would glue us together as one nation. Moreover, we always hear that the Kurds are ready to die for Kurdistan if they were under the leadership of the mythical Barzani, but the question is whether Barzani and his family are ready to die for Kurdistan? I doubt that, because Barzani had the support of Kurdish people, at least in Iraq, but we Kurdish people never had his trust. It's like the way that people say in their prayers that God is with them, but never occurred to them to ask whether they are with

God, too. That is our problem. We are with our leaders, but our leaders have never been with us."

Sardar was tired, but he wanted to continue the discussion. He looked at his friends. "I learned a lot from my many years in the mountains, while we were fighting the Iraqi government," he said. "They used all kind of weapons against us; their atrocities against Kurdish people were beyond imagination, yet we kept fighting them, and I don't think for one minute that the government in Iran, Syria or Turkey were more aggressive toward Kurds than the Iraqi government was.

"You see what I'm trying to say. Despite, all the effort of government to destroy us, we succeeded in bringing down the government. Imagine if all of us had stood and stretched the war into Iran, Syria and Turkey. First, we would have brought the world's attention to our cause, and second, we would have sent a message to all those governments that however strong and mighty they may be, we would be united and we would win. But, my friends, that wasn't the case. Take the idea of Grate Kurdistan. Could it ever work? I doubt it, Kurds from Turkey want their won Kurdistan, Syrian Kurds want their own Kurdistan, and Iranian Kurds want their own Kurdistan. If that is the case, then can anyone tell me why it is so surprising that no other Kurds came to participate in our fight during those six or seven years?"

"So, we are fooling ourselves with the dream of the

Grate Kurdistan?" another guest said.

"No, I'm not saying that," Sardar replied. "I just said that if I told anyone any of this, I would be branded as traitor, but yes, that is the truth for me. it's a big, confusing dream, and no one will have an advantage in this except those who pretend to be the leaders."

The guests weren't happy with what they heard from Sardar, but they didn't deny that he was telling the truth.

Sardar lit another cigarette. "My friends, there is something else you will not like hearing," he said.

"Is there anything worse than what we have already heard." Kameran asked

"Well, I have been traveling a lot these days to see for myself the progress of the peace agreement," Sardar said. "But let me tell you, my friends, the next war is very close and this time it will be bloodier. It will be more destructive and there will be more casualties and more devastation of Kurdistan, our Kurdistan. And we have to fight alone."

"How? Why?" said several people at once.

"There have been a lot of military buildups along our borders by the Iraqi government, and there is no sign that there are good intentions on both sides," Sardar said. "Our leaders are busy with themselves, and meanwhile, the Iraqi government is busy with Russian buying more weapons. They are trying to win time to prepare themselves for the second round of destruction of Kurdistan, and our people are too naive to see it. As soon as the agreement comes to an end, they will attack us with all their mighty army." one of the women knocked the door and stepped in. "It's getting late. We should leave," she said. The guests shook hands and left. Sardar went home to his family as well.

Alone at home, he sat deep in thought. He was thinking about the good days when he was a boy; he didn't have any worries, and the only thing he needed was food his mother's love and protection. And now he saw that his mother was aging. Her smile had disappeared forever. His father's death has taken everything away, and he felt alone in the world, even though he still had his mother and his expanded family.

Kameran, his long-time friend, and his brother-in-law wasn't the same either. His father, Dawood was aging fast and his mother, Azra was very ill. Now they lived with Kameran and his wife Nasreen, to be able to take care of his mother Azra.

Sardar saw the once big family vanishing slowly right before his eyes, and that was the most painful sorrow he had to endure. His sorrow grew each day, and he knew all too well that more pain would come. He was terrified, but he couldn't stop it, whether he wanted to or not. He was frustrated with everything.

The Kurdish authorities' argument was that the Iraqi government wasn't willing to give any more to Kurdistan and they still hadn't come to a point of being able to solve the disputed city of Kirkuk.

But he didn't think it was true that there wasn't money. If there wasn't any money, how had the revolution lasted almost seven years without help?

There was money, it went into their pockets instead of rebuilding the destroyed villages, schools and hospitals, or into building roads to connect the villages.

They could easily build more schools, they could help the poor farmers with land reform and have better interaction with them. They could educate them about their rights as farmers and put laws into place to protect them from constant abuse and exploitation by the rich and powerful landowners.

They could have put in place laws to protect women from being abused by their fathers, husbands, brothers, uncles and other males in their families, but they didn't as if women didn't exist in Kurdistan.

They didn't do any of these things. Barzani was a rich landowner, and he was surrounded by many other powerful men like himself. The farmers and their suffering had never crossed the minds of the leaders. Building schools was the last thing would ever worry about.

The rights of women and girls weren't a subject for discussion. Women were treated according Islamic laws and they didn't want to change that.

Sardar's brother Saman had finally found a beautiful girl to marry. She was from the town of Halabja. He moved there, and began his own business there.

The entire family was very happy for him. They had been afraid that he would never overcome his father's death.

One day, about six months before the final year of the anniversary of the agreement. Sardar asked Kameran to bring the family and come to his place; he wanted to talk to him. Kameran saw that Sardar wasn't looking very happy, so he asked him what was going on.

"I'm worried that the war will start very soon," Sardar said. "I've noticed more military buildup in Kurdistan. There are a lot of military activities going on, and we don't know anything about it and no one will tell us what is happening."

"So, what do you think will happen?" Kameran worryingly asked.

"I believe soon the war will be at our doorsteps," Sardar replied. "Probably one day we will wake up to the sound of tanks roaring into Slaymany! That is what I think."

"What can we do?" Kameran asked again.

"Well, for now we have to wait and see," Sardar said. "But I was thinking, while we are waiting, we should prepare ourselves a little bit, save money and things like that. By the way, did you check the KDP's headquarter?"

"No, I didn't, but I'll do that tomorrow."

"I don't think that they know anything, and even if they knew, won't tell you," Sardar said. "But I was thinking that we should sell a few things. As you know, we still have three houses we don't need, in addition to my house, your house and Nazanin's house. We could put the money aside in case we need it in the future. At least we would have money in hand if we needed it."

"It sounded very good and rational to Kameran, so he agreed. "If you like, I can get started as early as tomorrow," Kameran said. "But what Auntie Shereen think about it?"

"I have already talked to her," Sardar replied, "and she too, think it is a good idea. We should sell the extra houses and have the money, instead watching Arab soldiers destroy them."

Within a few weeks Sardar and Kameran had sold the three houses. They also sold Saman's store; but they kept the other houses and the other store.

Five weeks before the anniversary of the March 11, there were rumors that the army would soon attack Kurdistan any day and that they would start the war again. It was frightening thought to think about, because people they knew the pain it will cause.

Sardar and Kameran had already made their preparations for anything that might happen. They thought they would know within days and waited for the signal.

Sardar's mother had decided to stay and brought her daughter Nazanin with her two sons to stay with her. Kameran's parents, Dawood and his sick wife Azra moved with Nasreen and her two sons.

Sardar and Kameran weren't sure if they would take their families with them if something would happen. They had a lot of talk about it. Salma and Nasreen wanted to be with their husbands this time, but Kameran and Sardar wanted them to stay where they were. No one agreed on anything yet.

THE EXODUS

It was late February, 1974. Slaymany, "the city of victories and sacrifices," as they called it, was quiet that cold night. Its people slept deeply and without fears. They knew that while they slept, the surrounding high mountains had stretched their protective wings over them, like eagle's wings protecting its chicks. Slaymany was many centuries old. The city surrounded by mountains, looked like and ancient Roman coliseum.

Aram woke up in the middle of that February

night. He sat on his bed half awake and half asleep. He heard a noise, and at first, he didn't understand what it was. Then he wrapped his thick blanket around himself and listened carefully. The noise was coming from the street. He opened the door and ran to his parents' room.

He knocked the door; his mother woke up first, Aram whispered, "Mom, it's me. Wake Dad up and come out."

Salma came out and she saw her son with his ear pushed up against the main door. He was listening to the noise coming from the street. "Aram, what are you doing?" she shouted. "What are all noises?"

"I don't know, Mom," he said, "but there are many people outside. Let me open the door and see what is going on."

While they argued about whether to open the door, Sardar, half asleep and with a blanket wrapped around his slim body, came out of the room. "What are you two doing there? "he said.

"There are a lot of noise out there," Aram said. "It sounds like a lot of people. I think they are fleeing! by now Sardar was fully awake, and he went straight to the door and opened it.

There were hundreds of people on the street and they appeared to be going somewhere, but they looked as though they didn't know exactly where. Their faces were not clearly visible in the darkness of the chilly night. They were carrying their few belongings on their shoulders. Women carried small children and babies on their backs. The older children walked slowly behind them, staying close to their parents in order not to get lost in the crowd.

"Sardar! Sardar!" Kameran shouted. He had come out too. He still was on his night robe, and next to him stood Nasreen, his wife. "Are you ready to go?" he was waving to Sardar to come over to his place.

"To go where?" Sardar shouted back.

"You must have been sleeping the whole night and didn't hear the news," Kameran shouted again. By now the crowd was getting larger and noisier. Sardar asked his wife and his on to go inside and prepare themselves to leave. He wrapped the blanket around himself again and crossed the street through the crowd to Kameran's house. "Kameran, what is going on? What news?"

"Well, yesterday, I heard from our Kurdish radio station that Barzani ordered the Kurdish delegation to leave Baghdad as soon as possible and join their brothers in the north," Kameran replied. "The Iraqi government had turned their back on the March 11th agreement. There will be war as you predicted, my friend. We have to prepare ourselves for a very long and bloody war."

Sardar looked at him and in a very worried voice, he said, “but what will happen to all the children and women? Who is going to take care of them while we aren’t here?”

Kameran put his arm on Sardar’s shoulder and told him not to be worried about them for now. He, proudly said, “the revolution will take care of our families while we are fighting the enemy.”

Sardar was in fact very suspicious of all Kurdish leaders and their ability to protect defenseless families. “Listen to me,” Sardar said, in a disappointed voice, “I don’t doubt the revolution, but I do doubt the leaders. You know very well that they already sent their families abroad, and what will happen to other people’s families is not, and never will be their concern.”

“I know, but do we have any other choice?”

“Did you check the news with the KDP’s office here in Slaymany?”

Kameran knew that Sardar was right, he turned away and told Sardar not to be too worried.

Sardar looked at Kameran’s face and he immediately knew something was wrong. Even with the very little light in the house, Sardar could see that Kameran’s face had turned pale. “What! don’t tell me they already closed their offices? He asked.

Kameran felt stupid in front of his friend. He knew

that would prove that Sardar was right from the beginning. “Yes, it’s true. They close their offices two days ago.” Kameran said.

Sardar was angry and raised his voice. “How they could do such a thing? They just left without putting out an evacuation plan in case there was an attack?”

“So now we have to set our own plans to take care of our families.” Kameran said. “But don’t worry. we’ll stick together and we’ll be okay, and those leaders who left these defenseless families to the wolves, one day they will pay for that.”

“What are we going to do?” Sardar asked.

“We will leave as soon as possible,” Kameran replied. “I have decided to take my family with me, and you too will take yours,” Kameran said.

“But what about the rest, my mother and my sister Nazanin?” Sardar asked. “They wouldn’t leave that house for one day. it’s all they have left! I can’t take that from them, you know that, Kameran. And what about your parents?”

“I don’t know. I asked them and they answered the same way you just said,” Kameran replied. “They don’t want to leave, but I won’t leave my family here. it’s not fair to them either!”

“You prepare yourselves and I’ll go and talk to my

mother," Sardar said and left in hurry.

Sardar was very worried. He didn't know what to think. He went home and saw his mother was sitting quietly on a chair. He approached her and put his arms around her. "Mom, I don't know what to do. Please help me, Mom," he said in a sobbing voice. He explained the situation.

She looked at him. "Listen, my so," she said, "this house, is the birth place of your father. We celebrated our marriage here, and I gave birth to all my children here. Don't forget that you and your children too, were all born in this house. All my memories, both bad and good, still live here like the air I breathe, I'll not leave this house, my son, but you take your wife and children, and your nephews, Nazanin's boys too and leave as soon as possible. Go prepare yourself, son and don't worry about us, the rest of us, we all will stick together as one family. Kameran's parents and Nazanin will come here and we all live in this house and take care of each other."

Sardar asked Salma to gather whatever they could bring, including some warm clothes for the road and some food.

Shereen gave some money to Sardar and told him if he needed anything, he knew he could ask his father's friend, uncle Baram in Qaladze.

After an hour or so, Sardar and his family were ready for their journey. They would have to walk the entire way to Qaladze, because in this chaos there were no vehicles to take anyone anywhere. It seemed that everyone was leaving. Kameran and his family were ready to leave too. Salma and Kameran ran to their parents to say good-bye. They cried a lot, they kissed their hands, hugged them for a long time and then they left.

Salma came back to her house, she bent down and kissed the threshold of her house. She said good-bye to Shereen, her mother-in-law. Then she turned away and sobbed.

“I’m not worried, you know,” Kameran said. “We are one family together and we will go through this together. We have already been through a lot, but in the end, we will find our way home.”

Sardar was worried from the very beginning. He didn’t want to be like sheep following other sheep. He was very much mesmerized by the naiveté, yet the fearlessness of his long-time friend, Kameran. He was very happy to have a friend like him. He understood Kameran’s naiveté and courage made him an easy target for others to take advantage of him. But Sardar also knew that Kameran would take a bullet for him or any one of his family.

It was about two o’clock in the morning when all of them were ready. Kameran checked very one of them to make sure they had what they needed for a few days until they were in the safe place.

As soon as the two families came out of their homes, they melted into the crowd within minutes. From time to time, Salma looked back to see her home, until it disappeared in the darkness of the night.

"Look at this wave of people. it's getting larger and larger by minute, as if the entire city was on move," Sardar said. He waved his hand over the crowd. "It reminds me of the exodus of the Jews out of Egypt, fleeing from the tyranny of the pharaoh. The only difference was that the Jews had Moses to deliver them to freedom, but the Kurds are on their own and their leaders are not Moses-like men. They are businessmen, and businessmen look for profits, not sacrifices."

Kameran was very quiet, and he didn't reply to Sardar's comments. He just let him pour his anger instead keeping it inside. They walked through the night in one single column to keep an eye on each other. They didn't care how other people planned their journey, but for them, staying together was essential. The boys had taken the lead, and the two men brought up the rear, they kept the girl, Bayan and their wives in the middle.

There were many other families on the road, and from time to time someone passed by them and greeted them warmly. By the time they reached the foot of the mountains, it was just before dawn.

Kameran asked the boys to stop. "We will take a break here. And sons, we can't go on like this, we are going too fast."

But they'd reason to go fast; they must reach the mountains before daybreak. They knew what their enemy too well. They knew well what will happen if the jet fighters started bombing. They knew that they didn't have any protection here and they would all be easy targets.

The sun rose slowly behind the mountains and gave people hope for another day. As the sun rose, the two families saw there were many other taking a break as well. "I can't believe my eyes," Kameran said. "We have been walking as if we were sheep. We didn't notice that the entire city is out! What are we going to do? There won't be enough room for all these people in any nearby village. We have to continue our journey till we reach the nearest Peshmarga base, they will tell as what we should do. What do you think Sardar?"

Sardar shook his head, "I don't know what to say." "Don't worry about finding a place now," Nasreen told her husband. "If you could, go gather some wood so we can make a fire and make some tea. You know those kids are hungry."

The boys and their fathers all went to gather wood.

Even that wouldn't be easy, because of this time of year it was difficult to fine dry wood. It was still winter. But they came back, lucky enough to have found few tree branches. Quickly Sardar tried to make a fire and after few tries, he succeeded. And then the boys took two big kettles they were carrying and left in search of water.

Slowly the sun lit up the whole mountainside, and then they could really see how many people had already left the city. "This is not a good," Sardar said and shook his head. "If the rumors are true, we will be dead before we even have time to drink some tea."

"Why?" Kameran quietly asked.

"Well, according to the report you heard on the radio, the Iraqi army has been on the move for a few days already, right?" Sardar said. "As you know, every time the army advances, they have air raids first to clear a path and make it easier for them to move. Well look around. What do you see? You see nothing but defenseless people. A raid would kill half of them."

"That's true, but what can we do?" Kameran asked. "We? Who are we?" Sardar replied in an angry tone. "They should have thought about that before they encouraged people of to flee!"

"Who do you mean by 'they'?" Kameran asked.

"The leaders, those who always pretend to be the protectors of those defenseless people," Sardar said

Kameran noticed the tone in his friend's voice, and he knew that he was right, but he didn't want to admit it. "I'm sure nothing will happen. We will rest a little more and then we will continue on the road." he said.

They boys came back with their kettles full of water. "Dad, I think people have started to do back to the city," Aram told his father. "We saw many people packing back up and heading home."

Sardar stood up and looked around. "What the hell do those people think they're doing?" he cried out loudly. "Have they lost their minds? Why they are going back if they know the army is heading toward the city?"

Salma, Nasreen and Bayan were busing preparing some breakfast for all of them to eat. Salma told her daughter to take care of the fire while she went to talk to her husband. She went over to Sardar and took his hand. "Don't worry, we will be okay, we are all together," she said. "Come and have something to eat, and then we can all decide what is best thing for us to do."

He kissed her on her forehead, "You're right, my dear. I shouldn't be so worried and make all of you worried, too."

Twenty-four hours after the two families left their home in Slaymany, they arrived in a village behind the mountains. They were extremely tired; they were covered with mud to their knees. They were soaked in sweat and the cold February breeze made their bodies shiver even more.

There were many other families who arrived before them and many single young men wandering aimlessly through the village. Many other were gathered in front of the village's mosque.

Kameran told the boys to stay with the family while he and Sardar went to see if they could find a space in the mosque. Traditionally, mosques, besides being for the religious purposes, are also used as guest houses for travelers who needed shelter for one or two days.

Sardar and Kameran found the mosque were overcrowded with young men, mostly students. There was no place for one more single person in there.

Sardar looked at Kameran; he had a worried look in his face. He didn't know what to do. "Let's ask someone in there if they know who is the responsible in this village, or who could we talk to," Kameran told Sardar. "Maybe we could get some help."

"That is a good idea," Sardar replied. They went into the mosque. The air inside was too thick to breathe, because there were too many people in there. Wet clothes were hung everywhere to dry, and the stink of old wet socks irritated their eyes. Some of the people were still sleeping; others were gathered in small groups, engaged in heated discussion without end.

Sardar saw two young men, eighteen or twenty years old, sitting close to the door, who looked like brothers. "Do you see those two young men?" Sardar said.

"Yes, I see them," Kameran replied. "They look very familiar; do you think they are Baker's sons?"

"I think they are," Sardar replied. They walked toward them and when they were close, "Hewa?" Sardar said to the older one.

"Yes, what can I...mammosta Sardar?" He said, and grabbed Sardar's hand and shook it. How are you?"

Sardar and Kameran greeted the two brothers; they all knew each other. Hewa and his brother Hawar were the two sons of their friends. "We left Slaymany yesterday and we are trying to get to Qaladze, but it seems we are stuck here," Kameran explained to them. "We don't have a place to stay yet, and the kids are very tired. They can't go on." "Are all the family here with you?" Hewa asked.

"Yes, they are outside," said Sardar.

"They will be happy to see you here," Kameran said

They all went out, and Hewa said, "I believe I can do something. Come with me. We will find a place for tonight."

The two brothers found the rest of the family standing and shivering in front the mosque. They looked tired and hungry. However, when they saw Kameran and Sardar come out with the two young men, they greeted them; they too recognized who they were.

"Come with me I'll take you to the man how is responsible in the village." Hewa said. "There are few Peshmargas there; they arrived yesterday. I think they represent the KDP, so you could ask them if you want."

He led the two men to the house of the Imam of the mosque, where the Peshmargas were staying. Sardar turned and looked at the family for a long moment. He never saw his family so helpless, so desperate and then he turned to Kameran, "If anything happens to anyone of them, I'll chase those shameless leaders, I promise you that." He said.

They all stood in front of the house while Kameran went inside. There were few women working and few children played nearby. Kameran greeted the women, and asked if the Imam was at home; he wanted to talk to him. One of the women ran to another room, while the older woman stayed and continued working, "yes, he is here," she replied with an unwelcoming voice, and she pointed to where the young woman had gone. "She went to bring his to you."

"Thank you!" Kameran replied. It didn't take long

before an old man in his fifties came out, wearing the white beard and turban that indicated his religious authority in the village. He approached Kameran and stretched out his hand; Kameran grabbed it in both hands and shook it.

"What can I do for you, my son?" the Imam asked.

Kameran quickly understood that he wouldn't get any help form him. It was relevant that the Imam and the people in the village were tired of all the people they had already sheltered and fed. "We are two families, and just arrived from Slaymany," Kameran said. "We have been walking more than a day and we would appreciate it if you could find a place to stay for one night. We will leave early in the morning." Before the Imam had time to answer, two young armed men came out. They greeted Kameran warmly and asked him if they could be of any help.

The Imam explained to them what the young man needed, and he added that he didn't have any room.

One of the armed men respectfully asked the Imam for permission to take care of the man and his families. "Come with us," he said to Kameran.

Kameran followed the two men out of the Imam's house. "There is the rest of my family," he said and pointed to where they were standing.

Sardar was talking to the two brothers when he

saw Kameran wave to him to bring the family and follow him.

The two-armed men introduced themselves as Peshmarga, and said they were going to Qaladze. They had been waiting for a vehicle to take them there.

The two-armed men went to two or three homes until they finally found a place for the two families. They apologized that they couldn't do more for them. Then they left.

The next morning around seven o'clock, the two families slowly woke up to the sound of their hosts working. These villagers were usually up very early in the morning, but they had let their guests sleep a little longer. The families slept the whole night after the long journey along the muddy roads and through rugged mountains. For the first time, the younger children were feeling homesick.

They had breakfast and with their good night's sleep, they felt refreshed and ready to take to the road again. They thanked the family and then they left.

In front of the mosque Land-Rover was parked and many children surrounded it. Sardar looked at Kameran and said, "do you thing that thing is going somewhere?"

"I don't know," Kameran said, "but let's go and find out. If it's going somewhere close to where we want to go, we can ask if it's possible to go with them."

Hewa and his brother was there too, and as Sardar and the families approached, they greeted each other warmly. “Good morning,” he said politely. “Did you sleep well?”

“Yes, we did, thank you,” Kameran said. Sardar was eager to know when the vehicle was leaving and where it was going. “Do you know where this is going?” he asked Hewa.

“Yes, I do,” he replied. “He has been doing trips between villages every two or three days. Today he is going to Chwarta, but there is no room left; he is already taking two other families. Why do you ask?”

“Well, we wanted to leave as soon as possible. You know we don’t want to stay here.” Kameran replied.

We are leaving too,” Hewa said. “We have been here two days, and it is time to continue.”

“When do you leave?” Kameran asked.

“I don’t know yet!” Hewa replied. “We have to wait for my father.”

“Okay! We are leaving today,” Kameran said. Then he shook hand with the brothers and wished them good luck. When the two families were alone, Kameran gathered them. “Listen to me, everyone,” he said. “Sardar and I have a little experience on these roads. I know where to go, but before we go, I must tell you that the road isn't easy. We have to go through many more villages. That is good in some ways, because we might get some rest somewhere.

"We must all stay together, whatever happens to us. We have stayed together before, and we will get through this too. We have had worse time and we always stayed together."

Sardar told the children to go and refill the water containers. Kameran went to the little store in the village, he might find some food to buy. The rest of the family helped to pack their belongings. The boys came back with their containers full of water, and Kameran came back, too. He bought two dozen eggs and he left them at the store to have them boiled. He also bought a bundle of fresh-baked breads, some tomatoes and some onions. He handed all the food to his wife. "This will help us on the road," he said.

They gathered together and Kameran counted them all, as if he were counting sheep. He was laughing as he counted and the children made the sound of sheep when the counting came around to them.

Around noon, the two families were on the top of the hill, when the boys, who were ahead of the rest of them sighed many groups of people dispersed here and there. They stopped and let the rest of the family catch up. "Why are you stopped, guys?" Sardar asked the boys.

"Come here and see. Look at the people over there," the y said.

Sardar and the rest of the family hurried to see what there was to see. They saw hundreds or more people sitting in small groups and they seemed to be having dinner. "They, too have been walking for many hours, like us," Salma said.

"You are right," Sardar nodded.

The men took the lead, and they descended from the hill toward the people. They greeted the first group and put down their belongings. It was a nice day; the rain had stopped during the night. It was the end of winter and the days were getting warmer very days, and spring was just around the corner. But the soil was still wet and muddy. And the weather was very cold at night. That was the typical of Kurdistan's climate.

They spread themselves around to find anything, rocks, wood to sit on, because the ground was muddy. Kameran asked the boys to go and search for some firewood. They were about to go off to do that when the man at the neighboring group told them that it wasn't necessary. "There is a fire, you can use it if you want," he said.

Kameran thanked him and asked the rest of the family to sit close to the family. The women took out the food they had with them and prepared the eggs, the tomatoes and the green onions.

Nasreen approached the neighboring woman and quietly asked her if there was any water around. The woman understood that Nasreen needed to go to relieve herself.

"Yes," she replied. "Wait, I'll come with you."

Nasreen motioned to Salma and her daughter, Bayan, to go with them. They all quickly ran and disappeared behind some bushes.

They sat there quietly and ate what they had brought from the village. "That is the best meal I have had in years! Thank you, Kameran. It was a genius idea," Sardar said.

They finished eating and soon the aroma of fresh tea filled the air. Salma and Nasreen served tea. First, they offered some to the two neighboring men. They accepted the offer with great joy. Sardar took out his cigarette packet out and offered it to the two men, but they thanked him and told them that they were not smokers. They drank tea and smoked. They stayed there about two hours and then they noticed that people starting to move. They too packed up their belongings and soon were on the road again.

By the evening the sky began to turn gray and they knew that rain was unavoidable, but they were close to their destination.

They came down from the hillside toward the town of Chwarta and hit the pavement for the first time since they had left Slaymany two days ago. The hard part was over and from now on, there was a good chance they could travel long distances in vehicles, if they were available. The town was crowded with people from other big cities and towns. One could see the differences between townspeople and others by the way they dressed.

Many stores were still open. The teahouses were open and they were crowded with people. The two families walked through the crowded streets, noticing that people looked at them and examined them closely as they went by. They recognized many people; many travelers greeted each other.

"When did you leave the city?" someone shouted from the other side of the street.

"Did you see any Iraqi army?" another one said.

An armed man approached them. He recognized their muddy shoes and their few belongings and knew that they had come from far away. He greeted them politely and asked if they had any relatives in the town.

"No, we don't," Kameran replied.

"Okay, if you don't mind, come with me. I'll take you to the KDP's office. They can find you a place there," the young man said.

They followed the young man through the crowded street until they arrived to a big two-story house. He stopped in front of it and asked the two men to follow him inside, leaving the rest of the family outside.

Kameran told the boys to stay with the rest of the family while they went inside. The boys nodded.

All three went in. inside the house there were many rooms with signs on the doors. The young man asked them to wait while he went inside one of the rooms.

I hope he can find something for us for at least one or two days," Sardar said. "I wished my father's friend still was alive, he could have helped us. You remember when first time we came to this town."

"Yes, I do," Kameran replied and was quiet for a while. He remembered that day they were with Sirwan. "Don't worry, we are safe, even if they can't help us, we are still together, remember?' said Kameran.

"Yes, you are right. We have walked for two days and we could walk another two days."

The young man was gone for a bout fifteen minutes and then he came back. "I'm really sorry to have taken so long," he said. "You are lucky. I found a place for you and your families. this morning we were ordered to empty another school so we would have more room for the people fleeing their homes. We have already placed many families in one school and now we have the second one available. As you noticed people keep coming every hour." All three men came out and the rest of the family followed them.

"Sorry if it's not quite what you're used to," the man said, and led them to the school. He found an old man who was the responsible for it. He greeted all of them and opened the school gate for them. They went in. "You can take any room you like," the old man said.

The young man shook hands with the men and said, "If you need anything else, I'll be in the office."

"This is very good. Thank you very much," Sardar replied.

The young man was about to leave, he turned and said, "by the way, if you would like to have a bath, we have a public bath open till very late. It's just down the street, not far from where we met."

"Thank you again," Sardar said.

Late that evening, after they ate and rested, the boys asked Sardar if they could go out for a walk and see what was going on in the town. "Be careful, son, and don't be late, please." Kameran told the boys.

"Don't worry, Dad, we will be just outside the school," Awat answered.

The three young men went out. It was dark, and the cloud covered most of the sky. The air was fresh, but the cold breeze of late February forced many to leave the streets and go home. There were still many people, mostly the city people, walking aimlessly or gathered in the many small teahouses, drinking tea and playing dominoes.

The three young boys walked slowly and Shwan took out his cigarette and offered them around. They walked in the town back and forth and then they walked back to the school. They talked about school and teachers. And of course, they talked about girls, their favored subject at that tender age.

They stopped under the streetlight. Aram looked at them. "Are you going to join the rebels?" Aram asked.

"I don't know yet," Shwan replied. "I have to see what would happen. You can't just go and ask for a gun and be a Peshmarga. it's not that easy, is it?"

"Yes, but I thought you might know," said Awat.

"I don't know. I have to ask Uncle Sardar. I don't think he will allow any of us to do it." Shwan said. "And just because my father was killed by one group, it doesn't mean that I have to take up arm. I have my own opinion and I do what I think is right."

Sardar came out and opened the school gate. He stood in front of gate and looked one way, and then to the looked the other way. He saw the three men walking. They seemed to be engaged in a very serious conversation, probably about girls, Sardar thought. He was happy to see them becoming men. Then he called out to them. “Aren’t you tired, guys?”

The boys interrupted their discussion. “We will talk more about this later,” Shwan told them. “If you are thinking about becoming Peshmarga, we should talk to Uncle Kameran and Uncle Sardar.” The boy slowly turned and walked back to the school.

The next morning, Sardar woke up early and without waking the other, he went out. It was a rainy day. The streets weren’t as busy as the day they arrived, but the stores were opened.

He bought some eggs, tomatoes and a bundle of fresh-baked bread. And as he was on his way home, he saw two big pickup trucks in the street. A few men gathered around the trucks and they were talking to the drivers. He approached and greeted them. “I wonder if you are leaving for somewhere today?” He said.

“Yes, today at nine. We are going to Qaladze,” one of the men answered.

“Do you have room for two families?” Sardar asked with a great anticipation.

“Yes, I believe we could squeeze you in,” he replied with a laugh.

"Do you want me to pay you now or later?" Sardar said.

"No, brother," the driver said, "you can pay me when you take your seat. don't be late, be here at eight-thrifty. What was your name?"

"Sardar," Sardar replied, "Thank you very much. See you soon."

He couldn't believe his luck. He rushed back home to tell the good news to his family.

He opened the gate and went in. "Get up lazy people," he shouted happily as he went into the room. "We have to go! The truck is waiting for us! Come on people!"

Salma said, "What is going on with you, Sardar?" "Nothing dear!" he said. "Just get the children ready to go and make some food. We are going to Qaladze!"

"How? When?" she said.

He told them all the story and they all jumped for joy. Quickly, they prepared some food and ate. Then they went out to, where the vehicles were parked.

The two trucks drove along the mountain's muddy road, their engines roared as they climbed up. Thirty or more people were squeezed into each truck; there were a few crying babies whose mothers tried to in vain to comfort them. The trucks rocked violently, heaving people from right to left. It made many sick to their stomachs and it was especially hard on those babies.

Many people were getting sick and vomiting; they had to be helped. It wasn't a comfortable trip by any mean, but they had little choice. They were all tired walking in the mud. The trucks made few short stops on the road so they could stretch their legs. They passed through many small villages. A few passengers got off and that gave the others a little more space.

Slowly people left the trucks, until only few families remained. It was early evening by the time the two trucks arrived at Qaladze.

The trucks went through the crowded streets of the city until they reach the city's terminal. The passengers got off and most of them disappeared quickly.

The two families stood there for a while, looking around, breathing the evening fresh air. The street lights were on. The city had the look of an army city; some Peshmargas they saw walked the streets, and others were in pickup trucks, fully armed.

"Well, we are here!" Kameran said.

"What do we do now?" Salma asked nervously.

"We go directly to Uncle Baram," Sardar said. "They live on the other side of the city. It's twenty minutes walking."

"Don't worry, I know what to do," Kameran told them. "Just follow me, I'll let you know what to do." he asked them to take their belongings.

They walked for a while. Kameran stopped and asked an armed man if he could tell them where they could find KDP headquarter. The young man immediately knew these people weren't from Qaladze. He greeted them warmly and asked them to follow him. "It's here, just at the end of this street," he told them, pointing in the direction they were going.

There were many people gathered outside the building, and they could see many others coming out or going in. "Why you bring us here?" Sardar asked.

"Well, I don't want to walk another twenty minutes," Kameran laughed. "Kak Sddiq is here. He may drive us there. Yes, he is here and he is responsible for the entire city! He told me himself that if we come here, we could contact him first."

"I see, Mr. Smart," Sardar said and laughed too. "But when did you talked to him?"

"You know, I have always been smart all my life," Kameran chuckled. "I talked to him two months ago, the last time he was in Slaymany."

They waited outside the KDP building while Kameran went in alone. He asked where he could find Sddiq and someone pointed to his office. Kameran quietly knocked the door on the door and a man's voice responded, "Come in." Kameran opened the door. Sddiq was busy, his head bent over his desk and without looking up, he said, "Have a seat, please."

"Good afternoon," Kameran said. The voice was very familiar to Sddiq, so he looked up and saw Kameran standing there. He stood up and went toward him. They shook hands and hugged each other.

"What I surprise!" Sddiq said with a big smile on his face. "I was waiting; I knew you would come. Welcome home, son! But where are the rest."

"They are outside waiting." Kameran said.

"Let's go and meet them," Sddiq said, and he put his arm across Kameran's shoulder. The two men went out and found the whole family standing there tired, exhausted and hungry. Sddiq approached them and greeted them one by one. "You are very tired. Now I'll send you to Baram's place. Get some rest, eat and sleep. Tomorrow we will talk more." he called two armed men over and asked them to take the family to Baram.

The family followed the two men to the vehicles. They all climbed in and they drove off.

The vehicles stopped in front of a big house, well-guarded by armed men. Kameran gave Sardar a surprising look. They were frightened at first. The two men opened the doors of the vehicles and let the families get out and take their belongings. One of the men rang the doorbell. They waited a while and then another armed man opened the door from the inside. After they greeted each other, the man who rang the doorbell told the other man that this family was sent by kak Sddiq, and that was it, he didn't need any other explanations. The man left the family in and the two other armed men, shook hands with Kameran and Sardar and then they left.

Baram's son heard the door opened and when he looked he saw Kameran and Sardar inside the house. He shouted, "Dad, Uncle Kameran and Uncle Sardar are her!"

His father was in the living room, when he heard his son, he ran to the door. There he found the two families, standing, but he never had seen them like that! They had always been well dressed and well fed, but now they all looked like vagabonds. He couldn't help bursting into tears as he ran toward them with his arms opened. "Welcome my dear family," he said. He hugged all of them and showed them to the living room.

Baram was now the military commander of the Qaladze region' he had around two hundred men under his command. He was living with his big family of seven children and his wife Galawej. He now was one of the hardcore Kurdish patriot, yet everyone in Qaladze knew him for his honesty, and his disagreement with the KDP. He wasn't afraid to criticize them and he was a powerful man. The KDP, had known him for very long time, they knew him well for his honesty, always straightforward and never afraid to say his mind. Therefore, he was very much respected by everyone.

"I'm very happy to see you all well and alive." he said. He ordered the guards to leave the room and he asked his wife to prepare food for the family.

The family first needed to wash and change their clothes. Baram's family did everything to make them comfortable as possible. After they washed up, they sat on comfortable mattresses and ate, exchanging small talks. When they were done, Baram asked his wife to take all women and girls to leave. When the men and boys were alone in the room, Baram looked at them and said, "You have all grown so much that it's hard to recognize you." he took out is cigarettes and offered them around.

"You haven't change a bit, Uncle Baram," Sardar said. "Except for your mustaches," he chuckled.

"Well, it's necessary to have big mustaches if you are the leader," Baram said, laughing.

They talked about the situation in Kurdistan and

what they would have to do if they were obliged to engage in war.

After a while, Baram looked at his watch and said, "It's late, and you all tired. Go get some rest and we will talk more tomorrow." he stood up and left.

After breakfast the next morning, the men went back to the living room, where the tea was served to them nonstop, following the tradition among Kurdish people to have and serve tea continuously, especially when one has guests. A large samovar in the living room ensured that they had fresh tea at all time.

In the living room, they sat on comfortable mattresses, leaning on big pillows. That is another tradition in Kurdistan: people don't use furniture, especially in villages. Instead, most people seat and sleep on comfortable mattresses. "What are you going to do?" Baram asked them.

"I don't know yet," Sardar replied. "I have to wait a few more days to find out the Iraqi government's intention, and more importantly, which I believe, is what Barzani intends to do. You know me, Uncle Baram. I'm not jumping into anything if I'm not sure about it, especially if what I do will affect my family. My family is all I have.

Baram listen to him carefully. He always respected their opinions. "But today it is not easy to make any decision," Baram said. "We find ourselves facing an enemy that is strong militarily and financially. Most importantly, they have an international voice and support from other countries. We don't have that, and we will never have the support of others. We are all alone with our convictions, our mountains and our arms to fight the enemy."

"We have a leader who will lead, young men ready to die, and the rest of Kurdish people are behind us. We will defeat the enemy." Kameran said.

"But we don't know if our leader will really lead us." Sardar said. "We don't know if our men are really ready to die, and I'm not sure even whether Kurdish people are behind us. I'm worried about all these things." He stretched his leg and lit a cigarette.

"Here is another thing you won't like hearing, Sardar," Baram said. "For the last three months or so, Barzani and his advisers have been engaged in serious talk with Iran to try to convince them to support us. However, of course Iran can't and won't support us unless they consult with 'Uncle Sam' in Washington."

Sardar's face changed quickly. He was afraid of something like that. And he wasn't in a mood to accept it. "Of all the Kurdish leaders, Barzani shouldn't let Iran be involved in Kurdish affair ever again." Sardar said. "Not after he witnessed the distraction of the Kurdish republic of Mahabad in Iran and public execution of the president and his ministers in Chwar Chra square in

Mahabad. Barzani remembers his own exile to Russia, and he remembers the inhumane treatment the Russian people suffered under Stalin's regime." he was furious, but his voice was quiet."

Kameran didn't want to dispute that Sardar was right, but he still wanted to know something. He looked at all of them and said, "So what can we do? Or what can our leaders do to make it right this time?"

"Excuse me, respectfully ask that I might say something in quiet voice," Shwan said.

"You are like a son to me, Shwan," Baram said, "and I would like to know what the younger generation has to say."

"I know that the situation in Kurdistan is very fragile, and I think, it needs thorough examination. Kurdistan is not an isolated island, but rather a vast territory with hostile neighbors, most of them allied with one of the two superpowers. Anything that happens to Kurdistan will affect the entire region. Do you agree with that?" Shwan said.

Baram listened to the young man's discourse carefully and he nodded.

"As we all know," Shwan continued, "Iran is very important to the United States, and Iran's decision will affect American economy and its foreign policy. That is why, if Iran agrees to support the Kurdish war against the Iraqi government, it will mean that on the one hand, the US is agreed on that support, and on the other it means that the United States will have provoked the Soviet Union." he paused. "Therefore, America will do everything it can to get Iraq back under its control, no matter what and no matter what the price. I don't know if you follow me!" he said with great confidence and certainty. They all sat listening quietly, and Shwan took that to mean they had no objections.

"The US will never allow Iraq to be destroyed by any foreign or domestic power, and especially not by a group of armed men in the mountains of Kurdistan. As far as the US is concerned, Iraq, Iran and Turkey are much more important than the Kurds. Don't allow yourselves to be fooled. The US knows about Kurdish problem in Turkey and Iran, and they never had any intention to help Kurds, because both Iran and Turkey are US allies. And again, as far as the US is concerned, if the people of these countries stay under totalitarian regimes with dictator leaders, that is better than them having democratic governments. Because in this way the US will have benefit of cheap oil on the one hand and selling armaments to the dictators on the other. If the US is ready to help us Iraqi

Kurds, then why they don't help Iranian Kurds first?"

"You are arguing like your father," Sardar told him, "and moreover, if the war starts, it won't be a war for

Kurdish people, and we will never benefit from the Iranian support. The US has known about the Kurdish problem for decades now, and they have never cared about it and they will continue not to care.

"I'm afraid if we accept an offer from the Iranians, once we get in the middle of it, Iraq will find a way to turn things around. We all know about Iran and Iraq, they always had border conflicts. What if Iraq and Iran began talking in the middle of our war, doesn't that idea send chill to your spine?"

There was complete silence in the room. Some of them took their pillows and changed their position from one side to another, making their seats more comfortable and others got up and went out.

"I hope that will never happen, but it is true and it gives me chill in my spine." Baram said.

Sardar was warming up to the discussion as he smoked like a locomotive, he asked them again, "What will happen if things don't go as planned? Do you think our leaders think the way I think? Do they prepare for the worst? I don't want to scare you" he licked his lips" but as we all know; we aren't just fighting Iraq. We are also fighting the communists and armed militia who sold their souls to small Iraqi government. And don't forget the fact that our leaders still think as feudal. They believe neither in democracy nor freedom for all. Our leaders see Kurdistan as a farm, and what is on the farm belongs to them. They see people as tool that will get them more power. We also still suffer from the most dangerous disease, ‘brother-killing’ the disease that had been planted deep in Kurdish soul by our leaders. Their lust for power gone beyond any discussions and arguments. They use people as their tool for the job.

“There were as many Kurds killed by the Barzani and Talabani clans as there were by the Iraqi army! And they still didn’t come to any agreement. They still kill each other.

“Their conflicts have never been about ideology or who is more capable to ran a country, but rather about which clan will control which territories. You see, Kurdistan suffers from a disease that has no cure; leaders who refuse to admit their crimes against their own people and refuse to end brother-killing. So why we are fighting? And who are we fighting for?”

The discussion interrupted when Salma knocked on the door and came in. “Excuse me for interrupting you, but I need to talk to Sardar.” She said.

Sardar got up and went to his wife. “What do you want my dear?” he said. She took him out of the room.

Farther north, closer to the borders of Iran and Turkey, where Barzani clan had its territories and where the KDP was headquartered, cities and villages were getting more crowded. And the number of Peshmarga force were increasing by the day.

War was inevitable, and the smell of it filled the air. Everyone was concerned about it and people were on the verge of panic; they knew well from bitter experience what the war mean to them. They began to conserve as much as food and fuel as they could.

The Kurdish authorities prepared as the best they could militarily. But as far as the people were concerned, the leaders were indifferent. In Qaladze, there were many university, collage students and government employees who had left their cities and towns and now didn't have a place to live. They have been housed in empty schools for the most part. The Peshmarga's families didn't have a safe place to stay while their men out fighting. There was chaos in every quarter.

The KDP managed to organize themselves and rally the people behind them. Portraits of Barzani were everywhere. Everyone had a picture of him and every store hang a picture of him. Not having a picture of Barzani in your home was considered unpatriotic, and you would find yourself under watchful eyes. Barzani had become 'the Father of the Kurds."

Baram had many more talks with Kameran and Sardar. He told them it was up to them to decide what they want to do. But in the end, they decided to join

Baram and support him. They thought it would be better to be with him than anyone else; at least he wasn't ignorant about the situation in Kurdistan and moreover, he was real uncle to all of them.

Kameran already got a Kalashnikov with many magazines full of ammunition. He was busy to recruit other young men for the honorable cause.

Aram, Awat, and Shwan were all aware of what was going on in their lives. They have seen the suffering of their families and what the Kurdish people had been through, and they wanted to participate in the struggle of their people against tyranny and the enemies of their nation. They talked to their fathers about joining the fight and take up arms. Sardar was opposed the idea. He told them they were too young to be involved in such war.

Aram argued a lot with his father. "The war doesn't choose its victims, Dad," he said. "Besides, this is our war too. We all have duties toward our people, and if we don't fight, who will?"

"I know, and believe me, my son," Sardar said, "but it's too dangerous. I don't want anything happen to you guys, that is all." but in the end Sardar and Kameran agreed to let the three young men and Baram's two sons to join them.

Meanwhile, people from cities and towns were

joining the forces, tribes of Barzani's rivals were joining the government to fight Barzani's clan. The communist party threw its support to the Iraqi army and declared it was against Barzani, the 'agent of imperialism,' as they called Barzani.

The headquarter of the communist in Slaymany, was covered with placards glorifying the honorable war against imperialism and its agents in the high mountains. Now the communist party, like Talabani many years before them, took up arms and become the guardians of the city.

Kurdish people like every other nation has its diversities, whether it is tribal, religious, political or ethnicity. And often conflicts rise among them and they manage to settle their conflicts by peaceful means, but however, in the time of war, when one group takes arm against government, the other group or groups side with government to fight their rivals. Nonetheless, that is what happened in Kurdistan now. Many Barzani's rivals sided with government against Barzani and his allies and swore to fight against him till the end.

A week or more had passed without any major incident; still there was no sign of war. Sardar and Kameran stayed at home with their families. Most of the time they sat in front of the big radio and listened to the news. But there was no good news; mostly there was patriotic songs, most of them praising the beloved leader, Barzani. "You look tired and bored," Kameran said.

"Yes, I'm and I don't have any other choice." Sardar replied. Suddenly the radio host interrupted the song for breaking news. Kameran and Sardar sat frozen.

"Iraqi jet fighter raided the Halabja territories two hours ago, and Iraqi government had declared war against defenseless Kurdistan," the report stated. Kameran's face turned pale as he realized the bitter reality of war and the devastation it would bring on innocent people.

Sardar sat motionless, not noticing the cigarette in his hand until it burned his fingers. He sighed, he was thinking about his brother Saman who now lived in Halabja. They thought Halabja was safe, but they were wrong. In war, there are no safe place.

"I'm going to see Baram," Kameran told Sardar.

"I'm coming with you." And rushed after him.

Instantly the news spread across the city. Everyone was talking about the war; the Iraqi army put their plans into action. They began by moving most of their forces closer to the Kurdish territories to make it easier for them to move around in the region.

The war that everyone had been waiting for had arrived in full scale. All Kurdistan declared the enemy's territory. Every village, town and city in Kurdistan, along with any vital infrastructure. Was a potential target.

Bombing soon became a daily routine. Trees burned in the mountains, roads and schools were destroyed, and many people were displaced from their homes. everything signaled the brutalities of the Iraqi regime.

The Peshmarga were called immediately. They were transferred in every vehicle or animal that could take them to the mountains. The commanders had reasons to believe that there would be attacks on Qaladze soon.

Baram was a respected member of the KDP. He was one of most fearless and courageous army commanders. He was posted at KDP headquarter and met frequently with groups of other Kurdish commanders. They planned defense strategy for their territories, guided Peshmarga, gave instructions, and explained where to move the heavy machine guns.

At a time like that, Baram need men to trust, and luckily, he was surrounded by courageous, young, and intelligent men.

Sardar and Kameran caught Baram just as he finished a meeting and was going out of the building. They pushed through the crowd until they were in front of him.

"What are you doing here?" Baram asked.

"We were looking for you," Kameran replied. "We need to talk to you."

Baram didn't know what to expect. "I'll be with you shortly. Go and sit in my office."

After a while Baram walked into his office and found Kameran and Sardar waiting impatiently to talk to him. "What is going on?" he asked them.

"Don't worry, I have good news," Kameran said. "We have decided to join you. Our team is now under your command."

"There is no one as trust worthy as you," Sardar said. "You always been like my father, my father loved you as his own brother, I trust you with my life and the life of my family and if I would die, I rather die with you."

Baram didn't noticed that tears were running his cheeks, he got up and embraced the two men, "what I'm today, what I have today is because of your father," he said in sobbing voice. "I rather die than to betray the trust your father showed me. You are my sons, and always will be."

Baram was happy to hear that, because he knew them well, and they were the kind of men Baram needed. They were family to him and he could trust them with his life. Baram was a good man, and his love for Kurdistan was beyond question. He was always ready to give his life to the Kurdish people if it was necessary. But he never forced his political ideas on anyone else, especially not on his children.

They were free to choose what they thought was best for them.

At dawn, the entire family was awake. The women and girls were busy preparing breakfast for the big family. Salma, Nasreen and Baram's wife seemed worried and distressed. Their faces had gone pale, and they answered only with nods or by shaking their heads when anyone asked them something. They were in no mood to talk. Even the noise of the children or the radio irritated them. Each one of them was aware of why they were so sad, irritable and scared. Their husbands and their beloved sons were going out to fight, and they knew death wasn't something you joke about.

Their silence was broken when Salma suddenly burst into tears. Nasreen hurried to close the door and asked the girls to take care of the kitchen. The three of them sat on the floor of the kitchen and cried softly together. They understood each other's pain; they were all mothers and wives.

After the three women poured their sorrows and pains out, they came out of the kitchen and served breakfast.

The men ate with grate appetite. They were not worried. They appeared not to fear anything, and it was almost as if they were about to leave for a wedding party. The men well-armed and well dressed. They said their good-byes in private to their families and the families of their friends.

Salma took Sardar into their room. She had tears in her big dark eyes. She hugged him and put her head on his chest. He gently stroked her long, dark, thick hair and then he held her head with both hands and kissed her on the lips. “I love you more than anything in the world,” he said. Then he turned and ran out of as he came out, he saw his daughter Bayan standing motionless, tears running on her cheeks. He slowly walked toward her and pulled her into his rams and held her tight for very long time. He kissed her forehead and wiped her tears. “I love you, my princess, I love you.” He said and let her go.

Salma came out, her eyes were all red. Her son Aram was standing, she ran to him and glued herself to him, “come back to me, my son, come back to me.” she said and quietly sobbed.

Baram was already outside. “Hurry, there is no time!” he shouted at his men. They all went out of the house, yet they didn’t drive away. The whole family burst into load sobbing.

The war took off at full speed. There were battles all over Kurdistan, and the mountains were on fire from the continuous bombardment. Life for many people, especially poor villagers, became unbearable. The Kurdish armed forces depended on the villagers for food, shelter and their animals for transportation.

Moreover, they were used as informants in many cases; nevertheless, they were often accused of spying and were tortured and sometimes killed.

The death toll on both sides increased by day. One thing that made the situation more difficult was the militia forces called the *"Jash"*, those who sold their souls to the enemy. They were Kurds too, and they knew the territory very well. Moreover, many of them had been Peshmarga before.

The war spread quickly to every part of Kurdistan. Every day many Kurdish children were becoming orphans; many young girls who had married just few months ago would soon become widows. Many families were destroyed by the relentless, pitiless, and unjust war. Many dreams were shattered. Hope was lost in the murky cloud of the war. Love was replaced by hatred; brothers became enemies.

The price of everything was skyrocketing. People couldn't afford to buy food. Smugglers sold their goods for three or four times the usual prices.

It was now almost three weeks since Baram and his men left home. They had been in three or four fierce fights. There had been two casualties and five wounded, and his men were tired, but their morals were high. These men were mountain lions, and they had no fears. Baram stood with his men on the top of a mountain; he was watching with his binoculars. It was quiet and there was no movement anywhere.

The men had dug bunkers into the ground, laying rocks around the bunkers to protect themselves. They were spread in small groups all around the hills and mountaintops, and each group had its own guard and a man Baram had chosen to act as lieutenant.

Each group was provided with a military radio to enable communication among the groups. And most importantly, each group had a small radio to listen to Kurdish music and the news.

Baram's group was made of Kameran and his son, Awat, Sardar, and his son, Aram with his nephew Shwan, Baram's two sons and about twenty other men.

Baram had a reason not choosing any outsider for his group. It often happened that someone would wake up during the night and kill his friends while they slept, then ran away to surrender to the Iraqi authorities and receive a large compensation for each Peshmarga he had killed.

The KDP had bases in many villages. Each few days, three or four Peshmarga went down from the mountain to the closest village to bring up supplies for their group.

"Who is going down today?" Sardar asked.

"Me and whose turn might be, I don't know," Awat answered. Two other men raise their hands to indicate that it was their turn to go to get supplies.

Awat made sure he was ready, took his rifle and jumped on the back of a mule. He pulled another mule behind him and began making his way down the mountain. The two other men followed close behind on the back of their mule.

Baram woke up soon after the men left. He sat up on his bed, which consisted of three or four blankets, and he yawned and stretched. "What time is it?" he asked.

"It's seven," Sardar answered.

"Did you send the guys down?" he asked.

"Yes, sir," Sardar chuckled. "It's a beautiful day."

The rest of the group woke up slowly to the sound of a beautiful song on the radio.

"Nothing is missing except my wife next to me," Kameran declared.

They laughed and one of them said, "That is true!"

"But what about me? I don't have a woman!" Shwan said.

"Don't you worry, my friend!" Kameran said. "A handsome man like you won't stay single long. The girls will kill themselves for you, and you tiger, can choose the one you like most."

"I'll find him a good woman," Sardar said. "In fact, I have already found him one! She has flesh enough for two, knows how to cook, and throws her sandals on you when you come home late!" they all laughed.

"Thank you, Uncle Sardar," Shwan answered. "With an uncle like you, I don't need any enemies! You must be thinking about the lady in the bakery." They all laughed even louder.

"I'll give him my daughter in marriage. If he wants," Baram said seriously.

There was silence. It was not usual for a man to offer his daughter to another man, but this confirmed that Baram liked Shwan. Shwan represented the best of all qualities in a young man; and Baram was known as being a liberal and open-minded man.

Shwan bowed where he was standing, then he looked at Baram. "Nothing would give me more honor than to be your son-in-law," he said. Then he turned to his uncle and said, "you see, there still are people who think about me!"

Peshmarga forces were spread all over Kurdish territories. They were on every mountaintop, on the hills and in many villages and towns. The forces were growing larger day by day. More and more young people joined up. The Iranian border with Kurdistan territories was opened, and the supply of food was becoming more reliable every day. Shipment of small American-made artillery began to arriving.

Leaders both majors and minors made frequent vacation-trip-like to nearby Iranian cities and towns. The quality of the radio reception began to improve thanks to new equipment received from Iran. The life of the leaders changed from good to better. Many of them sent their families to Iran to be sheltered from war. But corruption began hatching in some of them, slowly but surely.

It was already mid-spring; the snows were melting, and little streams began appearing here and there. Their sweet, fresh waters ran down the hills and mountains. The grasses were green and tall; the shepherds let their livestock out to graze.

Sardar was standing on the edge of a big rock on top of a mountain looking at the green fields below. "This view looks like a bride in a green wedding dress," he said to Baram, who was peering through his binoculars, watching the other side.

"You are in love with this land, aren't you?" said Baram.

"Yes, I am, and I always have been. Is there anything more beautiful than this land?" Sardar didn't wait for a reply, but continued, "All the beauty you see here, or in any other part of the world, for that matter, will continue to be destroyed by the stupidity of mankind. Soon we will see trees burning on the mountainsides, the pastures will be destroyed, the animals will be killed by artillery shells. Women will no longer wear colorful dresses, girls no longer sing when they go to spring to fill their water pots. We will make many more children orphans, and many more young men will die before even getting married." he sighed. "I love this land, that is very true."

Kameran who was sitting on a rock facing Sardar and listing to his speech and admiring him for everything he was, got up and said, "And it's our job to protect it from all kinds of threats; Iraqi, Turkish, Persians, you name it."

Sardar got up, went toward him and kissed him on the cheeks. "If there were more men like you, we would have our country by now," Sardar told him.

Baram was still standing and looking through his binoculars. Suddenly he lowered them and said, Hush!" Everyone froze. "Do you hear choppers?" he said.

They all Listened carefully. "Yes," Sardar said, "there does seem to be something, but I'm not sure what it is."

Kameran switched the radio off and took up the communication radio. He quickly established contact with the other groups, telling them to be ready. The buzz of several choppers could be heard approaching, but so far there was no sign of them. Baram was confused. "Choppers never attack alone, without infantry," he said. "What is going on?"

"I think they are attacking the other side," Sardar suggested. "That is why we can't see them. We can walk over there in about an hour. Do you want us to go? I'm sure there aren't enough Peshmarga there."

Baram stood there without saying anything; then he came down off the rock. "Kameran call the other groups to get ready. "We are going to the wedding," he said.

"Send someone after the boys who went to get the supplies, they aren't far." Baram said. And someone ran shouting to get the boys back. And when they heard they turned around and galloped back.

Within minutes, they were on the road; and the two hundred men weren't walking, they were galloping like horses.

Less than an hour later, they had nearly reached their brothers on the other side of the mountain. A group of eighty or so Peshmarga had been attacked by army, Jash and choppers. They were trapped where they were and they were bragged by the enemy.

Baram contacted the leader of the group to let them know that they were on their way, and to avoid confusion between Peshmarga's forces and the Jash. They raced on, flying over the mountain like eagles, until their brothers could see them coming to their aid.

They shouted and counter-attacked the enemy. They had the advantage of the mountains; the army and the Jash were on the middle of the mountainside, trying to climb it, but the new enforcement sent a chill up the enemy's spine.

Baram sheltered himself with the commander of the other group behind some rocks so they could plan their strategy. Baram divided his men into four smaller group and asked Sardar, Kameran and other lieutenants to take their men to designated places, which he pointed out to them.

In minutes, they were in their places. All the men had regrouped and filled their magazines.

The choppers swooped over their heads, firing many rounds from their heavy machine guns, and turned to come back for more.

Far away, six or seven Russian-made MIGs and French-made Mirages dropped their bombs onto the mountains, burning everything in sight. It seemed that the entire mountains were on fire. The jets made one pass after another without pity. They didn't discern among rebels and innocent children or women as they bombed villages and towns.

Sardar could see that the battle wasn't on one front. The jets were bombing the mountain where the Peshmarga were fighting with army and Jash. "What did we ever do to Russians and the French that they should be so cruel to us?" he shouted to the man next to him. "Damn them both! They knew very well that Iraqi army would use all these weapons to fight Kurdish people! I don't understand. Both those countries tell the world they are the socialist, protectors of the repressed! Aren't Kurds repressed enough? Or is this all just game? I have to leave it for history to judge."

"I don't know," the man said, "all I know is, I'm not going to die before I kill as many Arabs and Jash as I can."

"I'm with you," Sardar replied.

Four angry choppers, two from the right and two from the left, pelted the Peshmarga's forces with machine-gun fire, but there was no chance to respond to them.

"Help! My brother is hit!" someone shouted.

Sardar crawled like snake in their direction; he found a young man was hit in the shoulder, and the other one was pressing his wound by putting his hand on the injured man's shoulder. "Let me see," Sardar said. The man lifted his hand from the wounded man's shoulder. Sardar looked and said reassuringly, "It's nothing." he took out some bandages from his bag, which carried with him no matter where he went and bandaged the man's wound. "There you go," he said. "Now go back and kick some more ass."

"Thank you, brother," the young man said and grabbed his gun again.

The fight was fierce; the enemy thought they could just come and take the mountain, and if they didn't capture all the Peshmarga, they would at least kill them. But they were dead wrong.

Baram's men would sing in every battle; it would reduce stress, they said. Sardar, Kameran and Shwan were singing together, Sardar stood, pointing his Kalashnikov downward, and each time he saw a soldier or a Jash, he sent a round flying bullets to them, killing them. He sang even more as they fell.

"The choppers aren't giving up so easily," Sardar told Kameran. As they were fighting, someone else shouted, "We have one dead.

The scene was tragic. There were many wounded; probably many had died, Sardar thought as he hurried over to help. Baram asked his men not to waste their ammunition, because he didn't know how long the army would hold to fight.

The choppers hovered over them, firing rockets that smashed into trees and rocks. Sometime they heard the cry of a Peshmarga who had been hit or killed. They were able to push the enemy back to the slope of the mountain, but they couldn't stop the choppers. It was still before noon, and the choppers might fly until late afternoon. That could mean a total loss for them. Time was against them; they knew well it wasn't good to start fighting so early, but after all, they couldn't choose the time.

Two choppers were flying in their direction, and they were flying very low. Baram shouted to all the men to hid themselves from the choppers; the men fanned out. Sardar had been checking on his son from far away, and he was terrified for his safety. The image of his son's dead body came to his mind, it was an unbearable thought. He couldn't imagine what his mother does if...he stopped thinking about it, for it was too painful to bear.

Sardar managed to get back to Kameran's group and asked what they were thinking of doing. "It's too difficult to attack with these choppers over our heads. We can't move," Kameran said.

Aram was lying on the ground. He appeared losing patience with the choppers, and the helplessness of the situation. No one was firing on the enemy, who was advancing quickly. If they didn't do something right away, they would be doomed. He looked at the rocket launchers next to him and didn't move for few seconds. And then like a crazy man, he grabbed one of the rocket launchers and loaded a rocket into it. He looked up and saw the two choppers on the right coming right at his position. He was ready to die, but he didn't want to stand there and be killed. He lifted the launcher to his shoulder.

Sardar froze as he saw Aram takes aim with the rocket launcher, Kameran saw him too, and together they shouted, "Aram! Nooo!"

But it was too late. Fire came out the other end of the launcher and the rocket was flying toward the target like two lovers running into each other's arms. Then there was a load explosion as the helicopter was hit. It was down! The moral of the Peshmarga lifted instantly as the other helicopter veered away and disappeared. Now the army and Jash were left without protection and at the mercy of Peshmargas.

Under the protection of the choppers, the enemy had advanced to the middle of the mountain. Now there were no choppers to protect them. Baram stood up and commanded, "Kill them all! Do not leave prisoners! They are all ours! As he fired on the enemy, the other men gathered their courage and they too stood up, and attacked them from all sides. They were descending from mountain toward the fleeing enemies. The army and Jash were on the run. They were leaving dead and wounded behind.

"Kill them all!" Baram was shouting.

"Slaughter them all!" someone else shouted. The enemy was running for their lives. Baram and his men were jumping over the bodies of dead enemy. Twenty or thirty bodies were scattered on the ground. The remainder of the enemy, those who could run fast, managed to reach their trucks and other vehicles, and they drove away.

Baram ordered his men to stop pursuing the enemy; he was worried the enemy would come back.

"What do we do with all the bodies?" Kameran asked.

"We will come back later with more men from the village and bury them all," Baram said.

Aram was sitting on a rock smoking when his father approached him. "You scared the shit out of me, son." Sardar said, tears running down his cheeks. He grabbed him and embraced him. "You are my little lion, you know that, son? You are the first Peshmarga to hit a helicopter with a rocket!" he was sobbing. "That bastard" he pointed to the crashed helicopter… "is the first plane to fall in this war." he cleared his throat. "You saved our lives today, and I love you, son."

The men did what Baram told them to do and slowly climbed the mountain again. Each man had more than one weapon to carry; they had also gathered all the magazines, ammunition boxes, and communication equipment. They climbed proudly.

From time to time one or two Peshmarga came to congratulate Aram for his courage and his quick action. They reached the top of the mountain. It was now too late for the enemy to make a comeback. Baram gathered his men and asked them to check how seriously hurt the wounded Peshmargas were and help them to get on the mules they had with them. They had five dead and nine wounded. Among the wounded were Awat and Shwan. However, their wounds were not serious.

Baram chose few men to take the wounded to the nearest village. He and five men took the dead back to Qaladze. The rest he ordered them to go back to their posts in the mountain. At the village, people rushed out to help. It wasn't long before fifteen or twenty men were washing and preparing the bodies. Then they laid the five bodies on the back of a tractor. Then Baram and his men left to escort the dead men to their families in Qaladze.

Baram went nonstop to Qaladze. At the next village he found a truck, and with it, the trip took less time. He reached Qaladze in less than a day.

When he arrived, he stopped the truck in front of the KDP headquarter. Within minutes, hundreds of people had gathered. Many were in tears; other cried loudly; still others beat their chests as if the entire city was in mourning.

Baram handed the bodies of the five Peshmargas to the authorities and asked for permission to go and see his family. Next day he was back with his men. They gathered in the village and headed to their posts on the mountain.

The news of the battle spread quickly through-out the region; it had two major strategic effect on both the enemy and Peshmarga. It sent a clear message to enemy that their air force was not immune to destruction by Peshmarga. It also gave the courage and lifted moral among the Peshmarga forces.

It was several months into the war, and the Iraqi army was using every weapon they had in their disposal. The Peshmarga forces, with the help of Iranians, were able to push back the powerful Iraqi army.

Baram and his men were ordered to change their location many times. They lost many men and had many wounded, but they were still the best and most well-known groups in the region.

Baram's group, they were now stationed close to Bahdinan province. It was considered by many to be the most dangerous territory of all, because it was where Barzani had his headquarter and all his family and relatives. The Iraqi army tried continually to capture it, but their efforts were in vain. For four months, Baram's men during many dangerous and bloody battles, they lost many friends and saw many others wounded. They were tired and need a break from fighting, but in the war, there are no breaks. The enemy wouldn't take a break until they destroy Kurdistan. So why would Peshmarga take a break?

One morning Baram's son Bestoon and the two other boys, Diar and Ako, asked their mothers if they could go out for a walk. They promised to be back before the lunchtime. Their mothers agreed gave them little pocket money and sent them on their way.

The tree boys walked to the busy marketplace downtown, laughing and teasing each other. The marketplace place was crowded with people that morning. Most people were looking for vegetable and meat or anything else to take home for dinner or supper.

Suddenly, they heard airplane roaring over their heads, high in the sky. They looked up to locate where the sound came from, but they didn't see anything at first. Then the sound of the plane became louder. The crowd became terrified and tried to find someplace to hide, but it was too late. There was a deafening explosion.

Diar and Ako had been holding hands. Suddenly Diar felt like he couldn't pull Ako anymore, and when he turned, he saw he was dragging Diar's headless body. He dropped Diar and fell next to him. He felt his back burning, and he reached around and tried to touch it, but his hands burned too. A chemical was burning his back. Diar had died instantly. When sharp metal debris had cut his head off. Ako was burning, and he breathed heavily, his eyes scanned the area looking for someone for help, but there was no one.

Everyone had run to hide. He was crying, but he tried to see if he could at least find Bestoon he looked one way and then the another, and finally he spotted him across the way, laying on his stomach. His head was split opened and he could see his brain was hanging out of his skull. Ako stopped moving. He closed his eyes and whispered, "Mom...mom..." Then he went silent and died, too.

There were many, many dead bodies on the streets, and many more were injured, yet no one dared to come out from their hiding places. They feared the plane would come back and drop another bomb. Time seemed to stand still for about twenty minutes. The bodies lay on the street, and the only thing one could hear was the screaming of the injured men, women and children.

The Iraqi army had dropped a Napalm bomb on the town of Qaladze and another one on the town of Halabja. Qaladze had the highest number of casualties, because there were more people in that town and the bomb was dropped in the middle of the populated area.

The town now seemed like a ghost town. Three or four hundred of corpses were scattered on the streets of the town. Slowly people started to come out. It terrified them to see all these bodies on the streets. A few men ran to assist a man who was still alive, but badly burned. Others gathered their courage and came out to see who they could help. Gradually the whole town seemed to be there, but it was too late for any real help. Those who needed medical care were sent to hospital, but there was only one hospital and few doctors. They lacked medical supplies. Even if they had had enough doctors, they weren't trained to help with these kinds of injuries, those caused by the Napalm bomb. Most of the injured were dead within few hours.

The wrenching sound of crying men and screaming mothers filed the air of the town. People beat their chests in lamentation; others were just paralyzed by the scenery. Nasreen, Salma and Galawej ran barefoot like crazy to the site of the bombing. They turned one body after another to find the tree boys., but there seemed to be too many bodies. They continued until Salma and Galawej heard Nasreen screaming, and then they understood that she had found the boys. They ran to her and knelled down with her. The three small bodies had been laid side by side to make it easier for relatives to find their loved ones. Nasreen was quiet; she was not crying; she was just looking at them. Diar had no head, Ako's body was totally burned and Bestoon had been hit in his head and his stomach.

"We will never see them again," she softly said. "We will never see them marry. they're gone. We will never see their children, they..." She burst into tears and wailed loudly.

"I don't know what we have done to those Arabs to

deserve such a death," Salma said. Galawej stood up and asked the two other women to stand up as well. Then she asked two or three men to help them carry the bodies of their sons. "Let's go. We will take them home, sisters," she said.

It seemed there were more dead bodies on the streets than living people. The sound of the roaring jets had created panic in the city. Most people didn't know where to go or where to hide. There were many young university students in both Qaladze and Halabja who fled the cities and sought safe place. The army knew about that through its many informants: that is exactly why they targeted those two cities with their Napalm bombs,

The dead were countless, four to five hundred. The injured were taken where people could find anyone to assist with their wounds. They took them to hospital, clinics, school, government buildings and private homes. Thousands were injured.

The cries of mothers, daughters, sisters, and wives, the wailing of fathers, husbands and brothers, were reaching the skies. But there was no god to answer them. "What we have done to deserve such cruel punishment?" someone cried out.

"God, if you exist, bring death upon all the savage Arabs for what they have done to us!" someone else shouted.

"Where are my children?" A woman sobbed softly,

asking people to help her find missing children.

It was a painful scene to watch. No one could stay there and watch without bursting into tears. It was horrible to see so many dead bodies laid down side by side on the streets. People gathered to find their loved ones, and many families had found their dead relatives; a huge parade of crying people followed those who carried the bodies. Yet half of the bodies were still there, no one knew them.

Half of the those who died in the bombing weren't from the town of Qaladze; they were university students from Slaymany and there were single young men. They had fled Slaymany because their university had been closed. They had been called up for military service, but they hadn't responded to the call. Instead they fled to another cities and towns to be safe. They didn't know that their short lives would end here.

It took everyone in town an entire week to bury all dead and to make sure all injured were cared for. After that, people mourned their dead for weeks, and the town seemed like a ghost town. People walked around looking more like dead than alive.

Baram and his men left their post to come back to Qaladze. He did everything to help his friends in the time of need, despite his own loss, but his friends were inconsolable.

The three families were heartbroken by the loss of their young sons. Sardar and Kameran were mute, as if they have lost their ability to speak. Sardar especially walked as if he were a dead man among the living. His guilt haunted him day and night. It was his idea to include his nephew, Diar when they left, and now he was dead. He didn't know how he could face his sister, Nazanin. He was smoking two pack of cigarettes a day. They buried the three boys next to each other in the cemetery in Qaladze.

Shwan was about to lose his mind. He had lost his little brother and he didn't know what to do or think. One thing was clear, he wanted revenge his father's, his grandfather's, his nephew's and his brother's deaths.

Baram came to Sardar's room. "Sardar, my son," he said. "We are going back tomorrow. If you don't feel like to coming back yet, that is okay." Baram never got an answer. He waited for a while and then he left the room.

Next morning, they woke up like it was any other day, but it was different day in some ways. Salma came to her room, where Sardar was lying on their bed. He sat up when Salma came in. she approached him, took his head, and pushed it to her belly. Stroking his hair gently, "Do you want to go back with them?" She whispered in his ear, "You could stay one more week if you wish." she sobbed quietly.

"I want to disappear and never come back," he said in a choked voice, "never come back to this barbaric world, where the substitute for justice has always been cruelty and destruction. I want my father and my family back." He burst into tears, too.

She didn't answer; she softly sobbed and again pushed his head against her belly.

The rest of the family was in the living room having breakfast, when Sardar and Salma came in. "Come on, Dad, have some breakfast and let's go," Aram said. He stood up and hugged both, and whispered, "I love you very much." Then they all sat and ate their breakfast.

The news of the bombing by Iraqi army of the two Kurdish cities, Halabja and Qaladze, with the deadly Napalm bombs spread fast. People panicked, because there was no safe place anymore. The fear of another attack by Napalm bombs made people desperate to hide, to go anywhere as long as it was safer than Kurdistan. The leaders had no plan to help people, and the world was ignorant about what was going on in Kurdistan or perhaps no one cared about a bunch of armed men fighting for freedom.

Two weeks after the bombing, Kameran was feeling somewhat better. But the loss of his young son has taken toll on him and his family. He and Sardar sat on a rock one evening. Kameran stared out at the horizon, then he turned to Sardar. "Do you think the world knows about us?" he said in a serious tone.

"Yes, I am sure that in this very moment while we're talking, the world is aware of us and our situation." Sardar said, "but unfortunately, they are indifferent. Otherwise they would have done something to help us."

Kameran was startled. "But why?"

"Well, today the world means the Russians and the Americans," Sardar said, "however, they know well what is going on in Iraq. Russian sell weapons to Iraq, that mean they are aware of the conflict between Iraqi government and us, but as long as there is profits to be made, they don't care how many Iraqi die.

"Nonetheless, what the Americans concern, they are busy with their own war in Vietnam, and their involvement in central and south America They are in deep shit there and they don't know how to get out. So, do you think they care about us and how many Kurds or Iraqi for that matter, die!" he sighed and lit a cigarette, "don't you think that they have spies everywhere? Even they have spies among us here in Kurdistan. So, they are aware of the situation, but as long as there is cheap oil to get and markets for their weapons, Kurds are not in their minds as much as Kurdish people aren't in the mind of our leaders.

The two friends were still talking wen Aram and Awat came up to them and asked if they could sit with them. "Do you have cigarettes?" his father asked.

"Since when father asks his son for a cigarette?" Aram said. He took out his cigarettes, and gave it to him.

"Where is Talabani now? Sardar asked with a sarcastic smile.

Kameran turned to him and said, "Talabani? Well, he is in love with Ba'ath party. So, if he is not with Iraqi Ba'ath party, he is in Syria."

"He is really smart as a fox. He knows exactly what to do to stay alive," Awat said. "And I'm sure that when everything is said and done, whether for bad or for good, he will come back and make peace with all the other parties. Who knows? Maybe he'll be a minister one day, somewhere in Kurdistan."

"We have to wait for that one. Meanwhile, while we are fighting here, he will be in Syria watching the situation closely," Kameran said.

Winter was approaching. In the high mountains, there were already a lot of snow and most of the road were impassable. But that was at least partly a good thing for the Peshmarga, because neither the army nor the Jash could advance in winter. Nonetheless, the plane could not fly either. Fighting continued almost everywhere though. Now it was mostly Peshmarga on the offensive, attacking small military compounds. Those surprise attacks on government buildings and the Jash center became nightly routines for Peshmarga stationed closer to the cities. The Iraqi army was under a great deal of pressure from both sides. On the one hand, the Peshmarga forces were pushing them more and more, and their casualties skyrocketed. Their side had lost more than forty thousand soldiers, with many thousand inured. But on the other hand, their army officers had begun to want to finish the war once and for all.

The war continues. Human casualties were on the rise on both sides. Iraqi army was defeated in every possible way, and they knew that they didn't have the capacity to continue another year.

The casualties among Kurdish people were grate; many families had lost at least one of their sons.

The Kurdish leaders, like those of the Iraqi army were feeling unrest among the commanders, the Peshmargas, and the average people.

Most people were not satisfied with the way was handled by the leaders and commanders. The entire Peshmarga forces was tired, exhausted and many of them were living in complete destitute.

The Peshmarga forces were mostly the poor villagers, farmers, artisans, craftsmen, government employees, and students. None of them had the same income that they had before the war, and many of them had their families with them, or the family left behind in the village with relatives and friends.

Both sides sought a solution, but neither of them trusted the other to start a constructive dialogue.

Sardar and Kameran and their family continued living with Baram's family. They money they had brought with them almost gone, and they now live on what Baram had to offer. Baram too was feeling the pressure. He didn't work for such a long time that his business had come to a complete standstill.

One day in late January of 1975, Kameran and Sardar were sitting together close to their bunker in the mountain. They had just finished early morning guard duty.

"I don't think I can go back to sleep," Kameran said.

"Me neither. Why we don't go sit and watch the snow fall?" said Sardar. They sat on a bench they had made from old trees under the roof of their bunker.

It was snowing. This time of year, in the Kurdish territories, it was usually quite cold. Fuel was almost as precious as gold. Kameran took two blankets and handed one to Sardar. The other one he wrapped himself in. he took out two cigarettes and said, "let's have one of these last few smokes." he shook the nearly empty pack. "We will let time to be worried about it."

"Well, it has been few months, and we haven't received any aid from the father of all Kurds, Barzani," Sardar said. "As you know, we can't live like this forever. it's been almost a year since we started living with Uncle Baram. All our money soon will be gone."

"Yes, I know and I feel the same way," Kameran said, "but do we have any other options?"

"Baram is running out of money too. He hasn't gotten anything left for his big family," Sardar said.

Baram came out too, he saw the two friends. "What are you doing out there?" He asked.

"Just talking." They replied.

He continued talking to them while he emptied himself. he was shivering with cold, then he brought a blanket and sat with them. "So, what is up with you old men?" he chuckled.

"Well, we were talking about our situation, our money situation," Sardar said.

"Money! No one has money anymore."

"Why? I don't understand how all those people go back and forth to Iran. How can the leaders afford to go to Iran for vacation?" Kameran asked.

"What do you expect, Kameran?" Sardar said.

"Well, if I'm ready to give my life and the life of my family, I suppose someone should at least help me to help my family, is it too much to ask."

"My friend, as long as the revolution run by deep-pocketed politicians, you and I'll be used, and that is how I see it," Sardar said.

"That is true," Baram said. "We are in deep shit. Let me tell you. We do all the fighting, and if we win this war, we, and those brave men you see sleeping in this cold winter with two thin blankets are the losers! The leaders, their families, relatives and friends will take over.

"The saddest part is that even the traitors, even the Jash, will be heroes. But not you or me. Now if you excuse me, old men, I'm going back inside to sleep a little more." he went back to his cave-like banker. Both Kameran and Sardar sank into deep thought. They stayed out in the cold of that winter day for many more hours, almost without feeling the cold. "I can't decide whether to go back to Slaymany or not," Sardar said. "We just buried our sons here. It wasn't fair to them that we even brought them here. But what can we do? Go back to my city? Surrender to the Iraqis and the communists? Let them make fun of me and my family? No, I would rather die here than to go back there."

"You are not alone, I am with you, we will make it together, or we will die together." Kameran said.

Shwan came back from his guard shift, "Can I sit with you?" He said. They nodded, and as he sat down, he said. "What is wrong, Uncle? you don't seem well."

"We were talking about our families and our future; it seems there is no light at the end of the tunnel," Kameran said.

"No shit! What tunnel, there is no tunnel, no light, but darkness out there," Shwan said and chuckled. "I heard what you saying Uncle, Me, too I am thinking about our families. You know better than me, there is scavengers out there looking for poor and defenseless farmers. Well, last week I was talking to Aram about going back to Slaymany, or going somewhere else. I'm telling you, I was very serious and I almost decided to leave this week. And now I see that I am not alone. You are angry too."

Sardar surfaced from his deep thoughts. He looked at Shwan and said, "If I were you, I would have left this place a long time ago."

"Yes, maybe," Shwan said, "but my concern is not the same as yours! There are things going on among Peshmarga, at all levels, and some of things are unacceptable. There are behaviors are not how some who fight for his people should behave. Do you remember, Uncle Sardar, last month when Aram Awat and I went out for a mission?"

"Yes, I remember well," Sardar answered. "What happened?"

"On our way back here, we have to stay in many villages and share quarters with our Peshmarga brothers. What we saw was heartbreaking. One day we were in the mosque in a village. We got called to go outside and see the public trial. And the trial was of a man, who had been accused, by whom, we didn't know, of being a spy, reporting to army and Jash, the nature of Peshmarga's activities. We have never seen a spy, and we also interested in seeing how our system of justice was working.

"We ran out..." Shawn's eyes suddenly became moist. He closed his eyes and tears ran down his cheeks.

Sardar and Kameran were stunned. Their jaws dropped as if there were no muscles left in their faces. They have never seen Shwan upset, and especially not crying. They were very curious now to know what happened.

"Well," Shwan said, "there was no such thing as justice. We ran outside, and there was a crowd of Peshmarga and villagers. A young girl fifteen or sixteen years old, and a boy eleven or twelve years old, were wailing loudly. They were lamenting and beating themselves, throwing themselves at the feet of two Peshmarga who were dragging and pushing an old man, probably fifty or sixty years old. The two children begged them not to harm their father. They ran to people in the crowd, pleading with everyone to have pity on their father. They were saying 'he has done nothing! He is not a spy; he is our father!'

"They were crying, but no one came to their rescue. The young girl threw herself at the feet of the man who seemed to be the commander. She said, 'Please Kak Ahmed, don't kill our father! You know he is innocent! it's Sharif Khan who should be killed. He always wanted our land to add to his, he took from poor people! You know the truth, Kak Ahmed! Please don't let them kill our father! I kiss your feet!'" Shwan wiped his eyes with his hands.

"No one dared to help her. The two Peshmarga dragged the old man along. They made him to take of his clothes in front of the crowd on that cold winter day. The poor man was half dead; he couldn't move to undress himself, so the two men tore his clothes off. Then they poured cold water on him, and then the beating started. It was horrible to watch! Aram wanted to intervene, but I grabbed his arm and told him to shut his mouth if he wanted to live.

"The old man couldn't even take four or five lashes. He collapsed on the spot. Then Kak Ahmed proudly announced, 'this is the fate of everyone betray the revolution!'" Shwan was sobbing the entire time he told the story of the old man, and he wasn't alone.

"So, what happened then?" Sardar asked in a sobbing voice.

"They killed the poor man with a bullet in the back of his head, execution style," Shwan said, his voice almost a whisper. "But the saddest part was that everyone was aware of the truth, and no one could tell it. The truth was that Sharif Kahn, the landowner, wanted the piece of land that belonged to that poor family. Sharif Kahn asked the poor man to sell it to him, but he refused. So, Sharif khan took a different road to solve the problem. He was a powerful man with a lot of connections among the Peshmarga forces, and he used those connections to accuse the old man of being an informant. It didn't take much to convince the corrupted leaders. For what Sharif Khan could put in their pockets, they killed an innocent man, this innocent farmer lost his life because of this bloodthirsty land-owner."

Sardar lit a cigarette and handed it to Shwan. "Here you go. This will make you feel better, my son."

He took a deep puff from the cigarette and blew the smoke into the cold air. "You know, the painful part was that the old man's oldest son was a Peshmarga with Barzani, and he was killed in battle just before the March 11, 1970, agreement. And anyway, the old man couldn't speak a word Arabic. I don't know how he could even be a spy," Shwan said.

Kameran looked at him and patted him on his back. "You haven't seen enough yet to understand all of this. But, I hope you will live long enough to understand the corruption among the leaders who supposed to set an example for the inexperienced Peshmargas and lead young men to build a better society. What I have experienced during my time hasn't been much better than what you have seen.

"You haven't seen the way some commander behaves when they go into a village. Many time we have seen that kind of scene again and again, and it doesn't show any sign of change."

"I saw the one incident, and I am sure you have seen enough of the same kind of cruelties. But I would like to know more about why that happens," Shwan said.

"Most of the time, when we enter a village, we all know the procedure," Sardar said. "The responsible of the group will send for the man whose job is to find a place for the Peshmarga to stay in the village. The man was chosen by the villagers to be the spokesman of the village. He finds places for the Peshmargas to eat and get some blankets to take with them to the mosque or to the mountain, depending on the time of the year. But some leader won't go to the mosque to sleep with twenty or thirty men in a mosque full of flea or to the mountain to be killed by a traitor. No, he will choose the cleanest and most well-furnished place and of course, the one that also has the most women, if you know what I mean."

"That is the way they do business." Kameran chuckled.

"Then if the leader wants to have a woman, who will stop him from having as much as he pleases?

Sometimes if he wants a certain woman, but she is married, he will make sure her husband is sent on a mission from which he will not return. Then he has free rein.

“And don’t even talk about money. They can have as much as they want. They need only ask, and if asking doesn’t get it for them easily, they will threaten people or even kill them. The way they killed the innocent old man you just told us about.”

“My friends, don’t try to change anything, because those people are more powerful than you and I.” Kameran said. “However, Kurdish society isn’t ready to change any of that, so we have to accept things the way they are if we want to live.”

“That is terrible. So, we just let them do as they want?” Shwan asked.

“What I want to say is that we can’t do much, but we don’t have to lean back and do nothing,” Sardar said. “We must not be like them; maybe in this way, we can bring up a generation that is less corrupted. Right now, the top level of our leadership is corrupted. The Barzani family, the Talabani family and other powerful families are all corrupted.”

“We have to acknowledge and accept the fact, that half of our society is illiterate,” Kameran said. “Religion is rooted deep in the mind and souls of the majority, and they follow it blindly. They have no idea what it has done to our society. Islam took the region and especially Kurdistan backward. Islam has forced our people to live the life of nomadic Arabs, a life in total ignorance and it was the religious leaders who led people into the darkness.

"All religious leaders like all politicians; they all promise a better life. Politicians, on the one hand, promise poor people a better life here on earth, but they never deliver on their promises. They only bring more misery to the people. On the other hand, religious leaders promise the poor people a better life after death, but they also lead the people to believe what they want them to believe. They make people accept the slave life they are living. And the two works to reinforce each other. Religious leader makes people accept the ignorant, bloodthirsty, hypocritical political leader. Both sides are in the union, and ultimately what they want is to make people obey them." Sardar paused.

"Another thing, is that we are living in a society like any other, half men and half women, however, our mothers, grandmothers, daughters, wives, sister...etc. had never been recognized by neither religious nor political leader. They don't believe in equality for men and women. You can't even mention the subject; it's enough to create a riot in our society. it's taboo.

"They want a society in which, women produce many children possible, cook and clean, raise their children, take care of their males and be quiet That is what religious men and politicians want.

"So, if half of a society has been discredited and accused of having no ability to be part of the progress, and if that half has been pushed back behind the walls of every home, then our society is not going to make any progress.

"Women in our society weren't respected. They are shoved into forced marriages. They have paid the price of honor killings, they have been circumcised by men, which must be the most terrible pain they must go through they have always belonged to men like any other piece of property. Don't be fooled by the promises they are selling out to you about the new society in Kurdistan. It's the same old shit, painted by the new leaders with the same empty ideas of the old leaders. Nothing has changed, and it won't change as long as men lead the way in the liberation of our mothers, wives and sisters. Women should ask for their rights and not make men ask for it for them. Men only ask for things that will keep them comfortable.

"In Kurdistan women, still are subject to forced marriage. They are stoned or burned alive. Nine – or – ten – year – old girls are pulled out of school and forced to marry men older than their grandfathers… these are men who already have three or four other wives. Marriage is still being used to settle the account between two families. That is our society, and if you are going to see any change, we must change ourselves first. That is what I believe."

Aram and the other returned from their trip to the village, pulling the two mules now loaded with supplies. "Are you still here?" Aram asked. "I thought you would be frozen solid when we got back."

"Did you see your girlfriend, the baker woman?" Shwan asked.

Aram laughed, "Do you mean your girlfriend?" I think you miss her."

"That is true," Sardar said. "She was your, Shwan!"

"Okay, I miss here, and if we were at the old post we could have been married by now." Shwan said. "But the problem was, that each time I asked her to marry me, she had the same answer."

"What was that?" Kameran asked.

"The problem is, she wanted to marry, when we have our country." Shwan said and everyone laughed.

"Well then. My son, you will never have a chance to marry her, because we will never have a free Kurdistan."

That winter was very difficult one for all Peshmarga forces. The Iraqi army was on the offense again, as if to prove their strength. There were air raids almost every day and too many land attacks to count. Peshmarga casualties were innumerable.

Baram's group had had little rest in the last three months, and his men were tired. The long winter had taken toll on them. However, they maintained their enthusiasm for the war and Kurdish victory.

They have seen the failure of the Iraqi army in their attempts to defeat Peshmarga's strongholds in the mountainous terrain with its rugged roads.

Kameran and his friends were given a new mission and marched down the mountain from their old post, their guns slung over their shoulders. A few of them at the end of the column were singing, while others talked among themselves.

They took a break half way down, gathering in tight cluster because they knew Baram was going to say something to them before they reached their new post.

"All right, men, listen to me, all of you." Baram said. "We are headed to the village, and some new brothers will take our place here in the mountain. Where we'll end up, I don't know yet, so be patient and don't do too much joking around."

They couldn't refrain from making jokes or fooling around a little. That was their way to reduce their stress and fatigue. Some of them did this now to show Baram they would go right on with it, no matter what he said.

"You are incurable." Baram said and laughed. "All right! Let's go, ladies!

Baram was still commander and he now had more than two hundred men under his command. They all came from different background and tribes, they even had many Armenians and Jews among them. However, Baram loved them and respected all of them for who they were.

Despite telling them not to joke around too much, Baram himself loved to crack few good jokes and when someone told a joke, he laughed with all heart. He always told them that a good laughter was good for health and moral. They slowly came down and they had all their belongings, their blankets, tea and cooking wares, and ammunition boxes and headed to the village to exchange posts with the new group. His men were overjoyed because they were going to have an opportunity to wash up and eat something different. They could even buy some new underwear and other personal items before they left for their new destination.

They reached the village, and Baram ordered his men to set guard in place. The other group was already there. They had bought a few sheep to be slaughtered and cooked, and they too replenished their personal supplies. The two commanders, shook hands and then all the men did too. The hand shaking went on half an hour or more, some of them recognized each other, friends found friends. It was a good day, and then in the late afternoon the two groups said their good-byes. One group went up to the mountain and the other took the road out of the village.

After they were far away from the village, Baram asked his men to take a short break. He gathered them and said, “Listen to me carefully, we are going to Penjewen. It’s far, few days walking and it’s dangerous. There has been a lot of fighting there. Peshmarga forces were driven out of there last month, but they recaptured it last week. The territory is very important and we must keep it under our control. There are more Jash there than in any other place. They are very familiar with the territory, but we aren’t and that shouldn’t stop us from giving them a good fight. So, let’s go!”

After three days walk, they finally they arrived in the new territory that they would have to protect from enemy. It was late afternoon when they arrived. There were Peshmarga from all over Kurdistan, and when they saw the size of the force that was present, they understood the importance of that area.

Baram ordered his men to rest for the remainder of the day. Tomorrow they would resume their duties, but today they were too tired. Baram conferred with the commanders. He learned about the ferocity of the Jash in Penjewen; the Peshmarga had suffered many casualties in the last three months.

That night Baram slept little; he paced in his quarters for a long time, worrying about his men. They were brave men and had fought like lions, they were the best of the best, but war has no pity on anyone. The more he thought about it, the more he worried. Finally, he sat in a chair, worrying no less, and woke up early morning to discover he still had his muddy boots on. Someone had come in and covert him during the night as he was slept.

He saw that it was late, around seven o'clock. Kameran brought him a cup of fresh tea. "Good morning." Kameran said.

"Good morning! I slept like a baby," he said.

"Good, I came in and covered you last night. I think you are fresh and ready to talk to you men."

Baram gathered his men and assigned them to their posts and duties. His men adapted well in their new territory. It took time for them to get to know the other groups and make friends. But in general, the time flew. In their first three weeks there, they were engaged in four battles with the Jash and the army, and they were victorious in all of them.

Baram was given supreme command over the entire forces. He was responsible for more than eight hundred Peshmargas, but because of his expertise and fearlessness, he was exactly the right man for the job. The men all loved and respected him, and they feared nothing if Baram was their commander. Baram's men made life for the Jash in the region very difficult. They searched for them and chased them out of their homes.

One beautiful morning in mid-March, just after the anniversary of the March 11 agreement, a messenger came to the camp seeking Baram so that he could deliver a letter to him from Qaladze.

Baram was very surprised. He knew the man well, but they both pretended they were strangers. He knew immediately that the letter was from Sddiq. He shook hand with the messenger and thanked him, and the messenger mounted his mule and slowly rode away.

Baram sat on a rock outside of his camp and looked at the envelope for a long time. Then he put it inside his pocket to read later. He looked out across the valley, getting greener by the day. He was worried because Sardar and his group hadn't come back yet from a mission to the town of Penjewen.

Kameran approached him and said, "are you worrying about Sardar and his men?"

"Yes of course, I'm! I don't know what could have happened to them, but I hope they're all alive. Come and sit." he said. He stood up and took his gun off his shoulder and hung it on a nearby tree branch. He took out his prayer-beads and his cigarettes, offered Kameran one, and lit one for himself. He sat back on the rock. "Do you remember why I chose you to be with me?" he asked

"Yes, I do. Why?" Kameran said with a surprise.

"Well, I trust you, that is why I took you with me. We're one family. Today I received a letter from my friend Sddiq you all know him well. We don't have any secrets. We always tell each other everything." He paused and took a deep puff. "Sddiq and I have a code so we could communicate with each other when things start going wrong. The code allows us to do this without letting other know what we are saying to each other, and today I have..."

Baram was interrupted by a guard shouting that Sardar and his men were back. He and Kameran jumped from their places and ran to their friends. Ten or fifteen men have been out on a mission under Sardar's command, but now they were back. A couple of men lay across the backs of mules, and several others walked haltingly. There were no casualties, but there were five injured. The medical team was there in minutes, a doctor and few men with little experience in hospitals and that was all they had, but it was enough to do the job this time.

Sardar was wounded on his right side. The bullet

had penetrated between two ribs but didn't went through any vital organs. He's lost blood, but otherwise he was okay. Shwan and Awat had leg injuries, but their wounds were not serious. Two other men were badly injured; one had a wound in the back and the other had an injured thigh that was so bad they couldn't save his leg. He needed more treatment than on-site doctor could provide, so Baram ordered his men to quickly prepare a group to take him to Penjewen, where they'd people to help the wounded man without being caught.

The doctor stopped the bleeding and gave him other treatment to help him survive the trip. Within minutes they put the two badly-injured men on mules and headed toward Penjewen.

Sardar and his men had been successful in their mission despite their injuries. They had killed two Jash leaders and their men, along with government official and his men.

Next morning Baram came to where Sardar and Kameran were resting. "How are my lion today?" It's so unlike you to stay in bed, Sardar. Come on let's go for a walk," he said. Sardar stood up with a little help from Kameran, and the three of them went out to the same rock where, the day before, Baram had been on the verge of sharing the contents of Sddiq's letter with Kameran.

The Algiers Accord

The 1975 Algiers Agreement, commonly known as the Algiers Accord, was a treaty between Iraq and Iran whose intention was to settle the disputed land and sea borders in Persian Gulf. This included navigation rights on the Shat Al-Arab water way and several other issues such as Arab-populated Iranian province of Khuzestan. But the main reason for Iraq was to end the Kurdish rebellion.

Saddam, Vice-Chairman of the Revolution and Mohammad Reza Pahlavi the Shah of Iran attended the OPEC summit in Algiers on 6 March 1975, where they agreed on an agreement and signed it with mediation of Houari Boumedienne. The president of Algeria.

The meeting in March led to several agreements. One was that they would return to the tradition of being good neighbors. Joint borders would be made more secure, and the two countries would try to cooperate with each other. Another agreement stated that they would each provide patrol or other means of watching the borders for any 'infiltration of subversive nature'.

What they meant by the latter was the Kurds, the enemy of both Iran and Iraq. The Kurds weren't mentioned in the agreement, but each country had prepared a deadly plan for their Kurdish minority population.

The Algiers accord was probably the most kept secret political game played by Iran, Iraq and many other players against the Kurds in the history of the Middle East. Its details, contents and consequences remain an enigma for Kurdish people. What led to the Algiers accord and why the countries involved were in denial, is a mystery?

The disasters that that followed the accord were too costly for Kurds to forget, and the players, all Kurdish leaders included, were too guilty to allow them to escape the eventual punishment. It had a devastating consequence on the lives of millions of Kurds in general and Iraqi Kurds in particular.

It was an act of evil intention by Arab leaders to save another Arab dictator leader from being ousted. There were no good intention or real effort to solve the problems between the two countries. It wasn't an accord that would particularly bring the Iraqi and Iranian governments and the Kurds together, either. It wasn't an accord that sought a peaceful solution to their problem.

Instead, the Accord was about the superpowers and their allies settling their accounts. It was about the United States wanting to pull Iraq out from under the Soviet-Union umbrella and put it back under their won umbrella. It was about the United States having more access to rich deposit Iraqi oil, and about turning American economic downturn that had resulted from the disastrous war in Vietnam.

The consequence of the Accord would lead to eight long years of destructive war against Iran in what become known as the First Gulf War, and the gulf war would lead to even more devastating Second Gulf War. The end result would be the fall of Iraqi regime and with it, millions of innocent people would be killed. Many millions would be displaced, hundreds of thousands thrown into prison, and thousands executed for no reason than being innocent.

During Iran-Iraq war, Iraq used many lethal chemical weapons which had being forbidden by the UN. The entire international community knew about Iraq's use of chemical weapons, and they were aware of the systematic ethnic cleansing of Kurds in northern Iraq, but not only they didn't try to stop it, they participated in it as well.

Baram, gathered his men to tell them the heart-breaking news no one wanted to hear. "Listen," he said, "we don't have much time for discussion. We have reason to believe that the Iranian are about to withdraw all military support for our struggle for independence." their eyes stopped blinking, they suddenly froze. Baram was not surprised by their reaction, because he, himself had the same reaction when he first read the letter.

He continued, "OPEC, had its annual meeting in Algerian capital city of Algiers, and during that meeting, the Algerian president, Boumedienne, invited the Shah of Iran and Vice Chairman Saddam Hussein to have private talks about their borders and to seek a peaceful solution to their conflicts. The two leaders agreed and Shah invited Saddam to visit Iran. He has already been in Tehran."

Sardar looked worryingly at Baram, "What the consequences be for us?" he asked. "We have to continue fighting, right! I don't think there is one single man who won't continue fighting! This is our fight. Probably Barzani's is over, and they can all leave if they wish, but we must stay!"

Kameran looked at Sardar. "I wish all Kurds had the same enthusiasm as you. People aren't united. They must have a leader. Believe me, if Barzani leaves today, tomorrow there will be just me and you left.

You talk as if you don't know the mentality of people."

"My friends, that is not all," Baram continued. "Barzani is disparate, he's called all leaders and military commanders for a meeting, and he'll give his advice to them. The situation is very fragile; no one knows what will happen tomorrow."

"Are you going?" Sardar asked.

"No, I'm not," Baram said. "I don't want to be told 'the revolution is finished now go home'. I'll stay right here with you. We should figure it out for ourselves. We are the men who fight, not run."

Few days later the heartbreaking news of the 'ash batal...literally, the mill is closed, go home', but in this case meaning the revolution has ended and time has come for everyone to put down the weapon and go home, had spread throughout the entire country. There were celebrations in Iraq and Iran for their gains, in the agreement, but mourning in Kurdistan.

"Do you remember what I told you, Kameran?" Sardar asked.

Kameran nodded. He didn't have the energy even to open his mouth. "Does anyone know the contents of the agreement?" he said finally.

"Well, according the BBC, Arabic Radio, the two sides had meeting in Tehran and they appeared they solved their conflicts, that is all we know." Baram said.

"But what all these had anything to do with us?" Kameran asked.

"It has everything to do with us." Baram replied. "My friends, the agreement was mainly about the Kurds. They don't want to tell the world the true picture, but we all know the bitter reality."

Sardar lit a cigarette and inhaled the smoke. Then he let the smoke out into the air. "I think I know where all this will lead," he said. "It's true Iran and Iraq have had their differences and disputes regarding waterway borders, but that has been going forever.

"But I can see how this time it's about us, the Kurds. As you know Iran has its own problem with its Kurdish population, even though the Kurds in Iran have been quiet, not rebellious like we are in Iraq. But Iranian must be afraid that our success in demanding out rights for autonomy will influence the Kurds in Iran. Nonetheless, neither Iran nor their protectors, the Americans, want Iran to go down in a conflict that will last forever."

"Barzani had a meeting with his advisers and military commanders. He told them to go home, as simple as that." Baram said. "Barzani explained to them that Iran has given as options concerning our future. We can lay down our arms, surrender to Iraqi army, and go back to our families. Or we and our families can take refuge in their country, God knows for how long! Or if anyone who wants to go abroad, Iran will facilitate their departure. They will give people's name to European and other countries and tell them to take us as refugees. Iran has already pulled back their military support, and they have closed their borders. There are thousands of families and wounded Peshmargas in Iran already, and no one know what their futures hold."

"Did Barzani explained what he and his family are going to do?" Sardar asked.

"No, of course not, it's a secret," Baram replied.

The Algiers agreement was like a huge asteroid that has fallen on Kurdish people without warning. It had hit Kurdistan in the middle of the night while people were in their deepest sleep. Its impact was visible on all fronts and in many countries. The celebrations of its positive impacts were reflected in the smiles of the Iranian delegations returning with the signed documents, proving that their winning hand was hidden in their briefcases. Iran was the biggest winner in the game. They now have their waterway borders extended far into Iraqi waters, and they also have the two Iraqi oil-rich islands in the gulf.

The Iranian soon packed their belonging and went home. Now the Kurds had just few days to decide what they wanted to do. Within twenty-four hours, thousands of Kurdish rebels came down from mountains with their rifles hanging on their shoulders. They were exhausted, disappointed and angry. They didn't have any idea what was going on. Yesterday they were Peshmargas, and today they were surrendering to the government they had fought against for so long. There were rumors that many commanders had committed suicide out of despair. The Iraqi government declared amnesty for all rebels, and they were welcomed back as part of the Iraqi nation once again.

Baram told his men that they were free to do whatever was best for them and their families. But he asked Kameran and Sardar to stay with him: he had a plan. After Baram gave his men his speech, within few days the mountains, which has been their home for so long, emptied. Baram ordered his men to leave and said that anyone who wanted to take his gun could do so. Many left their guns behind, but others took them when the left.

It had happened so quickly, within few days, all that remained on the mountain were the autumnal trees.

Just few days ago the mountains had been crowded with young men, proudly sacrificing their lives for Kurdistan. Today they had left to surrender to the enemy they had fought for years. It was heartbreaking for all Kurdish people, and especially for Baram, Sardar and Kameran.

After most of the Peshmarga forces had left, Baram sat and talked to his friends and Kameran and Sardar were listing to him carefully, "What is in your mind, Uncle Baram," Sardar asked.

"I could go back to my family like anyone else; after all amnesty has been given to all except for Barzani and his family." Baram said. "But I want to stay for a while to see what will happen to all men who surrender to the government. Then I'll make up my mind. Meanwhile..." he paused for a moment "I'll collect as many weapons as I can and hide them in the mountains near Qaladze, because no one can tell when we will need them the next time. What do you think?"

Sardar was astonished, "It's genius! I'm with you. After all, I don't have the courage to face my sister, Diar's mother. She trusted me with the life of her son, but I couldn't protect him. Now he is dead and I'm alive. I'll stay with you." Kameran too agreed with the idea and wanted to stay, but he wanted to go, because his father was dead.

"What I was trying to say is we will all go home, but we need to hide the weapons first. Then we can leave." Baram said. "Kameran you go ahead and leave. Sardar and I'll do the job."

Aram, Shwan Awat, and Baram's sons were ready to go home. They and their fathers were the last ones left, but soon they would have to leave. Sardar talked to his son Aram about why he wanted to stay and the reason he couldn't surrender. He also told him to tell his mother not to be worried, because he was safer in the mountain that in Slaymany. Aram kissed his father, shook hands with Baram and they all went down the hill.

Baram and Sardar said their goodbyes to their friend Kameran. He went down the mountain slowly. He was angry and confused, and he felt helpless in the face of the disaster that Kurdish leaders had brought upon them. Slowly he disappeared into the valley below as Sardar and Baram watched him. He was the last man beside them to leave the mountains.

The two men, alone in the mountain, took a break and made a fire to prepare some tea. They had a month worth of supplies and ten strong mules with them. They sat next to the little fire they had made and sipped their fresh tea.

"We have thirty-five Kalashnikov, two heavy machine guns and a lot of ammunition," Baram said. "We will take them to the nearest village and then to Qaladze and bury them well. We should find a place in the mountain closer to Qaladze. I'm sure this is not the end. I think there will be some men who will not accept this defeat and soon will be back."

Thousands of armed men were on their way to surrender; others went to Iran. There were army along almost every road leading into villages and small towns. Army trucks would transport the surrendered rebels to their cities and towns after they registered and gave up their weapons to the army.

It took a few days, but soon the mountains were left as empty as a tree whose leaves have fallen off and blown away by autumn's wind. The mountains themselves seemed to feel ashamed, as if they didn't do enough job providing sufficient protection to their people.

Barzani fled to America. His tail between his legs. His sons and their families, other relatives and many other wealthy families went to Iran. There they were offered protection and political asylum. Some settled in the beautiful cites on the outskirt of Tehran. They bought nice big houses and had all help from Iranian authorities in case their money ran out. Meanwhile, thousands of poor families of Peshmarga were sent to refugee camps in the worst part of Iran. They live under intolerable conditions. The poverty, hunger and helplessness of the situation led many families to prostitution. They were hostages, and their lives were the ransom they were paying for the stupidity of ignorant, selfish leaders.

Kurdistan became a prison for Kurdish people. Thousands of families were exiled to the hot, burning, sandy and hostile desert of southern Iraq. Iraqi prisons were filled with innocent Kurdish people, most of whom couldn't speak a word of Arabic and had never been outside of their territories.

The Iraqi government had ordered a security zone to be built along the Iraqi borders with Iran and Turkey. The zone will encompass twenty-five kilometers of land from the border into Iraq. This mean Iraq would clean out the area, destroy every village and town situated on that line.

The destruction of Kurdistan had had begun. Just a few months after the Algiers agreement, they created a no-man's-land, and anyone seen in that zone would be shot without warning.

Military trucks transporting people from the destroyed villages, some to the south and others to the so-call modern villages.

'Modern villages' as the government called them, had started to spring up near small towns. They were just cement bricks stacked up, windows hole without windows, or doors. No sanitary or sewage systems in place. They forced villagers whose villages had been destroyed to live in those cages they called it 'modern villages'.

The destruction of Kurdistan was visible everywhere. For centuries, the farmers in those Kurdish villages had supplied themselves, the cities and towns with all kinds of food products, including fruits, vegetables, meat, dairy products and other crops. The entire Kurdistan had been living on the shoulders of the poor farmers. Now, the livelihood, not only the farmers, but nearly everyone else in the cities and towns was history.

The most difficult thing for the villagers, besides the fact that they lost everything, was to live in those prison-like houses and not be able to wake up in the morning, go to their farms to pick fresh vegetables, and work there until sunset. Now the only activity for many was to sleep and try to forget all they once had.

Cities and towns were overwhelmed with farmers and villagers, and that created a friction between them and the city people. The villagers were accused of being the reason for high unemployment among city people. They were being treated like second-class citizens; after all, they were nothing but farmers, many thought.

They had forgotten that the farmers were the backbone, the driving force of life in Kurdistan. They were cornerstone upon which all the Kurdish armed movement for the last century had been built.

Baram and Sardar were paralyzed by the quick collapse of the revolution of more than a hundred thousand brave armed men who had been ready to die. All hope was shattered within a day, and the destruction of Kurdistan continued forever.

Baram and Sardar were not the only ones who thought to hide weapons in the mountains. Many villagers who were lucky enough to live outside the no-man's-land zone and who were lucky enough to be spared being removed started to gathering weapons and ammunition and hiding them.

Those including Sardar and Baram weren't sure why they were doing it, but they were many of them, enough to begin another revolution. But they would have to wait.

Baram and Sardar sat there alone with no one around to bother them. They discussed their futures, made some food, drank and smoked. Then they went to work. They had gathered the weapons and ammunition, and they wrapped them with any plastic they could find and with whatever blankets they had. They put the bundles on the back of the mules and slowly went down into the valley, walking until late at night. They decided to stop for the night, eat and get some rest. The next day they came to the place in the mountains where Baram wanted to hide their weapons. They took the heavy loads off the mules' back and let the animals out to graze.

It was a hot afternoon late April, and they didn't want to be seen while they were digging, so they waited until the sunset to get started. They dug until midnight, when they finally had a sizable hole to fit all the weapons and the ammunition in, they took a break. They were sweaty and tired. First, they laid three blankets on the bottom, then a layer of plastic, and then the weapons. They covered them with more plastic and blankets. They threw the soil on top. Any extra soil was spread on the ground far from the hole to avoid bringing any attention to the dig. Finally, to finish the job, they laid some broken tree branches on their hiding place and fashioned a marker so they could find the place again. Then they gathered their tools and headed for a different place in the mountains where they could rest.

The two friends stayed in the mountains two more days and waited for something to happen, but all was quiet. They decided to go home. They pulled the mules behind them and headed down the mountain. When the passed by a village where Baram knew some people, he gave the mules to them.

Three days later Sardar was smuggled to Slay-many by some of Baram's friends. Late at night he carefully knocked on the door of his home and went in. Sardar was happy to be back home with his family, but the pain of losing so many friends and family was too much to bear. Everyone noticed that he wasn't the same man as before. His spirit was restless, his heart broken, and all his hopes vanished. He didn't have any desire to live. He had been willing to sacrifice his life for Kurdistan, and he wished he had died a long ago, before seeing the tragedies of the Kurdish people. He had been injured, but he was still alive.

He couldn't go out, because he didn't officially surrender to the authorities, so all the news that came to him was by Kameran or his son.

Azra, Kameran's mother was still alive, but she was very sick. He thought she was probably dying.

His wife Nasreen wasn't the same; she seemed to have lost the will to live. She wanted to die rather than see her family vanishing in front of her eyes. Awat, his son was on the brink of losing his mind.

Sardar's sister Nazanin was totally devastated by her son's death; she was still living with her mother and Shwan at the house they shared with Sardar, Salma and their son Aram.

Saman Sardar's younger brother, was still living in Halabja. He was married and had his own family.

Kameran ran his father's store, because he had not been able to get his teaching license back. It wasn't bad, but there were a lot of people to support, and the money wasn't enough for all. It was a good thing that they still had their home. Sirwan's home belonged to them as well, and it was standing empty. Kameran wanted to rent it out, but Sardar had another idea.

Eight months passed. The Iraqi government began carrying out their plans to remove all Kurdish villages in the belt line of the Iraqi-Iran border and the Iraq-Turkey border. Tens of thousands of poor villagers were forcibly displaced by the Iraqi army to southern Iraq, with increasing pressure heavier by the day. The Kurdish language had been banned from all schools, and no other political parties were permitted, not even the communists. The entire Iraq seemed like a big prison.

A new hope

1976 was the year during, which the Iraqi government thought it had, once for all solved the Kurdish problem. Saddam thought the government had uprooted the Kurds and that they were now under the government's control and left without no friends to turn to. Their leaders had fled the country and sought refuge in countries hostile to great Iraqi nation. Iraqi government developed even more plans to corner the Kurdish population and force them to be proud Iraqis who belonged to the great Arab nation. If they couldn't force them to do that, they could at least force them to obey Iraqi laws and forget their dreams about free Kurdistan.

But the Iraqi government was dead wrong, as soon as the imaginary leader, the 'Father of all Kurds' Barzani, had fled Kurdistan to the United States, a group of young, patriots gathered in the mountains of Qaradagh region, near Slaymany. They were armed with a new philosophy, new ideology and a new hope.

The existence of the new group, quickly reached the city of Slaymany and its surroundings. Young people were eager to know more about them and to find a way to contact them, because life for most people had become a kind imprisonment.

Many young men wanted to leave their families and join the new rebel forces. At that time Kurdistan was being marked for some of the worst destruction it would see. Saddam had already started his program of removal of many thousands of Kurdish villages.

The Kurdish languages was banned at all level of education, and no practice of any Kurdish cultural activities were allowed. Military service had become compulsory for all Kurds, and that was the main reason that pushed many young people to join the rebels.

Sardar was hearing the rumors of the new group, and he was anxious to know more about them. However, he still wasn't going out much; he got his news from Kameran and his son Aram and his nephews Shwan and Awat.

One day while Sardar was at home, anxious to hear more about the rebels, Kameran came to see him and tell him the good news. "Well, as you have been hearing rumors about the new rebels," Kameran said, "they aren't rumors anymore. In fact, there are a group of rebels already Qaradagh, the leaders of the group, as I heard, are a man by the name Aram, he is highly educated man, he has studied in Russia, I believe. And two other men by the name Aziz and Sirwan. They aren't many, but they are well educated and good patriots." He was quiet for a moment and then he continued, "they are aware of the Kurdish people suffering and most importantly, they are aware of the rivalry of the two clans."

That was enough for Sardar to make his mind, no matter how and where. He was suffering and losing his patience at home, he had to do something.

"Kurdistan is in my blood." he told Kameran. "I have plans, but I don't know if you would like to hear it."

"Go on, tell me what is in your mind." He said.

Sardar was quiet for a moment and then he looked at Kameran and said, "I want to sell the houses and the store. We are going to Halabja. We can take our families to Halabja to live there and you and I'll join the rebels. Do you hear me?"

Kameran was happy to hear Sardar's idea too. He was addicted to Kurdistan as much as Sardar was. He couldn't just sit and watch his country being savagely destroyed in front of their eyes. He promised Sardar to put their plans into action beginning tomorrow morning.

Both had discussed with their families on the subject, and finally all agreed to move to Halabja, where Saman was already living.

A few weeks later they had sold their houses and the store. However, Shereen demanded that they keep the big house, so they kept the big house, even they didn't know why they kept it, and they all made the journey to Halabja. With the money, they had gained from selling their properties, they were able to by a big house for all of them to live in together. The rest of the money they would keep for emergency or for the boys to do some business.

The two men had decided to join the rebels, and their families knew that they had no choice and reluctantly they agreed to the plan. Two weeks later, after they had settled their families, they left them again.

They left Halabja after the sunset. Sardar knew the road to Qaladze, and it took them around two weeks to reach their destination. They were very careful, because they knew they could easily have recognized as city men, and they didn't want to bring any unwanted attention to themselves. The journey took a little longer than it might have otherwise, but they have to stay safe.

As they approached Qaladze, they stopped and waited for it to be a little darker. They were able to enter the city without any difficulty, and soon they found themselves in front of Baram's house, where their families had spent more than a year there.

Sardar knocked the door and waited. Baram's son opened the door and was about to shout, but Sardar was quicker, "don't shout!" He quickly understood the situation; he let them in without making any noise. Inside the house, they hugged each other and shook hands. They went in and found Baram sitting with his family. He turned, and when he saw the two men standing there, he stood up and grabbed them. "What a nice surprise, guys!" he said. Quickly Baram asked his wife and children to prepare food, because he knew the two men were hungry. They sat, ate and talked. Baram asked them about their families and how they were copping with all the difficulties. And then he asked his wife to leave them alone.

"We're back, and now it's time to for us to go back to the mountain," Sardar said.

"What is going on?" Tell me...I'm dying to for some news!" Baram said.

"There are new rebels deep in the mountains of Qaradagh, and we want to join them as soon as possible," Sardar said.

"We sold our properties and settled our families in Halabja and they had enough money left so they don't need to be worried." Kameran said.

"I take it you want me to come with you and take you to our treasure in the mountain?" Baram asked.

"Yes, we do!" Kameran replied.

They stayed that night with Baram, talking for hours about the Kurdish cause, the failure of Barzani, and his betrayal of the Kurdish cause.

"What is your plans, uncle Baram?" Sardar asked.

"For the moment, I don't have any plans," he answered. "But I'm waiting. If there are rebels in any part of Kurdistan, it will not take long until they spread over the entire Kurdistan. it's like the forest fire, it spreads quickly. And when it's closer to home, I'll jump on board. After all, I'm still a Kurd. For now, I'll help you find the weapons" They rested, and in the early morning they packed a little food, water, few tools and they left before sunrise.

They passed through the village where Baram had left the mules a years ago, and asked the man if he could borrow few of them left. The man gave him six strong mules. They took the animals and headed to the mountain. By late evening they reach the mountain where they had hidden the weapons. They found the place. They rested, ate and then when it was dark they began to dig. They unearthed the weapons and then they took a break.

They were all silent. Sardar looked around him and sighed. He felt very emotional, remembering the year he spent in these mountains. He thought of all those brave men ready to die for a cause, all those mothers who would never be able to see their sons' and daughters' weddings, all those fathers who didn't want to cry over a son's dead body lest they discourage the second son from sacrificing his life for Kurdistan too. He thought of all the young girls who became widows even before they delivered a now-orphaned son, and he remembered his own son Aram, who was just a boy but wanted to die for the freedom of his people. He remembered all the suffering his people had faced at the hand of Arabs. "Kurdistan deserve one more chance," Sardar said suddenly.

"What?" Kameran asked.

"I wish I had died long ago and had not seen this happening to Kurdistan," Sardar said. They were all silent for a few minutes.

"So, you won't join us yet, uncle?" Kameran asked

"No, I can't come with you yet." he said. "I have to

return and do something else for now. You take the weapons...and good luck.

The two friends understood Baram's decision. They thanked him and loaded up the mules.

Traveling alone with so many weapons, they had reason to be afraid, so they walked slowly and tried to avoid stay close to any village. When they need food, one of them would go into a village to get some while the other waited at some distance. They were on the road for more than two weeks, but finally got close to Qaradagh territory. Now all they have to do was wait until sunset and cross the road to a checkpoint without been seen.

It wasn't difficult for the two men to cross the road into Qaradagh. However, the rebels were very curious about every new member who showed up, and about any passer-by they didn't know. The government was aware of their existence and their small numbers, and they did everything they could to silence the young voice before they reached the Kurdish population.

The small group of rebels was chased every day. Government informants were everywhere, and the with their remaining of Jash, were doing a good business informing on rebels' hiding places.

The two men approached the first village in Qaradagh and they were welcomed by the villagers. They rested for a while and then they asked for the direction to another village. They knew rebels wouldn't stay in the villages close to the main roads or towns, because then they would be an easy target for Jash and military attacks.

They continued their journey the whole day. By nightfall, they were in the middle of the Qaradagh territory; they decided to stay in the village for the night, but they were aware that they might be recognized as city people, so they were cautious.

They went to a house at the far end of the village to avoid being around too many curious people. They tied up their animals, and then Kameran quietly knocked on the door of the house. And old man opened the door and greeted him; he asked them what they wanted.

"We came from very far away, and we need to stay for the night, if you allow us," Sardar respectfully asked.

The old man welcomed them in. "You are very welcome, my sons! Please come in." he said.

"We have few animals. They too need some food," Kameran said apologetically.

"Salaam!" the old man called out.

A young man appeared. "Yes, father?" he said.

"Please take care of these men's animals, son," the old man said.

“The animals carrying very heavy loads, and we need help to unload them,” Kameran told the old man.

They all helped to unload the animals, when they had finished, the old man led is guests into his house.

“You seem to have come from very far away, my sons,” the old man said.

“Yes, we have,” Kameran said.

“Not to be disrespectful, but may I ask where you heading?”

Sardar looked at the old man, “In fact, we are searching for Peshmarga,” he said and was curious to know the old man’s reaction.

“I don’t know if there are any Peshmarga here, my sons. And if there is any, why you want to see them?” The old man asked.

“We want to join them.,” Sardar replied.

The old man called for some food, and another young man brought them what they had. “Now eat and get some rest, then we will see.” he said.

The two men sat and ate eagerly, as they hadn’t had anything since early morning, and while they eating, two armed men appeared at the old man’s home.

They greeted the old man and his guests, and they

too sat and let the two men finished eating. The two men understood that the old man was the rebels' informant and that he had sent his son to inform the rebels of their presence.

"Where did you came from?" the armed men asked.

"We are from Slaymany, but we came from Qaladze," Kameran said.

"Where do you intend to go, my friends?" the other man asked.

"We are not going anywhere now, because we have found you," Sardar said.

"Very well. If you have finished eating, we can go," the armed man said.

They thanked the old man for his generosity and left with the two-armed men.

They were taken to the rebel's leader, who was waiting just not far from the village with the rest of his group. They left the mules and the loads at the old man's house.

The rebels had no idea that these two men had just what they needed; the leader of the group greeted them warmly and asked them what they had with them and where going.

Sardar and Kameran asked the leader to ask his

men to help them to bring the load to show them what they had with them. The leader asked his men to do what Sardar asked them and when they came back with the loads and need more men to bring the rest, the leader was very much surprised. They were amazed to see so much weapons and ammunition. "What do you think?" Sardar asked them.

"Where were you able to find so many weapons, when we have to pay a high price for a Kalashnikov?" the leader asked.

"We were Peshmarga like yourselves when the revolution collapsed. We decided to hide some weapons for a day like today." Kameran said.

The leader asked his men to take the weapons and prepare to move. "We will move only as a precaution. We don't know if anyone has followed you, but if so, it's better to leave right now,"

"We keep two mules and give the rest to the old man."

Kameran's and Sardar's sacrifices for Kurdistan didn't make a big impression. Not because they hadn't sacrificed enough or their sacrifices weren't appreciated, but because too many people had told them the same stories and had then turned out to be enemies.

The leader was very frank and straightforward with the two men. What they had done, and what they had sacrificed, would not be forgotten. "One day this nation will remember you and many thousands of other young men and women who gave their lives to this land." he said, "but today there is an atmosphere of mistrust. The only way to stay alive is to be very careful whom we take. Our lives are in the hands of those we choose to guard us at night while we are sleeping. The government, meanwhile is willing to pay a huge amount for every Peshmarga, dead or alive. And don't forget we are just human beings. Money can lure anyone to sell their souls and honor for money. it's not important what we have done in the past, but it's important what we do today. We have neither the time nor the means to verify everyone's background. it's up to every individual to prove his or her trustworthiness and loyalty to Kurdish people."

The rebel's leader told them that they would be under watchful eyes as long as he didn't trust them, and he didn't apologize for that. It was the only way for all of them to stay alive. He gave them a choice: if they wanted to leave, they were free to do so, as soon as tomorrow.

The two friends were fascinated by the leader's frankness. They didn't feel insulted; on the contrary, they were happy finally to meet someone they could relate to. So, they told them that they were more than happy to stay and prove whatever they had to.

♣♣♣♣

Five months went by. The group grew larger and they were able to provide guns for all the men after several successful attacks on military compounds.

The new movement had to do a lot to regain the trust of the Kurdish people especially the villagers, because on one hand, the brutalities of Iraqi government and on the other, the stupidity of the Barzani and Talabani clans have killed the trust, and the hope in people to rise again. Therefore, the new movement has to educate the villagers and let them know that the monopoly of Kurdistan by the two rival clans was over, and Kurdistan belong to all Kurds. They have developed educational circles that designed to educate the rebels not just on how to fight the enemy, but also about Kurdish history. They learned about the role of Kurds in the world, the role of Kurdish leaders, and the effects of religion and religious clerics in Kurdish movement throughout history. It was a very good idea, Sardar and Kameran thought, and they became responsible for their education.

They were happy with the new philosophy. They were glad that this time the Kurdish cause was in the hands of intelligent, intellectual men that putting the interest of Kurdish people before their own interest.

They have found a new dream: to fight with a group of men they could trust, who fought for a free Kurdistan. However, they didn't know that soon their dreams would be shattered again.

While all this was going on, Talabani and his followers were founding a new political party in Damascus. Now they called themselves Patriotic Union of Kurdistan, PUK. They were preparing for an opportunity to come back and launch a new kind of armed resistance against the Iraqi government. But they too had to wait, because the time wasn't right. They would have to wait until the rival clan, the Barzani, was completely gone. Otherwise it would not be the best time for them to come back and try to bring together thousands of men and former Barzani's commanders who wanted to fight. Talabani and his followers could have come back and fought without help from other greedy self-serving countries. The could have come back at a moment when people were searching for someone to lead them to freedom.

They could have come back and continued what people, not Barzani, had already started. During this time, the Iraqi government was crying for help from left and right. They were on their knees begging, and with another push the Kurds could have reached something they had long been fighting for.

But they didn't come back. They were still ashamed of their ugly history and their betrayal of their own people. They were ashamed of their ignorance of what Kurds and Kurdistan meant to Kurdish people. They were ashamed of their many years of indulgence in the pleasures of looting and killing Kurdish people, and they were ashamed of all innocent people they had killed for the same reason the government of Iraq, Syria, Iran, and Turkey had done: because they were Kurds.

One day the rebels were in the mountain they had finished their circle as they had every week, but the leader, Anwar, seemed very worried, he asked his men to stay, "Today I have to give you some bad news."

The rebels were quiet, they thought probably their friends had been killed in some mission inside the city, "Have we lost Peshmarga...?" someone wanted to ask, but he was interrupted by Anwar.

"No, we haven't." he replied. "We will face many, many dark days from now on, because the traitor, 'Talabani' has decided to come back. He is going to clean Kurdistan of his rivals...wait and see."

"Is he in Kurdistan now?" Kameran asked.

"No, not yet, but we have reason to believe that he is on his way and he will be here soon. When? I don't know. Talabani's or Barzani's comeback, wouldn't and shouldn't stop us to do what is right. We will fight Iraqi army and their allies the Jash."

The rebels had divided themselves in many smaller groups of fifteen or twenty men and scattered all over the territory of Qaradagh, after all their number had grown beyond government's expectation. However, they all meet every month or so to exchange info-rmation about military and Jash whereabouts and to meet the new members of the rebels. One day in the middle of March, the rebels had a meeting the day before with the other groups as they had many times before. After the meeting, each group went back to their territory, unaware that they were about to face the worst battle of their lives. The Jash and the government had been informed that the rebels would have a meeting with their members in the mountains, but where? They didn't know.

However, Kameran and Sardar's group, of twenty or thirty men had stayed behind after the meeting. The next day, they heard the buzz of choppers were flying exactly toward their location. They could see Jash and army climbing up the mountain in their direction, so they knew there were being attacked and there was nothing to do but fight. The Jash, all of them familiar with the terrain, were advancing rapidly through the narrow passages. They attacked with ferocity, because each rebel's body meant gold in Jash's pocket. They were given a bonus if they brought back the actual dead bodies.

The choppers were flying law, the machine guns in the opened doorways of the choppers. The guns poured their anger onto the mountains where Peshmarga were spread around trying to find a safe place, shattering rocks, cutting trees and silencing Peshmargas. The choppers were very difficult to fight with. Their gunners fired rockets addition to the machine guns and they were very accurate.

Kameran and Sardar weren't very far from each other. Their commander was shouting to take cover, and there was chaos and confusion among the rebels. They scattered as they ran, and they appeared not to know what they were doing. Sardar ran to his commander to help him to gather the men as fast as they could and try to move quickly to higher ground, where the choppers might do less damage. Sardar then went back with a few other to join Kameran, who was attempting to provide cover to the others while they retreated. The commander began gathering the men for retreat, but just then he saw the Jash were now coming up both sides of the mountain. He had no choice but to stay where he was and fight.

Sardar told Kameran he should go to a location a little farther away. He wanted to try to defend their position so that the rest of the men could retreat. The Jash and army attacked from all sides, while the choppers shot at them from above. They heard the cry of many Peshmargas being shot or killed.

Sardar could see few Peshmargas reaching the top of the mountain. He knew if they could reach the point, it would provide some protection to them so that they could retreat. As he was about to move on, a rocket hit a rock just few meters away from him.

The helicopter had missed him, but Sardar felt sudden pain in his legs and his back. But he didn't have time to think about that now: the enemy was approaching. Kameran was still not far from him. Two other men on the other side of Sardar were aiming to kill, so as not to waste bullets. Sardar shouted to Kameran and others to be careful with ammunition. He saw Kameran searching to find a sure target. Then he stood up to fire a round at tow Jash who were very close to him. The two Jash fell and rolled away from them like a big ball. "This is for all innocent children you have made orphans!" he shouted.

Sardar felt tired, and he couldn't feel his legs. He didn't want to worry Kameran, who was moving away with other rebels to find a secure place for cover and to try to provide cover to their friends who were still exposed. Someone shouted to Kameran to retreat, and just as he did so, the man was hit by a rocket and was killed. Kameran waved at Sardar and shouted. "Move! Get up! Run!"

"No, you'd better go on ahead," Sardar shouted back.

Kameran saw that Sardar wasn't moving and he was pale. Kameran knew Sardar wasn't pale from fear, because Sardar wasn't afraid of anything. Kameran realized Sardar must have been wounded, and he immediately ran over to him. Sardar was bleeding, but he didn't know where it was comings from.

He tried to move Sardar to a safer place. He grabbed him and tried to get him to stand, but Sardar couldn't do it and asked him to stop.

“I’ll carry you, don’t worry,” Kameran said. “The Jash are still attacking. They won’t give up until they’ve kill us all.”

He changed his magazine and sent one more round out into the Jash. Then he grabbed Sardar’s arms, but because the ground was still wet and muddy, Kameran lost his footing and fell. At that moment, he was hit by enemy fire. He tried to stand up, but he fell again and started rolling down the mountain.

Sardar was angry. He knew his last brother and friend was gone forever. He took aim at Kameran’s rolling body, thinking he would finish killing him himself rather than watch him be killed and tortured by Jash. But he couldn’t do it, Kameran was his brother! How he could kill him? He leaned back on the that was giving him some cover and sobbed. Then he took his gun and shot blindly at the Jash.

Kameran’s body was rolling directly toward the Jash, who were now sending hundreds of bullets into Kameran’s already-dead body. The body rolled to a stop on a rock. Jash surrounded Kameran and continued shooting at him. They spat on him and kicked him, and they shot so many bullets into him that he looked like a fishing net. They took his body and threw it into the back of a truck.

The incident brought the fight to a halt. The Jash started dancing and singing, happy to have a body that would reap them their bonus. In that short moment, two of Sardar's friends grabbed Sardar and managed to pull him to safe place.

It appeared that the soldiers didn't want to fight, they were forced to, but the Jash were doing all the killing. It is hard to understand the mind of human beings, who could anyone have a job 'killing innocent people' to feed their families as the Jash were doing. They weren't fight for a cause as to free their people, but fighting for money.

It was getting late and the army wouldn't want to fight anymore, and they were retreating as well the Jash. They had many casualties, but the rebels had even more.

The attack should have happened the day before, while all the rebel forces were gathered in one place. Why hadn't they attacked yesterday, when there were more than two hundred rebels in the same place? They were well informed that a small group would stick around, and the informant has given them exactly the information they needed.

Sardar had been hit by the debris from the rocket strike, and he had more than fifteen pieces of metal stuck in his body. Nine rebels were dead, and almost all others had at least one or two injuries. The Jash had succeeded in killing Kameran and many others that day.

The only doctor and two nurses who were with the entire rebel forces, had come to help the injured. Those who needed to be evacuated to a more secure place where they could recuperate.

After a few months Sardar was back on his feet. He still had few pieces of metal in his body that would have to stay there because it was too dangerous to remove them and they didn't proper equipment to remove them. He had to learn to live with it. He now had a limp, thanks to his right leg being damaged by the rocket debris. He felt his life had been destroyed, but he was still one of the finest of the Peshmargas, and he still had hope that a generation in Kurdistan would live free. He clung to that hope even though he himself had few people in his family left to live for.

While young men were fight the government of Iraq and its allies the Jash and the hired militia, Talabani had secured the life of his family and other relatives in London and Damascus. Now he wanted to come back and end his long vacation. Perhaps he finally saw a light at the end of the tunnel, and he saw an opportunity to realize his life-long dream: to control and secure the Kurdish leadership for himself and monopolize it like all regimes in the Middle East. And like all the kings, presidents, and sultans who had come before him, to hand down the leadership to his son and grandson.

Or perhaps his guilty conscience was awakened when he realized that his host country, Syria, treated his Kurdish brothers and sister as if they didn't exist. The Kurds in those countries like Syria, hadn't been allowed to use their mother tongue, and their rights as Kurds were ignored. 'Kurd' wasn't a pleasant word, but it was rather an insult.

One of the Syrian Ba'ath party's leaders and the founder of the party, Michel Aflaq, had declared that the existence of Kurds was an absurdity.

Talabani was aware of the ignorant of the masses, he knew, he just need to blow the whistle and thousands of men will run to him and fight for him no matter what the cause might be.

In 1977 Talabani settled in the Qandil mountain. It didn't take long before he managed to gather around himself as many as a thousand young men. He was still popular among Kurds, especially in Slaymany and Kirkuk. That pose an enigma for Sardar. He just couldn't figure out! How could so many people be wrong? He struggled with that riddle the rest of his life.

The first thing Talabani did was to set up business as a tax collector so that he and his follower could collect taxes on the remnants of the poor villagers. For centuries, Kurdish villagers had traded goods across the Iran and Iraq borders. Collecting taxes on this trade provided a good income for Talabani. The villagers now had to content with this taxation in addition to usual assortment of bandits who continued to rob poor people. The only difference was Talabani did it in the name of Kurdistan.

Talabani and his followers did very well for themselves in the cool Qandil mountains. They built mud brick houses, a luxury compared to most villagers. He led the life of a wealthy landowner, surrounded by armed men ready to die for him in a minute...like the men who had been ready to die for the imaginary 'Father of the Kurds' Barzani.

The new of Talabani's return to Kurdistan was a shock for the rebels in the mountain of Qaradagh. The commander of the entire rebels was a man named Aram, as Sardar's son was called Aram. One day he gathered all his men to tell them the heartbreaking news. "My friends, prepare yourselves for the long-lasting and bloodiest brother-killing in the history of Kurdistan," he said and socked everyone. "Talabani has come back, and he is preparing himself for battle. He is already in the ring, waiting for his opponent, and the match will begin."

By now there were many armed group of Talabani's followers under the banner of PUK in other parts of Kurdistan. They armed themselves for the fight with Iraqi government.

However, many of them were bandits living on the poor farmers, collecting the taxes they had imposed on them. Some villagers had to pay two or three times in the same day to different armed groups.

Nonetheless, as soon as they found out that Talabani had come back to challenge them to another match, the Barzani clan regrouped themselves for the challenge. They too like Talabani, still had many followers among Kurds, and that was another enigma that shocked many. How could people be so blind as not to see the crimes and betrayals that the two clans had brought upon the Kurdish people?

The Barzani clan settled their armed men around the territory closer to the Iranian borders to make an easy getaway passage for themselves and their men in case of another betrayal. Even if they ended up having to run with their tail between their legs, it would be easy to get away if they were in that region.

As Talabani settled in, he finalized his plans to eliminate any threat to his reign. He made it clear that Kurdistan belong to him. He surrounded himself with men like himself, men who were interested in power. Talabani convinced both his followers and the bandits groups to join forces with him and fight for Kurdistan together. They all agreed to work with him under the PUK and Talabani's leadership.

While he was gathering all bandits and thugs, he also had plans for all his enemies and friends, whom he feared that one day, wouldn't be friends anymore.

Therefore, he had all planed in advance.

Then it was time for him to get rid of those of his closest friends who might pose the threat to him...to weed out his ranks of his perceived enemies. There were two or three men he feared most. One was his closest friend and his most loyal servant a man called Ali Askari. He had spent his entire life to serve Talabani and his family, yet Talabani feared him most. Therefore, it was time for Askari to go.

For his evil plan to succeed, he had gathered his forces and explained that unknown sources had sent them weapons and ammunition to help them to fight Iraqi government. Therefore, he needed brave men to do the journey to the border of Iraq and Turkey border and bring the weapons. He chose Ali Askari, his righthand man, his longtime friend, and few others as the leaders of the mission. The commanders of the mission, perhaps knew the intention of Talabani, they knew Talabani's plan wasn't to bring weapons but to eliminate the remnants of the Barzani clan, which spread on the Iraqi borders with Iran and Turkey. He wanted to kill two birds with one stone. However, that wasn't being a problem for the bandits, they wanted a piece of the pie. But they wouldn't have that piece if they wouldn't serve a man like Talabani.

Talabani, as he was deceitful, managed to gather around nine hundred young men and convince them to fight for Kurdistan. He reminded them of who he was right about Barzani's clan and their betrayal of

Kurdish people. Now it was time for all of us to unit and fight our main enemy the Iraqi government. He also convinced them if Barzani followers wanted to join us, they are welcomed among us.

Talabani was a smart man, he knew how to survive. Even before one single shot was fired at the enemy, his plans to eliminate those he thought pose a threat were in place.

Nine hundred young men were sent to the Hakkari territory, a triangle where Iran, Iraq, and Turkey meet. Nine hundred young men walked toward the Hakkari territory, and only one third of them escaped the fateful trap that had been laid for them in advance. The rest never came back. However, when the news of the failed attempt to eliminate Barzani clan reached the remnants of Talabani clan, he wanted to stir up more hatred toward the Barzani clan by accusing them for the massacre.

Sardar had lost his friend Kameran, and he had no idea what was going on with his family. Many months passed, Sardar and the rebel forces had many other bloody battles with the army and the Jash. They killed many of them and they noticed that there were more and more Jash, as if Kurdistan had become a Jash factory. The Peshmarga suffered many losses. However, their number were growing by day.

A year after the Hakkari tragedy, one hot day in July, Sardar sat with his friends after they had finished the day's educational circle. They were gathered under a large tree, and the smell of fresh tea filled the air. They enjoyed the camaraderie as they told jokes and teased each other, savoring their tea.

Through the narrow passage leading to the mountains, the guards saw two men approaching. From far away they looked like villagers. The guards shouted to the groups letting them to know that there are people were coming. Sardar quickly, sent few armed men, down the hill to meet them before approaching too close. Sardar stood up and watched the men approaching, and after a while they let the two men to come up to the mountain, where the rest of the rebels were gathered.

When Sardar saw them, he could see they were two young men, had small beards on their bonny faces. They looked exhausted. As they approached, the laughter and the jokes stopped. The two men exchanged greeting with the rebels. As they stood there one of them said, "We are looking for..." he was unable to finish. Sardar as if he awakened from a dream he shrugged. He was eyeing the young man, "Shwan?" he exclaimed. When Shwan heard his name, he turned and saw Sardar standing with his arms open, his Kalashnikov hanging on his shoulder and a walking cane in one hand. Shwan rushed to him. They hugged and embraced. Sardar didn't want to let him go, until someone shouted, "Let the man breathe!"

As if waking up from a dream, he released Shwan and asked him to sit. Shwan introduced his friend. "Uncle Sardar, this is my friend Zorab," he said. Sardar shook his hand and welcomed him warmly. Sardar's friends understood they were family, and they allowed the three men to go off alone together. Sardar let the way, walking with the help of his cane, toward an old tree trunk where he, Shwan and Zorab could sit and talk. Shwan, his face drawn with worry, sat next to his uncle and put his arm around Sardar. "I'm happy to see you again, Uncle Sardar," he said. However, he didn't want to start interrogating his uncle, and at the same time he wanted to tell him immediately about his son Aram...he wanted to deliver the bad news he had quickly. Like pulling a bandage of a wound, but he let Sardar start the conversation.

"Tell me, how are you doing?" Sardar asked. "You have grown so much! You are a handsome young man."

"I'm very well, and, how are you?" Shwan said. "But what is the cane for, uncle? And how is Uncle Kameran?"

It was a long time since he had heard Kameran's name, and Shawn's question made him burst into tears. Shwan understood that meant that Uncle Kameran had been killed. Tears ran down his cheeks, and he sobbed with Sardar quietly.

Sardar told him the story and explained why he didn't have the courage to tell his family. It would be difficult to tell Nasreen that her husband had been killed and his body taken by the enemy. "I just couldn't bear the pain. Do you understand, my son?"

Shwan turned his face away from Sardar; he tried to hid his face in his shaking hands.

"I have lost two of my friends and brothers." Sardar said and put his hand on Shawn's head.

"I have lost two of my friends and brothers too," Shwan whispered. He was afraid the news he had to tell Sardar.

Sardar heard what Shwan said, but he wasn't sure if he meant his father and his uncle or...

"Me too, uncle I lost Aram and Awat! I too lost everything, uncle!" Shawn's cheeks were wet with tears. There was no consolation for him. He had really lost everything and he left alone in the world. He didn't have any hope.

Sardar sat motionless. He didn't move, he shed no tears, and he didn't sob or show any emotion. He simply took one of Shawn's hands.

Shwan didn't understand why his uncle stopped crying. "Uncle, if you want to be alone, we could leave you for a while," he said.

"No, my son; don't go," Sardar said. "I'll tell you something. When I lost my father, I cried a lot, and it was the most painful experience anyone could have imagined. When I lost my friends, Kameran and your father Sirwan, I felt like a bird losing its two wings, but when I lost my son..." he paused. "Sometimes you express your pain with words, and other times you express it with silence. That is all I can tell you, my son."

"I wish I could understand," Shwan replied.

"Would you like to tell me what happened to them.?" he softly asked Shwan.

Shwan took out his cigarettes and offered them around. He lit his cigarette and took a deep puff. Then he said, "A year and a half ago, the three of us, Aram, Awat and I, decided to join the rebels. The situation in Slaymany and the surrounding had become unbearable for many young men, especially in Halabja So, we joined the rebel. We were like brothers until the Hakkari tragedy We were all together with this young man, Zorab…" he pointed to his friend who still was sitting quietly... "He really saved my life. I owe him my life..." he stopped, crying so hard he couldn't talk anymore.

Zorab softly patted on Shawn's shoulder, and he said, "I met Aram, Awat and Shwan when I first joined the rebels. We became very close friends, and then we decided to join the rebels who were going to Hakkari.

We thought we were fight the enemy. We didn't realize that the lives of many young men would end on the snow-covered mountain of Hakkari on that fateful journey planned by Talabani and executed by Barzani brothers." Zorab couldn't hide his hatred toward the Barzani and Talabani clans. Each time he mentioned their names, he hid the tree trunk with his fist. He stood up and lit another cigarette.

Shwan seemed calmer, he too lit another cigarette, looked at Sardar and said, "At that time of the year, around early march, the Hakkari mountain are still covered with snow, as you know. We weren't prepared for that kind of journey. We didn't have warm clothes or good shoes for walking in the snow-covered mountains, and yet we kept walking for hours— for days. We didn't see or hear anything that signaled danger.

"We went on like this for many more days. What little food we had was gone, but finally we were about to reach our destination. We were exactly in that area that is called the '*triangle*', where Iran, Iraq and Turkey meet, and we were happy, knowing we would soon be there.

"Then suddenly we found ourselves under a rain of bullets coming at us from every direction. We're in the snow, which of course had made us much more visible to our invisible enemy. We couldn't see anything. They were well hidden in mountains."

Sardar sat quiet and listen to the two young men

tell the story of their lost friends, he looked at them and said. "How did your commanders react?"

"They were as surprise as we were, I believe," Shwan replied.

"Those Kurdish tribes, which lived closer to the Turkish border, had been under the influence of the Barzani clan, and they were instructed by the two Barzani brothers." Zorab said. "They were told that a group of armed men, mostly communists, infidels and Iraqi spies, were coming to their area with the intention of taking their lands and killing their men and taking their women. They were told it was up to them to protect their honor, their land and their homes. That was one contingent of the enemy."

"The Barzani brothers themselves were ready too, with a group of armed men." Shwan began again to tell the story. "They were able to gather more than thousand hateful men for the slaughter of Kurds, and they were in place before us, well prepared. And it was clear that Barzani brothers had been informed before we reached their territories. Barzani brothers were the second enemy.

"At the same time, the Iraqi and the Iranian armies were informed too, of the march." Shwan continued. "They too were ready for the slaughter. No one ever knew how the two armies knew about the march. There was a theory that Talabani himself informed the two governments. Everyone was certain that Talabani was capable of doing even more than that. He is a second Saddam in the eyes of many. Another theory was that Barzani brothers who notified the two governments. In either case, it would be no surprise. Both were capable of massacring Kurds."

"We didn't have any chance to defend ourselves against so many enemies." Zorab said. "The Barzani brothers and their tribe allies were shooting to kill, they were not just shooting to kill, but seemed intent on eliminating every trace of those young men who had been lured into the trap. No one knew the real reason for what was happening, but everyone knew about the rivalry of the two clans."

"Worst of all were choppers of the armies of the two countries," Shwan said. "They were flying low hunting us down, and what was ironic was that those choppers have been the enemy of all Kurds. They have been used to kill Kurds of all allegiances, but in that particular day, they were targeting one and only one target, the young men from PUK. They weren't targeting the tribes, or the Barzani brothers' forces.

"That fact that made things perfectly clear for our group. We suddenly knew we had been misled and lured to our death, but it was too late. On those high mountains, the body of those young men were rolling down the hill like snowballs, as they been hit by bullets. There was no one to come to their rescue. Many who weren't killed surrendered. Some surrendered to

Iranian army, others surrendered to Iraqi army, and the rest of surviving men, arrested by the Barzani brothers.

"Most of the commanders of the march, were executed, and the simple Peshmargas like us, were imprisoned for about four or five months, then we were released like animal from a cage.

Sardar sat staring at the young men. They were sobbing when they told the tale of nine hundred young men who thought they were fighting for Kurdistan. But instead were being used by the two criminal clans to settle their old accounts. Zorab took out his handkerchief and wiped his eyes.

"How Aram and Awat killed?" Sardar asked in a chocked voice.

Shwan gathered his courage, "We were behind a rock trying to find a target to shoot at, but we just couldn't see any. They were well protected and they were on top of the mountain. They weren't in a hurry, they were there to kill and they took their time to do the job.

"Aram and Awat were little downhill from where I was standing when one of the choppers fired two rounds of machine gun fire on us. The first round stopped exactly where I was sitting, but the second one...both Aram and Awat were dead, their stomachs were ripped opened and..."

Shwan lost control of himself and turned to vomit. He looked at Sardar and then ran away. Sardar and Zorab let Shwan alone and let him grieve.

"Talabani had two things in mind," Zorab said. "First was to get rid of his friends inside his coalition, because he considered them a threat to his authority. The second was to eliminate his rival the Barzani clan once for all.

"Those who were killed in those mountains were young Kurdish men. Their bodies remained there without proper burial. They don't have tombs that their grieving relatives can go and visit. The Barzani clan use the same method as the Iraqi government. They too had killed many innocent Kurds in mass killing, but at least those who were killed by Saddam were buried in mass graves. Those men were killed by Kurds and they haven't been buried.

"The crime of Barzani and Talabani are countless, horrific, and barbaric. They are nothing less than the crimes committed by the Iraqi regime. The march started quickly, ended quickly and was forgotten, but one day both Talabani and Barzani clans will stand trial to answer the cry of many mothers."

Zorab and Shwan decided to stay with Sardar.

The First Gulf-War

Iran in late 1979 was riding a political roller coaster, and things weren't going very well for the royal family. They were about to lose over the fragile political situation. There had been much uproar in many parts of the country, and uprising was on rise.

The Iranian religious leader, Khomeini, had been for some time, provoking the Iranian regime by asking the religious leaders inside Iran to stand up against the royal family and topple the Shah, 'the puppet of the great

Satan, the United States,' as Khomeini called monarchy. His speeches were a wake-up call to all Iranians to topple the Shah's regime.

The Islamic revolution had started. Thousands of students stormed out onto the street of Iranian cites. Demonstration became increasingly bloody.

American had tried to stop the turmoil, but their effort was in vain. Consequently, the Shah fled the country. Ayatollah took control and put an end to the brutal regime. They also put an end to the Iran's alliance with the United States.

Sardar was with his men and listening to the radio. Every radio channel was talking about the Iranian revolution and its effect on Iran's relation with the world. However, no one talked about how this new Islamic revolution was going to affect Kurdish people. As if there was no Kurds living in Iran. All the news was about economy and Western interests in the region.

Sardar listened as everyone else, to all the news about the Iranian revolution. He was watching the situation closely. He had already told his men to gather for the today's educational circle. Sardar's group now numbered about a hundred men. They sat crossed legs under the shades of trees, with Sardar facing them. "We start, as usual with a minute of silence for our brothers and sisters who have died so that we will have a better future," he said. There was hushed quiet, a silence that somehow seemed filled sincerity.

"Thank you, brothers," Sardar said. "As you know we are going through a very sensitive time. I might call it a 'golden time' for us…for all Kurds. Iran, as you all know, is going through a period of political unrest. The world in general and the US in particular are watching Iran with their eyes wide open. We are watching too. Now here is the question I would like to ask today to start the circle. Why are we Kurds watching the Iranian revolution?"

"We have to, because it concerns us more than anyone else in the region. There are more than eight million Kurds living in Iran, and their future is now and will always be our future." A man said.

"That is true," Sardar replied. "Do you think that our brothers and sisters in Iran think the same way? Do they know how important the situation is for all Kurds?"

"If they don't know, then we are all doomed," another man said with a chuckle. "We might lose the best chance our people have ever had in their history."

"I believe it will be a good opportunity for Kurds in Iran to separate directly and declare autonomy for Kurdistan," someone else said.

"That would be a good idea, but it's very far that Kurdish people in Iran will do so!" Sardar replied.

"Why" is it not what we want?" Zorab asked.

"Yes, it is what we want," Sardar said, "but take a closer look at what is going on in Iran in general and in Kurdistan in particular. It has been few months since the revolution started in Iran. The Kurdish people have divided into many so-called political groups, and they have no concern whatsoever for anyone other than themselves. All the weapons and ammunition they took from the Iranian army when they fled the Kurdish territories have now found their way to the black market for sale. No one care about tomorrow, they want to be rich as quickly as possible!" Sardar sat down he had pain in his leg, and he was upset. "The Iranian Kurds are making the same mistakes as all other Kurds have done. The Kurds in Iran are being misled by the cries of religious clerics, just as Kurds in Turkey answered the cry of Mustafa Ataturk's call for in 1920 and 30s for all Turkish citizens to unite under Islam and fight the infidels. As a result, many Kurd in Turkey were misled into participating in killing millions of innocent Armenians. And when Ataturk finished his atrocities against the Armenians, he turned his back on Kurds and eliminated all of them. Today Kurds in turkey faced elimination, repression and destruction of their territories.

"Kurds have been turning to religious clerics to save them. it's the same situation now. Half the Kurds in Iran have allied themselves with the Shiite Muslims and Khomeini, hoping that they will free Kurdistan! And that is our incurable disease."

“What about the other political parties, didn’t they have their own KDP?” another Peshmarga asked.

“Well, that is another problem,” Sardar replied. “The Iranian KDP doesn’t have much power in Iran, because people there see what the KDP has done to Iraqi Kurds and Kurdistan. They have lost all hope in the KDP and its leadership. And the KDP in Iran is an exact copy of the same old KDP in Iraq. People don’t trust them, no matter who leads the party. The KDP has lost the people’s trust, and if there are no parties to lead people, then what we expect? We expect nothing but chaos, anarchy and looting. And that is what is going on in Iranian Kurdistan, chaos and looting.

“During the turmoil in Iran, anyone with a little sense, had thought it was a golden opportunity for all Kurds, and especially Iranian Kurds. The day the Shah left Iran, Kurds could have taken the opportunity to unite themselves as one nation, to reclaim their independence from the central government. There was already the Iranian KDP, under the leadership of Qassim Lo, and they could have united their forces with the Iraqi Kurds.”

“If Iranian Kurds didn’t trust the KDP and Qassim Lo, why didn’t they come and join us?” someone asked.

Sardar was looking at his men with much pride, he lit a cigarette. “The unity, my friends, the unity,” he chuckled. "I remember my father talking about Barzani when he came back from his exile. He had started the armed struggle against the Iraqi government. My first question was, has Barzani tried to bring other Kurds into his fold? And the answer was no. He never sent wise men from his entourage to Turkey, Iran and Syria to convince every Kurds that the struggle of Iraqi Kurds is and would be for all Kurds. Do you know why? Because all Kurdish leaders are territorial. They have their own territory just like most animals do, and they fight to preserve it.

"We all are contaminated with the same virus. I can't feel and understand your pain until I feel it for myself. We didn't feel the pain of Kurds in Turkey. We didn't feel the sorrow of Syrian Kurds, but after we tasted our own pain and sorrow, we realized what our brothers and sister had been going through, and then it was too late, because the disease of territorialism had spread through our blood. Religion, especially Islam, has corrupted our mind. And we've been misled by the leaders, who were already corrupted by Islam."

"I believe that anyone who decides to lead, no matter whether it's a group of people, a football team, a political party, or a nation, must be sure not to blame his failures on others." A young man said. "He can't expect anyone to come to help him during a disaster. He is alone because he has chosen to be the leader...and he must be ready to die along with those he leads.

"From the very beginning of Kurdish struggle, we have failed every time we have fought. Nonetheless, there wasn't a single time we condemned our leaders our ourselves for our failures. Every time, instead, we have accused the superpowers or the enemy. We have never accused our leaders of not being capable of a leader of our nation. Our leaders knew we were surrounded by hostile countries, and they knew that the superpowers wouldn't put their interests in jeopardy for a bunch of armed men, yet our leaders have put our destiny in the hands of Russians, Americans, Iranians and Syrians. And we have failed time after time." The man sat down in his place.

Sardar looked tired, but he wanted his men to know exactly what was going on in Kurdistan. "The situation among our leaders reminds me of a story," he continued. "A couple had a little child who was outside in the snow, and the child was almost frozen to death. If someone didn't hurry to put a warm coat on the child, the child would die. The parents had the child's coat in their hands, but they were fighting about who would do a better job putting the coat on their child. By the time they figured it out, their little child was dead. That is the problem with our leaders. "Every one of them thinks they are the true leader and rightful owner of Kurdistan, and meanwhile Kurdistan bleeds to death. This is our problem, my friends." Sardar said, his voice catching. He turned his face.

After a few minutes of silence, Sardar wiped his eyes.

"The fight hasn't stopped in Iran. Now it has extended to Iraq too, and some group of Iranian Kurds are fighting the Iraqi Kurds," he said. "A golden opportunity has become a bloody war, and what has amazed many, is that each of those Kurdish political parties has flown a large Kurdistan flag…they all say they believe in the great Kurdistan."

Attack on Peshmarga suddenly declined in the middle of August, 1980. the rebels were happy to reorganize themselves, and they watched the situation very anxiously. In September of 1980, Sardar and his men were in the mountain waiting for some new. Finally, the news everyone had been waiting for arrived. Iraq finally launched its first attack on Iranian soil, and Iran had responded.

"I think this is better than anything that has happened for our people in a century," Shwan told Sardar.

"You are right, my friend, but..." someone replied. "Don't tell me 'but,' please!" another one said.

"Two regimes…the two enemies of our nation are fighting, and we may have a chance to reach our goal," Zorab said.

"That is true," Sardar answered with a sigh. "But the war isn't the Iraq and Iran war."

"It doesn't matter whose war it is," Zorab replied. "It's not our problem; our problem is, how can we mobilize ourselves against the two regimes? The American may help us to regain our freedom."

"Look, my friends," Sardar said, "how the war started is more important to me than the war itself, I'll explain to you why. When Khomeini came back, he told the world that they will change and the west will no longer be the master of the destiny of the Islamic world. The message had terrified the west and the American, and everyone searched for a solution to stop the lava of the Islamic revolution from reaching the neighboring countries. So, the cause of the war wasn't the hostile history of the two countries, but rather the west and America's fear of losing the holy oil in the region.

"They have tried many plans, but none of them worked. Believe me they even thought about helping Iranian Kurds to weaken Iranian regime. However, they had better idea much better than helping Kurds and create a headache for themselves; their friend Saddam, the man whom the Iranians and the Algerians helped in 1975, the American turned to their friend Saddam. After some negotiations, finally, they succeeded in convincing him to invade Iran.

"The Americans reminded him about the Algiers Accord in 1975, in which Iraq lost a lot in the settlement over the border waters dispute. Iraq gave up too much to Iran then, and now it's time for Saddam to take it back. Of course, the US and he west will help him with heart and soul. They don't object to a war with Iran.

"These were the reasons the US and the west didn't need to do the job themselves. That is why they used Saddam Hussein to do it for them and that scares me to death."

It was now three years since the war had begun, and there was no end in sight. One day, Shwan came to his uncle and said, "I want to talk to you about something, Uncle Sardar."

"About what, my son? Tell me," Sardar replied.

"As you know, we still have the old house in Slaymany. I was thinking about selling it. it's an empty house and no one live there. All the rest of the family still lives in Halabja and I may have something in mind for what to do with the money. What do you think?"

"Well, it's your house if you asking me, and you can do with it what pleases you, my son," Sardar said. "But it is dangerous to go to Slaymany. How do you plan to sell it?"

"I have friends who could do it for me. I don't need even to be there," Shwan answered with a smile.

"Go ahead and do it, son." Sardar patted on his shoulder. "But you didn't tell me what you will do with the money, are you in love, son?" he laughed.

"Maybe!" he laughed too. "I would like to go Halabja and visit the family, in any case."

"You want to go to Halabja?" he said and was quiet.

"Yes, uncle," Shwan replied. "I would like to go Halabja. And while I'm not here someone will come and give you the money. Then you can keep it with you until I come back." Two days later Shwan left.

The situation was a little better in most parts in Kurdistan. The attacks on the rebels were less frequent. Sardar and the other leaders in Qaradagh decided to take the fight to the enemy. They decided to move their forces closer to the towns and villages where they thought they might find where the Jash and the hired militias, which created by the Baathist, where hiding.

After a few weeks, Shwan came back from Halabja. Sardar greeted him, and he was impatient to know everything about the family. Hoping Shwan quench his thirst, the two men sat to talk about the family. Shwan told him everything Sardar wanted to know, but it wasn't enough. He wanted, or rather he wished that Shwan would tell him that everyone was still alive and well, including his father, his uncles, Sirwan, Kameran..., but there was no more news to tell.

Sardar was quiet for a while, sunk in deep thought.

He was thinking about the old days when he and Kameran planning their lives as one family. Now Sardar has no one to gather together and call the bird's nest. He was sickly, reduced to skin and bone, and his leg was getting worse by day.

He didn't know how to find courage to face wife and his daughter, his sister, his sister-in-law, and his mother. He was the cause of all the tragedy he had brought upon his family, and he had to live with it by avoiding any contact with them. He has to live with it until his death or if he was lucky to be killed in battle, but now he had to wait.

"So, did you find a girl to marry?" Sardar said with a smile.

"How do you know that I'm searching for a girl, uncle?" Shwan asked.

"I'm your uncle and I know when my nephew wants a woman," he replied and laughed.

Shwan laughed too. "I have found a nice girl from nearby village, and probably you have to go and ask her hand from her family for me. Especially, now that the two regimes are busy fighting each other in this brutal war."

"I'm happy for you, son." Sardar said with his eyes already moist. "It's good to have a woman, son. I'll do everything for you, and I'm sure you will be a good father and an excellent husband."

Then the war was in its fourth year. The Kurdish rivals in Iraq as well as in Iran, were as busy as ever, hunting, accusing and killing each other. There were more than ten different political parties in Kurdistan and there were many confusing agreements between one group from Iran and another group from Iraq to fight another group in Iran and Iraq. It had become so complicated that no one was able to keep track of who was really fighting whom, or for what.

In the middle of that brutal war, which hundreds of thousands of people had lost their lives, and the turmoil and the animosity between the Kurdish groups in both Iran and Iraq, suddenly Turkish Kurdistan gave birth to another Kurdish political force, the PKK. A socialist party, the Kurdistan Worker's Party, under the leadership of Abdullah Öcalan. The Kurdish people in Turkey had hope that this party will unite all Kurds under one party and one leadership to fight for Kurdistan, but over time Öcalan has shown his real intention toward Kurds.

He began selling socialist ideology to Kurdish people who had been contaminated and brainwashed with religion, and as if the socialist ideology has succeeded anywhere else in the world. He ran his party with an iron fist, as Talabani, Barzani…etc.

First thing Öcalan did was to eliminate his rivals in Turkey and in many other countries. No one could criticize him without risking his or her life. He was like Saddam, Hitler, and Stalin all rolled into one. In Öcalan's mind, there wasn't room for discussion or criticism. You either obey or you are a traitor.

Soon, he dropped his pants and knelled...just as brother Talabani had done nearly a decade ago...in front of his master, the Baathist. He asked Assad for forgiveness and in return, Assad allowed Öcalan to stay in Syria and open a military training camps. Meanwhile, the Kurdish people in Syria weren't even allowed to give their children Kurdish names, and they weren't allowed to register as Syrian nationals. Öcalan bowed to a dictator to allow him to fight for Kurds, while denying that Kurds have any right to exist in Syria.

Hasn't Talabani or Öcalan seen how the Kurds in Syria have been treated? If they have, then why do they always go to Syria? That leads many to believe that Syrian regime, might have been the friend of Kurds, and Kurds have been blind not to see it.

Öcalan might not have seen the reason, why Syria is helping one group of Kurds and eliminate another. As we know, Syria and Turkey share the Euphrates river, and the two countries have always had a problem with their borders and the Euphrates river. Syria using Öcalan against Turkey to reach its goals, but Öcalan can't see that. He too has to wait until he is thrown out.

Now Iran Iraq war had turned into full-blown war,

and now half of the world was involved in selling weapons to one side or another. Iran had accused Saddam of using chemical weapons, but international community wasn't hearing Iran's cry. They just wanted to prolong the war to sell more weapons and destroy Iran at any price.

However, UN and its allies knew well the profit of the war and not just the war, but the aftermath of the war. The two countries would eventually destroy each other, one way or another, and then they have to be rebuild. Who is going to profit from the rebuilding of the two ruined countries? Those who started it.

Life for Sardar wasn't easy. He blamed himself for what had happened to his family, and he had lost every hope for redemption. He was falling apart physically; he had been injured too many times. He was still alive, but he didn't want to be alive, and he began to say that he was living only to suffer and for no other reason.

He was all alone in the world. He had lost all hope for humanity, and he couldn't find a light in anywhere or anything. That was why he had decided to continue the fight in the mountains of Qaradagh. He was now one of the most respected leaders, and he was loved by all his friends. They too understood him and his pain.

In the shadow of the war, the Iraqi army was obliged to reduce the size of its military presence in most part of Kurdistan. And that gave the rebels a chance to breathe. That might have done some good, but many golden opportunities had passed them by. The many Kurdish armed factions didn't notice that most part of Kurdistan had been emptied of the Iraqi army, because they were still too busy in their bloody brother-killing.

It was during the middle of the war when things went from bad to worse. This time Barzani's son had renewed his loyalty to the Iranian regime and promised Iran he would help its military invade Kurdistan without any objection. The Iranian were waiting for such a chance to engage the Iraqi army from different fronts, and with the help of Barzani's armed forces, the Iranian were able to capture many parts of northern Iraq.

The response by Iraqi army was quick and swift. While most of the poor families were sleeping in so-called modern villages, the Iraqi army raided their homes and made people get up and leave. Between six and eight thousand innocents, unarmed poor Kurds from Bahdinan region were put into military trucks and driven away to the south of Iraq. They were held as prisoners for a while, and then they were all massacred and buried in mass graves.

One day, Sardar was out, it was a little cold, but he preferred the cold weather over the hot. He was feeling a lot of pain in his leg. He sat down on a rock and lit a cigarette. He sighed; he was tired and worried, because Shwan and four other Peshmargas were out in Slaymany on a mission and they were already days late. He couldn't hide his worries, but he didn't want to worry his men, either.

Two of his friends came and sat with him and asked how he was doing. They knew he was worried. "How are you, Sardar? They asked.

"I'm good, but things aren't" he said.

"Why? What is going on?"

"The Barzani family has again joined forces with Iranian revolutionary guards," Sardar said. "You know the Barzani family allowed the Iranian army to cross the border, and they were leading the revolutionary guards into Kurdistan. The Iranian now have free rein to attack the Iraqi army on one front and fight the Talabani clan on the other. isn't that madness? isn't that stupidity? isn't that the biggest insult to all men, women and children who gave their lives to protect this land?"

"What do you expect from them?" his friend replied.

"You are right, my friend. I shouldn't care what they are doing," he said. "Today Barzani joined Iranian forces, and I'm sure tomorrow it will be the Talabani who join them. Just you wait and see."

Three weeks passed, and Sardar and his men still had no news about the five Peshmargas who went to Slaymany on a mission. Late afternoon, the guard on the top of the mountain sighted two men coming toward them he signaled the other to go and see who they were. When the men approached, Sardar could see they were his men who had been missing for more than three weeks...but there were only two of them.

Sardar was certain this meant that his nephew Shwan, would never come back and he would never see him again. And that turned to be true.

The two men told Sardar what had happened to them. After they had successfully executed the mission, they were on their way home when they were ambushed by the national guards. The three other Peshmargas were killed instantly, and the two others were injured, but managed to escape the ambush. They hid themselves in Slaymany and were treated medically until they could come back. They told the story, and they told Sardar that they were very sorry that they couldn't bring back his nephew's body.

Sardar was silent the whole time. He didn't cry; he just sighed, grabbed his cane, got up and walked away. His men left him to be alone.

Kurdistan's situation was deteriorating day by day, and it seemed no one cared about it. The friendly relationship between Barzani clan and Iran angered Saddam. In fact, Saddam was furious. He swore to put an end to the Kurdish problem, but he would have to wait a little more. The relationship angered not only Saddam, but also Talabani clan. Sardar was right about the Kurdish leaders and their stupidity. In 1984, the fighting among all the armed groups of Kurdistan rebels reached its peak. Then Talabani wanted to retaliate for Barzani's decision, and under the leadership of Talabani's PUK, established negotiations with Saddam regarding autonomy for Kurdistan under the federal government.

But the negotiations were stopped by the Iraqi government, for two reasons. The first reason was that Iraqi government was under pressure from the Turk. Turkey was constantly threatening Iraqi that if they allowed Kurds to have autonomy in Iraq, the Turkish government would cut the oil pipelines that went through their territories to Turkish port city of Jehan on the Mediterranean Sea. The second reason was that Saddam was smarter than the Kurdish leaders. He knew if he let the Kurds kill each other, he didn't need to fight them or negotiate with them at all. So, Iraq complied with the Turkish threat.

But now the Iraqi government resumed its attacks on Kurdistan with all the military force they have had at their disposal. The army was busy with the war with Iran, but that didn't stop them from fighting on two fronts.

By now the Barzani family and other political

groups who allied themselves with Barzani had offices in the capital city of Tehran and many other cities. But that wasn't all. The armed groups in Kurdistan, both in Iran and Iraq, were engaged in the worst kind of brother-killing. Almost every group was fighting a different group, whichever one was closest to their territories. In the middle of all this fighting, the most affected were the poor villagers again. They were punished by all armed group. One would enter one village today, and the next day another group would enter the same village. The second group would punish the poor villagers for letting the former group to stay and receive food. In addition to simple punishment, torture and summary executions were becoming routine.

The killing of innocent people by Kurds and the bombing of Kurdistan by both Iran's F-15 and F-16 and Iraqi's MIG and Mirage fighter jets all took their toll on the Kurdish people.

The Kurdish territories are both in Iran and Iraq were the easy targets for both armies. The Kurds were between the two fighting countries, and that is why it was bombed by both Iran and Iraq.

In late 1986, after Talabani failed to negotiate a deal with Saddam, now it became clear that Talabani had established a good relationship with Iran. Now it was Talabani's turn to be the agent of the enemy. This time the frustration and anger Saddam was feeling toward the Kurdish people was beyond measure. He again launched his attacks on Kurdistan. However, because he was busy with the bloody war and his hands were tied, and, he lost confidence that his army could do the job for him. Desertions were increasing every day. Therefore, he had greater plan to retaliate, and put an end to Kurdish problem once for all.

Sardar was still grieving his nephew's death, and the fresh memories of his lost family haunted him day and night. Sometimes he didn't even want to close his eyes, fearing the nightmares would come return. In them he saw the faces of his family, and the dreams made him feel like he was going insane.

One day, Sardar was outside sitting alone, as he now often did, smoking. Suddenly he felt a pain like electric current traveling down his leg from his spine to his feet. He put his cigarette aside and bent down to pull up his pants leg. He folded it up to his knee and saw that the large wound on his leg appeared to be starting to rot. He looked at the angry wound and thought he thought he was going to die. When he finished his cigarette, he went to find the doctor.

The young doctor looked at his leg and shook his head. "I'll be honest with you," he told Sardar. "You have about a week to get rid of this leg, or it will kill you. I'm going to send you to Slaymany. My uncle works in hospital there, he can't do the operation at hospital, but he will do it at his home. You will be safe there. The operation won't take long, but you have to stay few weeks to recover. Then you will come back to us, my dear friend."

Next day they arranged to smuggle Sardar to Slaymany, and several men volunteered to help him to the drop-off point. One man stayed with him in case anything happened. After he arrived to Slaymany, the next day he was operated and happy to have gotten rid of his rotten leg. He rested long time to recover and then he was back to the mountains with his friends.

Sardar was back without any incident. He felt better and was learning to walk with his new crutches he got in Slaymany.

But in was January of 1988, and Sardar by now felt like a broken man. It seemed nothing was left of the man he used to be; he was a dead man walking. He had lost a lot of weight. His long white beard made him look like he was a hundred years old. But however, he looked, he was still in the mountains, fighting with what he was left in him. But he was beginning to lose the desire to stay. He knew he wasn't the man he was before, even though he was still leader and was still respected as ever.

Still he was hearing a voice in his head that constantly told him to go back and see his family once more before he died. Shawn's death had taken away every hope he had left in him, but he decided he wanted to go home...if he had any home by this time. He was forty-nine years old. He talked to his men about his desire to go and see his family, and on the fifteenth of March, he pointed a man to be the commander in his place. He gave him a letter to be delivered his commander. He kissed all of them. He handed his rofle to one of his under-commanders, took his crutches and descended from the mountains of Qaradagh, headed toward Halabja.

From Halabja, Iranian could collect the military information they needed. During the first two weeks of March, Iran had begun launching attacks. For almost three days they had the area surrounding Halabja, and these attacks resulted in a massive retreat of Iraqi army.

Iraq was eager to retaliate. The cooperation between Kurds and Iranian army worried Saddam very much. His greatest fear was what would happen if the Kurds led the Iranian to the two dams in Dukan and Dar-bandi-khan. That is why Saddam must act, and act quickly.

This time Saddam wasn't planning to send infantry to Halabja. He planned to do something that would more easily break the alliance between Kurds and Iranian.

On the fifteenth of March, Iraq armed forces were ordered to leave the area surrounding Halabja, without giving any warning to the inhabitants. The next day the Iraqi air force began bombing Halabja and its surround-dings. And because of the previous Iranian bombing campaign, many people were still hiding, either in their homes or in those hiding places the government had left behind. They were afraid to come out. Then on the seventeenth the bombing stopped around noon.

Sardar arrived in Halabja early morning of the eighteenth. As he descended a hill and approached the town, it seemed different to him. He hurried his steps and tried to move faster. As he entered the first narrow street, he saw a few dead animals and felt a pain in his body. His entire body suddenly ached, but he didn't have time for pain. He approached the first row of houses and saw the body of a man who looked like a mummy. His fears increased, and he began breathing rapidly. There was another body, and another, people and animals lay motionless everywhere he looked. What had happened in this town, he didn't know, but he tried to ran. But even with the help of his crutches, he couldn't.

He came to the street that led to the center of the town. He saw a man kneeling over a woman's body, crying softly, as if he was singing to her. Another man ran helter-skelter, turning dead bodies and shouting, "has anyone seen my daughter?" Sardar noticed that town was full of journalists, photographers, and many other people who didn't appear to be Halabja residents.

The town seemed abandoned by its inhabitants, and it smelled death. There were dead animals everywhere. The photographers were busy taking pictures of the dead people who were scattered all around. The journalists interviewed witnesses and several people tried to help other find their relatives.

Sardar approached few people and asked what was going on, but it seemed no one had time to explain. He continued making his way through the crowd of people. He caught snippets of people's conversation and began to understand that Halabja had been attacked with chemical bombs. He began heading toward the area where his family lived, but he wasn't even hoping to see them alive after what he was seeing.

He passed a man with his son. They had just found the wife and two other kids dead. The little boy was clinging to his mother's dead body, crying, "I want my mom! Mom, wake up! Please, I want my mom!" it was unbearable. The man took his little boy into his arms and burst into tears. The boy was crying and tried to escape his father's grip, but his father squeezed his small body to his chest and walked away. The boy leaned over his father's shoulder and kept his eyes fixed on where his mother was laying, sobbing softly.

Sardar felt frozen. He had a lot of pain in his leg and his back, but this wasn't the time for pain, so he kept moving. Every so often he had to stop, and when he did, he didn't feel anything, as if his body had turned to wood. He would just stop and look around him. It seemed there was a cloud hovering over Halabja. At the same time, he didn't know whether to go back or continue his way to find his family. He was certain they were all dead, lying somewhere inside the house like mummies.

He sighed and walked a few more steps, slowly making his way toward his home. But then determination took over and he started running like madman with his two crutches. He suddenly felt he didn't have any time to waste. His family were probably all dead, but if they weren't, he knew they would want him to be there to hear their last words or their last wishes. At the very least, he could hold their hands.

He lurched along, sweating like a race horse. He was getting closer, and finally he reached the street where his family had lived for the last ten years. He saw other people searching for their families and their loved ones, just as he was.

He approached his home. The door was ajar. There was no sign of any kind of life...not a single sound. He knew what he was going to find. He could imagine them all in the basement, where they might have thought themselves safe during the bombing.

He stopped on the threshold of the front door, took a deep breath, and with one crutch pushed the door wide open. He stepped into the cold house. The smell of death was obvious, and there were signs that they had been in hurry to get to a safe place, the basement.

He approached one of the other rooms and looked

into it, looking for any sign of life, but he saw nothing. Then he turned to the stairs leading to the basement. But as he began to go down, he stopped, caught by the sound of people in the neighborhood screaming from their houses as they found the bodies of their loved one. He knew that he would soon be wailing for his loved ones as well.

He went down two or three steps and stopped again. He wasn't sure whether he really wanted to go down there and discover the unthinkable. His arms were hurting him; he hadn't grown accustomed to the crutches yet. He always had two legs and his pride, and now he had nothing, not even the courage to look at his beloved wife.

He went down the rest of the steps into the dark basement and stopped in front of the door that led to the room he thought they would have gone into. He supported his body on his crutches and with one hand opened the door. The buzz of a dozen of flies indicated the worst. There were no windows in here, but the light from the opened door dimly illuminated the room. The smell of dead bodies was unmistakable and overpowering. The air was heavy. Flies were everywhere. He stepped inside.

He sighed; he felt a pain in his heart that was traveling slowly up toward his throat, creating a lump there and then a flood of tears. The first body he saw, a foot or two from the basement stairs, was his sister

Nazanin. She was lying on the floor, her body folded, her head rested on her stretched arm. Her hair covered her beautiful face, he gently moved the hair from her face and saw that her eyes were closed. In her hand, she held a bunch of keys, probably the keys to the house. Her lips parted a bit, as if she was kissing death and finally happy to die and put an end to her long suffering. He sat down next to her, bent and kissed her.

Then he crawled along the floor of the basement to the wall, his brother Saman was leaned up against. He sat crossed-legged, his head tipped back a little, his mouth opened as if he was still crying for help. His two sons were on either side of him, their heads on his lap. It appeared they night have died before Saman and that he had taken both into his lap. They looked like they were sleeping. Saman had one hand on the younger son's head. Perhaps he was still comforting his little one when he too finally died. His other hand held his other son's leg. His son may have been telling his dad that his leg was hurting him, and his dad tried to comfort him, too.

Near Saman and his two sons, were Saman's wife, lying on her back with her three- or four-years-old daughter clinging to her chest. They looked like they were posing for a painter. The baby girl rested so peacefully on her mother's chest, it seemed it would be a grate sin to try to move them apart. He paused, looking around. He made out several other bodies in the dim light. He was quiet, but he felt overwhelmed.

He was very angry, but he tried to keep his anger under control. He knew this was the last time he would ever see his family, and that was why it was important that he take time to see them all. Near Nazanin lay the body of Kameran's wife, Nasreen. He crawled toward her. She had aged a lot. When he saw her, he couldn't hold himself back anymore, he began crying loudly. He remembered Kameran when the Jash took his body away. He wanted to tell her how her husband died, but he had never been able to find words to describe it. He bent over her cold body, grabbed her head, and said, "I'm sorry! I'm really sorry, Nasreen!" he kissed her and slowly laid her head back on the floor.

He turned to his right and saw his mother's body. The light from the door shone on her face and her snow-white hair. He crawled toward his mother, so overwhelmed that he felt he couldn't take any more. He beat on his chest and wailed. "I'm sorry, Mom, sorry I couldn't be here to protect you. I'm sorry," he cried beating his chest. He grabbed her head and put it on his lap and wailed. She too had aged a lot, but she had kind of smile on her beautiful face, as if she was telling the world not to be worried, she was in peace now.

He kissed her many times. "Mom," he said, "You have seen everything, and now it's time for you to get some rest and peace. Rest assured that if I ever loved anyone or anything it was because I loved you. I loved you more than anything, and still do." he burst into tears again.

He put his mother's head down. The air in the basement room was suffocating, as if there was no air anywhere. He crawled back to the basement door to see if he could get some fresh air. He sat down on the steps and lit a cigarette.

His eyes now accustomed to the dim light in the basement, and he looked at one body and the another, as if counting how many dead bodies were there. Then he saw his beloved wife, Salma, and his daughter. Salma the love of his life, was now lifeless. There she lay on the cold, cement floor of the basement with his daughter, Bayan, lying next to her on her side, just as she used to sleep. His daughter! He hadn't seen her grow up, and she had never had a proper education. She never had a chance to get married. Now she looked as if she was sleeping, not wanting to be awakened.

He threw his cigarette away and crawled to where Salma and his daughter were lying. He looked at his wife and remembered all those days when he waited for her to appear, just so he could throw a matchbox with a love letter inside to her.

He remembered Salma, Nasreen and Nazanin, the three girls going to school, giggling and whispering when they saw the boys. They were like sisters and were the very best friends. Now they had all died together, a few feet from each other, just the same as they lived in houses a few hundred meters a part.

He crawled to Salma and took her cold, lifeless feet

into his hands. He kissed them saying, "I hope you, too will find enough compassion in your heart to forgive me, my love. Rest in peace, the light in my life. I'll always keep a warm place for you in my old broken heart."

He approached his daughter, Bayan, who lay next to her protective mother. Bayan's thick, dark hair resembled her grandmother's...Sardar's own mother.

She looked very sad, but why not? She had grown to an age where she was too old to be married, and she didn't see her own father very often. She had lost her brothers. Why she should be happy?

He was about to lose his mind. He bent down and kissed his daughter, took his crutches and stood up. He looked around one more time. "I love you all. You are my lost family," he said. He hobbled around aimlessly in the dimly-lit basement, crying. He was all alone this time. There was not a soul around to comfort him or give him a shoulder to lean on.

A knock upstairs brought Sardar back to reality. He turned and slowly walked up the stairs. At the front door, he found two armed men. They greeted him, and respectfully asked him if there were any bodies in the house. He turned his head toward the basement...paused to be sure he could speak...then turned his face to the men and nodded. "In the basement," he said, and walked away as the two men went in.

The entire town was in pain. Everyone had sorrow and grief. But they had yet to come out and bury their dead. It took many weeks to bury all the thousands of dead. Sardar was there every day, watching the men lowering the wrapped bodies into the graves. In his old age, he had now buried the rest of his family in Halabja. There wasn't anything more terrifying than to lose so many people in one day. He had been robbed of everything and everyone. To whom would he turn for comfort? Who would have time for a man like him? Everyone else had the same story. He wanted to die, but death was still some distance away from him. He had to wait and suffer more; his suffering wasn't finished yet.

Those who died in the bombing lay out on the streets, inside the basement of houses, and rooftops. Those who hadn't died ran for their lives, some toward the Iranian border and others to the arms of the Iraqi army, right into their traps.

Halabja had finally found a place in the bloody history of humanity. The world was watching the bombing of Kurdistan unfold before their eyes. They might have been able to stop the massacres; they had the power to eliminate the evildoers. But they didn't stop it, because they weren't sure whether Saddam was a dictator, a criminal, or a mass murderer. Instead, they leaned back in their comfortable chairs and watched the massacre unfolding on their TV screens.

But that wasn't enough inaction. Instead of helping those who were wounded to rebuild their lives, they took some of them to European countries to be tested...not to find a cure for them. but to find out how effective the bomb had been on humans. There were no better subjects for the experiment than the Kurds, who had neither their own country nor anyone to represent them in the so-called the United Nations. The west world had invented the chemical, and the international arm traders had delivered it to Saddam. Saddam used the weapons on the Kurds, and now it was the Europeans' turn to examine the wounded to see the effectiveness of the lethal weapon they had produced.

The bombing of Kurdistan continued until late August of 1988, for a total of one whole year that Saddam bombed Kurdistan with chemical weapons. Thousands of villages were destroyed or burned down by the bombing, and no one helped or tried to stop Saddam from his madness. The true is that the world still needed a mad man like Saddam to justify their bloody inhumanity.

Thousands of innocent people died a horrifying death, while none of the Kurdish leaders not their families had so much as a scratch. Most of the Kurdish leaders had taken their families to the European countries long before the bombing.

The saddest part was that while the massacre in Kurdistan was unfolding, most of people weren't aware of the existence of a nation of thirty million people living in four different countries: Turkey, Iran, Iraq and Syria. The world wasn't aware that Kurds were the largest nation in the world without their own country. And had no representation in the world's communities. It was sad that thirty million people lived in the world without anyone being aware of them.

If what happened to the Kurds, had happened to Kuwaitis or Saudis, Americans and Europeans would have turned the world upside down. Within few days thousands of soldiers would have been deployed and the bombing would have stopped. But Kurds aren't Kuwaitis or Saudis, so why should any American and British soldiers sacrifice their lives for a nation that didn't exist in the eye of the world?

Sardar regularly went to the cemetery where his family was buried. He would sit near Salma's tomb, weeping softly and talking to her. He didn't know who should be blamed: Saddam, who used the chemical weapons, or the Americans and western world, who sold the materials and helped him to make them, or the Kurdish leaders who allowed the Iranian forces to march on the cities and towns of Kurdistan as if Kurdistan belonged to them. He didn't know. Most of the time he blamed himself for the death of his family.

Sardar wasn't ready to go back to his family's house. He needed some time to process his loss. His leg was getting better, and his wounds were healing slowly. He lived outside near the cemetery and spent most of his time there, and he didn't really care about anything else.

In the late September, the weather was becoming cold, so he couldn't stay outside any longer. He asked some people to come and help him clean his family's house; he needed his home.

It was agonizing to live in the house where everything still smelled like his family. Everything reminded him of them. He still had Shawn's money wrapped in a plastic bag. He took it out and looked for a good place to hid it. He found a small, locked metallic box, so he started looking for the key. He finally found it in a canister along with a few other keys, some matches and some prayer beads.

One of the keys opened the box, and he was surprised to find even more money in it. He sobbed at the sight of the money, because he knew immediately that it was his mother's idea. She had always wanted to keep some money tucked away for an emergency. He took Shawn's money out of the plastic bag, put it into the box with the other money, and locked it, pocketing the key.

He tried to live a normal life, but it was difficult. He was old and had only one leg. The thoughts of his family haunted him day and night. He couldn't sleep and was eating only once a day.

In the turmoil of the chemical bombing, with all the pain the Kurdish leaders and the world leader had brought upon the Kurdish people, with all the destruction within Kurdistan, with all the orphans children who walked on the destroyed streets of Kurdistan's cities and towns, with all the weeping mothers and daughters, and with all the sacrifices Kurdish people had made for Kurdistan and its future, hadn't stop them from killing each other. They insisted on looting Kurdistan, and their animosity growing.

All Kurdish political groups…or as they were starting to be called the political bandits, from Iraqi Kurdistan to Iranian Kurdistan to Turkish Kurds, were engaged in the worst brother-killing yet, and no one knew why they were going it. Everyone fought fiercely against everyone else all at the same time, and the poor people continued to pay the heaviest price. The leaders were getting richer and poor farmers were getting poorer.

Sardar was fed up with the Kurdish leaders and their constant infighting and accusations against each other for being spies. In fact, he knew all of them had been spies at one time or another.

The Second Gulf-War

Sardar tried to keep busy and put his life back together. Like many others, he tried to rebuild on the ruins of a city that was once rich and beautiful and full of life. Life for most people began to take shape again. However, the scars from the tragedy were inscribed on the hearts of everyone in Halabja and every Kurds with a drop of dignity...except the leaders.

He went frequently to the marketplace in the center of what was left of Halabja. He had made many friends, most notably a man who owned a small teahouse and had lost all his family in the bombing, sixteen in total. Business wasn't going well. The town was still in ruins, half of it have been destroyed by the bombing.

Every day, he took his crutches and slowly went out, taking the same route, he had taken for the last two years. The first place he went was the cemetery. Visiting the cemetery had become a daily routine. His teahouse friend often got there before he did, and they would greet each other as Sardar sat down among the graves of his family. His friend had lost all sixteen members of his family, old and young. He visited the cemetery every day, just as Sardar did.

Sardar would sit there repositioning a few stones, rearranging some flowers and stroking his hands along the tombstones. He would offer a cigarette to his friend and light one for himself. The two men would smoke, make some small talk and then they together they would leave to the teahouse.

This had been routine for some time now. Time was passing quickly. He managed to arrange his home with help of his friends. It has been almost two years since the tragedy. He was trying hard not to go mad, however, he was still not able to sleep well.

It was August 1990, a beautiful day, and Sardar had just finished breakfast. He took his crutches and went to cemetery, but his friend wasn't there. Then he headed to the teahouse. It wasn't busy, and a young man came up right away and put a fresh cup of tea in front of him. Sardar thanked him and said, "Where is the boss?"

"He went to try to find some sugar and tea. it's difficult to find any in this town, but he will be right back," he said.

The boss came in just then, when he saw Sardar, "How are you, my old friend?" he said.

"Well, as you see, boss, I'm still drinking tea," Sardar replied. "And what about you, boss?"

"It's difficult to find anything anymore," he said. Suddenly people were acting strangely, straining to hear the radio, as if there was an important new.

"What the hell is going on? Is it a chemical bomb again? Sardar asked. "If it's chemical bomb, please tell me! I have to run first, you know."

"Thank you! God, thank you!" a man came in shouting, throwing his arms into air, as if finally, God has answered his prayers. "Now it's time for Arabs to kill each other!"

"What is going on?" Sardar asked the man. The man hurried up to where Sardar was sitting, still waving his arms. "Iraqi army had crossed the Kuwait border and invaded Kuwait!"

It was very strange, Sardar thought. He couldn't help the joy he felt in his heart, and he didn't have such a feeling for very long time. What has happened to us? He wondered. He worried that he was feeling happy that others were suffering. Was it natural to feel like that? Or was it our so-called humanity that reduced us to being just selfish individuals? Have my losses made me seek revenge, and it doesn't matter who pay the price? He was amazed, but he was happy. "And do you believe it?" Sardar quietly asked.

"Yes, it is on the news! Listen for yourself!" the man told Sardar.

"No, I don't mean that it isn't on the radio," Sardar chuckled. "I mean that maybe the whole thing is a game! It's bullshit! How could Iraq invade Kuwait?" "It's true that Iraq has invaded Kuwait, and they are about to ravage the country." He triumphantly told Sardar. "I can't believe that for the first time Kuwaitis...Kuwaitis! ...fleeing their homes."

However, there was something Sardar didn't understand, it seemed beyond his comprehension. "How can this be?" he whispered to himself. "There is something very wrong with this picture." he was worried, but he couldn't put his finger on why. He tried not to think about it as he finished his tea and his cigarette.

The news of the Iraqi invasion of Kuwait was dominating all the papers, radios and TV stations. The entire world watched the events intensely, because it was Kuwait that had been invaded, not Kurdistan. Suddenly it seemed the entire world was busy. The international community held meeting after meeting. The future of Kuwait oil was in danger! That wasn't the same as Kurdistan's children been in danger! The Kurds could always make more children, anytime they wanted. However, the Kuwait oil wouldn't last forever, Sardar thought bitterly. The bombing of Kurdistan wasn't an important event for the world. Killing thousands of innocent Kurdish men, women and children was less important to the United States than the Kuwaiti oil fields.

"Are you celebrating boss? Sardar asked his friend.

"I think we are celebrating the invasion of Kuwait, aren't we?" he asked Sardar.

"I don't really care anymore who is invading whom or what they're doing it. Let the world do what it wants. Why should I care?" he said. He grabbed a chair and asked the boss to sit with him. "Let's talk politic now!"

Sardar was listening to the radio. He just couldn't understand how Saddam succeeded in invading Kuwait when he was under the watchful eyes of US, Israel and Saudis. He looked at the boss, "You know, boss," he said, leaning and whispering, I have asked myself the same question hundreds of time, and I just can't believe that Saddam was able to invade Kuwait without being allowed to. It sounds crazy, I know." he paused. "Listen, boss, if anyone looks at the map of the region, they can answer the mysterious question about Kuwait."

"What do you mean, old man?" the boss asked.

"Kuwait is surrounded by Persian Gulf, which has always been a vacation resort for American naval fleets. They have been in the gulf for eternity. That is one issue. Another is Saudi Arabia, Turkey, Jordan, and Israel, are all American allies. Think about Israel...the same country that was able to detect and destroy Iraq's so-called nuclear power plant."

Three men came into the teahouse. The boss rose and went to his customers. He greeted them and he served them. It was still hot in Halabja. Most people were at home taking their afternoon siestas, and the teahouse was almost empty. The boss came back and sat with Sardar.

"I'm not sure, boss" Sardar sighed. "But I know something is very wrong and that won't be good for Kurds. Just think for a moment and look at the facts. With all eyes on Kuwait on all sides, with all the spies and technology, with all the American forces in the region, how could Saddam invade Kuwait?"

"I don't know! Where are you going with this?"

"As we all know, the Iraq army has been dispersed

all over Iraq, and if Saddam wanted to invade, no matter how close Kuwait was to Iraq, Saddam would still need to gather his army. That would take at least one or two months." Sardar said. "What I don't understand is how Saddam succeeded in taking all his troops to the border of Kuwait, without being detected!"

"You know, old man, you are not bad, not bad at all!" the boss said.

"Well, I do my homework," Sardar replied with a smile. "But listen, this is not all. Let me continue.

"It's impossible for anyone to be foolish enough not to understand that everyone was aware of the invasion. The American, the Saudis, all must have been aware of the tension between Iraq and Kuwait in the last two or three months, prior the invasion. The Arab league meddling between them didn't help to loosen the tension. They all new when it would happen, they knew the devastation it would bring to the region and the world, and they didn't care. I may be crazy, but I need more than that to be convinced that US didn't know Kuwait was about to be invaded."

The boss was looking at him with amazement at how Sardar was putting things together. They sat there for long time and talked, while the boss serving the incoming customer from time to time. He liked Sardar, and enjoyed to have conversation with him.

Eventually, he got up and said, "I must go, old man. I'll be back later." he left Sardar with his thoughts.

Whatever the truth about the invasion of Kuwait, the Americans were busy comforting the Kuwaitis who now begged to be saved from the grips of the madman, which Kurds have been telling the world about his madness. But no one listened. Saddam was the same madman the Kuwaitis praised and helped for eight years in Iraq's war against Iran. And the same madman the Saudis and the Kuwaitis had worked for, arresting and extraditing any Iraqi soldiers who deserted, back to the Iraqi regime, where they would be executed. He was the same madman for whom the Kuwaitis had opened the doors of their banks for him during the war with Iran.

American were heartbroken to see rich Kuwaitis dispersed around the world. They must do something to help those defenseless Kuwaitis. The American responded to the cry of Kuwaitis, and they came to their help. American hadn't answered the cry of the innocent Kurdish children when they been gassed to death by the same madman. The American mighty forces gathered and forced the Iraqi army out of Kuwait. Thousands of Iraqi soldiers were killed, and the rest fled, with the American hot on their heel. The Americans fully intended to follow the Iraqi army until they got to Baghdad, where they would capture Saddam and bring him to justice. Of course, the American justice.

Meanwhile American pleaded with Iraqi people to revolt against Saddam. On March 7, 1991, the city of Slaymany was on the brink of a revolt. People from everywhere were attacking the authorities. They were fighting ferociously until the almost took power over the city. Meanwhile the leaders of the Kurdish rebels were waiting for the victory. After bloody fight between ordinary people and armed Iraqi forces, the Kurdish political leaders declared Kurdistan was free.

Sardar watched all this happened before his eyes, and he cried every time he saw the power of people when they came together. He thought his dream for the unity of his people was finally coming true, but he would soon learn this dream was short-lived.

Sardar woke up early one morning, as he usually did, he swallowed some yogurt with a piece of bread. He took his crutches and went out. After ha had visited the cemetery, he headed to his usual place, the teahouse. He was sitting there when the boos came in.

After they greeted each other, the boos grabbed a chair and sat next to him. "So, tell me, old man, what do you think?" he said. "Are we finally free from Saddam?"

"Take it easy, boss, take it easy! We are far from being free!" said Sardar.

The boss wasn't happy to hear that, but at the same time he knew that the old man was never wrong in his predictions. He hoped he would have some good news. But he also knew that the truth isn't always necessary the good news. "Why?" he said. "What is wrong, old man?"

"We are a simple people, and we are hasty. We do things now and regret them later," Sardar said. Lightning a cigarette. "Let me tell you, boss, this isn't the end, but the end will come soon. You know Saddam is still very much alive and his Republican Guards, too. What if the American want to remove Saddam, but they don't want to do it quite yet?"

The boss coughed and nearly choked when he heard Sardar's last sentence. "Are you crazy?" he almost shouted. "Why would the American not want to remove him?"

"Calm down, boss! I don't want to upset you, boss!" he laughed. "But let me ask you this. Which of the so-called the opposition leaders would you like to be the replacement for Saddam? If you answer this question, then you will understand why I'm worried, boss."

The boss was silent for a while. He lit another cigarette and said, "Well…I would have to choose a Kurdish leader." he replied.

"There you go! You got it!" Sardar shouted.

"Am I stupid for not understanding?" the boss said.

"No, boss. I didn't mean you are stupid!" he replied apologetically. "But if you want to choose a Kurdish leader, then tell me, which one would you choose? We have more than a dozen leaders, and all of them have claimed to be the right leader! Although we know for fact that none of them will agree to let the other to lead. How the devil are we going to agree who will lead a country so important to US and the west?"

The boss was silent. He understood what the old man was trying to tell him, and what he was trying to tell him wasn't good news. "Are you leaving boss, or you want to listen to more?" Sardar said.

"No, I'll stay," he said and grabbed his chair and coming closer to Sardar. "I have two new boys, and they are good workers. Business is picking up. I think I can relax a little bit and listen to your pessimistic discourses!"

"Now I am a pessimistic old man, boss" he replied. "First, you aren't much younger than me, second, allow me to inform you that I'm neither pessimistic nor optimistic. Rather, I'm realistic, my friend.

"As I told you, this country's oil is too important for the US. Iraqi people aren't...of course not. God forbid that the American help a country for the sake of its people. We have oil, my friend, and that is our curse." Sardar said. "The American won't allow Kurds to lead Iraq, because it would create a civil war among Iraqis.

As you know, the Arabs are the majority in Iraq; they would never accept a Kurd as their leader, that is one thing.

"The other thing is that the same American helped Iraq fight Iran! They helped Saddam to stop Shiite Islamic Revolution, and now the same Shiite in Iraq represent most of the Iraqi opposition. Their voice is the loudest among the Iraqis. Do not be fooled by American promises. Their promises go as far as their interests are kept safe. Otherwise, they are empty promises and nothing else.

"The US will never choose a Shiite leader to lead Iraq into twelfth-century. They might have said that about both the Kurds and the Shiites, but their main goals have to do with the leaders, whether Arab or Kurd. The US has never thought much about Iraq or Kurdistan as far as its people are concerned. Their goals have always been to control Iraq and its wealth for themselves. The leaders don't use reason; they fear reason. And because they are afraid of it, they have never conquered it."

The boss was sitting, he seemed he was afraid to breathe fearing he would miss a word. When Sardar lit a cigarette, he sighed and said, "So what are you saying, that maybe, just maybe, the US will let Saddam go? He asked.

"I'm not saying that," Sardar replied. "What I'm trying to say is that we shouldn't be so optimistic about all this uprising and killing and looting. I'm happy to see my people united, but unity hasn't come from us...it hasn't come from our long history of brother-killing. It hasn't come from the cry of thousands of mothers to stop the bloodshed of Kurd by Kurds.

"Unfortunately, it has come from the United States' desire to protect their interests in the region. Otherwise, Saddam is the same man who killed thousands of Kurds for no reason other than being Kurds. He is the same man who destroyed two countries and the lives of millions of both Iranians and Iraqis. Saddam is that same man. So why won't the Americans remove him now?" Sardar's voice getting calmer and he was almost whispering. "Can yo tell me boss?" he had tears in his eyes as he remembered his own innocent family.

The boss was quiet too. He realized what the old man was thinking about, and he was impressed by his discourse. He was also worried, but at least now he knew his options in case something happened.

"Old man, you aren't just an old man with one leg," the boss laughed trying to make Sardar laugh too. "You know too much, and you should be careful what you say in public." he took his chair and went back to work. Saying as he left, "I'll be back for more talking later, my old friend."

Sardar was happy that at least the boss was willing

to listen to him from time to time. It gave him the acknowledgment that he was still someone, not just an old man without any history.

The Second Escudos

Finally, Kuwait was liberated from Iraqi tyranny. The Kuwaitis celebrated joyfully, but Iraqi people went into hiding. Saddam's republican guards were allowed by the American troops to go back to Baghdad and resume their daily job of protecting their leader, Saddam, from evil eyes. And in this way, the American gave the green light to Saddam a free hand for him to destroy the Iraqi people's uprising and to reach the final stage of his criminal acts against Kurdish people.

It didn't take long before Saddam put his plan of retaliation into action. He launched continuous attacks on the Arab Shiites, killing thousands of them. Then he began his attacks on the Kurds. His frustration about the Kurds was beyond control. He ordered attacks on the Kurds using any weapon at his disposal.

The freedom of Kurdistan was short-lived. One day, Sardar woke up to the bad news. The Iraqi army was on its way to Kurdistan. Kurdish in many cities and towns closer to Baghdad had already fled their home. Slaymany was next, and within hours, people had begun fleeing to the mountains. Because Halabja was very close to Slaymany, people there quickly learned the news. Within a short time, half of Halabja was on run toward the Iranian borders.

Sardar came to the tea house, the boss was there, but he was preparing to leave. "What is going on, boss?" Sardar asked.

"The Iraqi army is on their way here. Go grab something and come with me. we're leaving, and I don't want to leave without you! Do you understand, old man?" he said.

"Where do you want to go?" Sardar asked.

"I don't know, I'll just follow the crowd," he said.

People in Halabja weren't like other people. They had already survived the worst tragedy. But they were so afraid of the chemical bombing that many didn't even care about their homes or belongings. All they wanted was to save their lives and the lives of their families.

Sardar remembered the night he and Kameran had fled with their families many years ago. He was terrified with the idea of leaving now without his family. However, this time he didn't have any family. He wished he was dead and had not lived long enough to see another exodus. But he had no choice. No one would stay in the city, and he had to leave now. He grabbed his crutches and went home. Half an hour later he came back. The boss was waiting for him in front of the teahouse. The two men, who lost their families in the worst tragedy, started walking along the dusty road. They had nothing else to lose, but their lives and their lives, they really didn't care much about.

"We have to hurry a little to catch the crowd." the boss said. There were thousands of people on the run; family with children following the parents, old men and women carried by their sons, babies crying on their mothers' arms. People were tired and hungry, but mostly they were afraid of the chemical bombing. That is why they wanted to reach the border as soon as possible.

Sardar and the boss were almost the last people in the crowd with the elderly, sick and people like Sardar. The boss was walking alongside Sardar. "I thought you were an old man," he said. "But you've proved that I'm actually not younger than you. I'm out of breath. Can we stop for a moment?"

"Yes, boss," he said. "and from now on you are the old man. Give one of your cigarette. I don't care if I reach anywhere at all." they stopped and smoked their cigarettes several people passed by. Looking at them as if they were two crazy men, standing there, smoking cigarette while no one else was taking time to breathe.

"You will come back and nothing will have changed! Today Saddam is looting your homes, but tomorrow it will be Talabani or Barzani! But don't worry, run along, my friends! don't mind us." Sardar shouted as people passed by them.

"That was good, old man," the boss said.

Within two days the mountains of Kurdistan on the Iran and Turkey borders with Iraq were covered with hundreds of thousands of men and women, old and young, and their families. Some were barefoot, other didn't have proper clothing, and it was cold and raining whole time. There was chaos among the people. Everyone feared another chemical bombing and they ran and kept running. They didn't know where they were going. Soon Iran opened their borders and let the refugees go inside Iran. There they set up camps with tents. Later Turkey also opened its borders.

By now Kurdistan and its fleeing people were the

main news in the world media. The entire world was watching the tragedy of many millions of Kurds on their big and small TV screen and were finally waking up to do something for them.

Sardar and the boss were standing in line to cross the border into the area where the UN had set up tents for the refugees. "Thank the UN, for their help!" the boss said.

"What! Thank them for what?" Sardar said angrily. "The UN, or as I call them the UC…it's not the United Nation, but the United Criminals, my friend…doesn't need to thank them. You see this tragedy? This is all because of those motherfuckers, those men with their expensive suits holding meeting and discussing whether Saddam is criminal or not. Those men have no conscience. Helped Saddam build his chemical weapon factory. Those men allowed Saddam to kill two million innocent Iranian and Iraqi people.

"Those men allowed Saddam to invade Kuwait, and the same men have now allowed this to happen. Now it's obvious they want to be praised and for us to ask for their pity. Then they can feel strong in front of millions of powerless people!"

Most people stayed as long as they could tolerate the horrible condition in refugee-camps under UN supervision. Then UN, realized that nothing could stop Saddam from his aggression, so they imposed a so-called 'no fly zone' on Iraqi air forces, meaning that Iraq had no permission to fly over the zone delimited by the UN. The zone provided a safe-haven from Saddam for the Kurdish people. But Saddam stood defiant to all threats of the UN and US.

Eventually, the news came out about the protection the Kurds were being provided by the UN and about the agreement of peace between the Kurdish armed factions, people started to go back to their homes.

Sardar and the boss went back to Halabja. The beautiful city they had left turned to a ghost town. The army wasted no time destroying whatever they could. As soon as they arrived, they took everything that would fit in their vehicles. They had done the same thing in Kuwait.

Sardar and the boos came back to the city. The old man's predictions had come true. The boss was too tired to rebuild his teahouse, but Sardar told him he shouldn't give up just like that.

"Boss, you aren't old enough to up your teahouse so easily." he said.

"What do you want me to do? No business will survive now, and I'm tired, old man!" he said.

"Well, Boss, how about you let me run it, and you just sit and give orders," Sardar told him. "Bring back those two young men and we will work together. I don't want anything, and you don't need too much, either, boss. The teahouse is everything we have! Not just us, the people in this town had nothing left. They come here to sit and talk. Why we want to take this away from them."

The boss looked at him. "Old man, since the day I met you, you have never told me anything that wasn't true, and now again you are right! Besides, what am I going to do if I don't work in the teahouse!"

They began to clean the place, just like everyone else who had to clean up their own stores and homes. Everything needed to be cleaned and prepared. After a while, the teahouse reopened.

Most people went back to their daily lives. It was quiet in Kurdistan. The tension and animosity between the different Kurdish armed forces had decreased, thanks to American efforts for meddling between them. They had created a provisional Kurdish government, and there was an election. It wasn't an election; it was rather a comedy. There was election, but there wasn't choice, it was already fixed. Fifty-fifty, between the two shameless clans of Talabani and Barzani. They had fought for more than six decades without reaching a fraction of what the US set up for them in days. That was the best proof yet of their incompetence and their inability to understand democracy. They were ignorant about what led to victory, and they proved to the Kurdish people that the only difference between Talabani, Barzani and Saddam was that the two Kurdish clan leaders spoke Kurdish, and Saddam didn't.

The UN put economic sanction on Iraq. They didn't allow Saddam to have control over its oil revenue. The UN was responsible for the so-called 'oil-for food' program, but in fact the program had many flaws. The sanction appeared to have no effect on Saddam, but had devastating effect on the lives of millions of Iraqis and on the UN's deep-pocketed members who were responsible for the program.

The imposed sanction on Iraqi people was called 'the sanction of mass destruction'. Every month, hundreds of children and babies had died from lack of food, clean water, and medicines. The death toll of people as a direct result of the sanctions was increasing daily, while those who imposed sanction on Saddam, both imposers the UN, and the imposed upon Saddam, were profiting from the sanctions. Many of the UN members were getting richer, while Iraqi mothers didn't have milk to give to their dying babies.

The so-called 'no fly zone' was initially set to protect the poor Kurdish people, but it turned out to be just an immense concentration camp. The UN's intention probably was good, and everything that appeared in the sky was good, but under the sky of the 'no-fly zone', was a hell. The UN has forced the economic sanction on Iraq, but every human with a little conscience knew the sanctions were the real weapon of mass destruction, the UN was looking for. It was a silent killer.

Under the sanction, Saddam had forced on all Iraqi another sanction, and finally the greedy, disgraced, bastard Kurdish leaders forced the poor Kurdish people to live under the worst human conditions. While they, the leaders had all the life's luxuries for themselves and their families. Most of them had already sent their families and relatives to foreign countries while poor Kurds were obliged to sell their belongings, furniture, cars and houses. In many cases people were selling their blood and organs just to feed their families.

After they reopened the teahouse, one day the boss came in and said to Sardar, "How are you today, my friend?" he stopped calling Sardar 'old man'.

"As you see, boss we are trying to make another day pass by without being told to go to hell," Sardar chuckled.

"Did you have anything to eat today?"

"Today!" he giggled. "Not yet, boss."

The boss went to the back of the shop and returned with a plate of food. "Here you go!" he said and put the plate on the table in front of him. "Go get some bread. This is something I cooked to see what you think about my cooking. I know you are a very good cook, but me,

I'm still learning. So, let's eat together.

Sardar was silent, but the food was too precious to say no to. He looked at the boss and hurried to get the bread. "You are a good man, boss," he said.

"What is new, my friend?" the boss asked.

"Well boss. What do you want to know? He said. "The sanctions are about to destroy what Saddam couldn't destroy. The entire world has finally come together to do something in the name of humanity and help the Iraqi people. They set the sanction of mass destruction.

"As you know, boss, it's now twelve years since the UN imposed the sanctions on the Iraqi. they had had little or no effect on Saddam. His gangs of criminals along with many international criminals and weapon dealers, are becoming very rich at the expenses of the poor Iraqi people. The death toll reached hundreds of thousands. Diseases among people is increasing, because of lack of clean water and sanitary systems. The mortality among newborn babies is skyrocketing, because malnutrition." he was quiet for a while. "Boss, as you see, Saddam still standing firm, defiant as ever despite all threats from the US." he said.

On September 11, 2001, the American got the taste of what many poor nations had experienced for more than hundred years. For the American, a crime wasn't a crime unless it was directed at Americans. The atomic bomb dropped on Hiroshima, the Vietnam war, the Korean war, various acts of violence in South America and Central America, all those atrocities weren't a crime against humanity, because they were committed *by* the United States and not *against* them. Now three thousand innocent Americans were killed in the most horrible death.

The attack on America was a crime and the responsible must be captured and brought to justice. For that reason, US and their allies invaded Afghanistan to catch Osama, but he was nowhere to be found. But instead of continuing to search for Osama, suddenly, the US linked Saddam and Osama together and decided to invade Iraq.

Sardar looked tired. He wasn't feeling well, and he was getting older. He didn't shave his long white beard and was so thin he looked like a skeleton in a suit, but his mind was sharp as ever. He still liked a good conversation with people.

He was in the teahouse one day when a man came in. Sardar recognized him; he had been coming to the teahouse with two other friends. Sardar hadn't seen him for a long time. He greeted him and said, "where are your friends, young man?"

The young man looked at Sardar and didn't answer. He went to sit in a corner of the teahouse.

Sardar didn't want to make him talk. The boss came in after a while and sat next to Sardar. "What is new, my friend?" he said.

"I don't know, boss," Sardar said. "Do you remember that young man, he used to come her with his friends?"

The boss looked at where the young man was sitting, "yes, I remember," he said.

"They were three friends, and now he is alone and looks lonely. I wish I could talk to him." Sardar said.

The teahouse was almost empty. There were four or five people were sitting and busy playing dominions. After a while, the young man took his coat from the back of his chair and approached Sardar. "I apologize for my ruddiness." he said. "I wasn't myself. You asked me about my friends."

"Here," Sardar pulled a chair. "Have a seat."

"Thank you," he said. He grabbed the chair and sat next to Sardar.

Sardar had changed a lot over the years, and his long white beard and long white hair made it difficult for people who had known him long ago to recognize him now. The tragedy of losing his family, sadness over the thousands of other families who had lost loved ones or were killed, and the years that his land and his people were ravaged by the war and the bloodsucking Kurdish leaders had changed his life. He wasn't the same man as before. Sorrows permeated his soul and was very visible all over him. He was also very old...around sixty-three, he couldn't remember exactly. His leg wasn't an issue anymore. He had grown used to it, and now it was almost as if he'd been born with only one leg. But he still had problem with his back. He was getting older and didn't feel well. He knew his time was running out, and he'd become a stranger to one and all. No one ever recognized him. He wasn't anxious to tell his story anyway; he told himself it belonged to him.

The young man sat down and said again, "you asked me about my friends." Sardar nodded.

"Well, one of them was killed, and the other one is still missing." he said. "I don't have any idea where to start looking for him."

"Did you asked the Kurdish government to help you?" Sardar said.

The young man chuckled and looked Sardar, "I have been visiting those idiots every day, but they don't have time for me. They don't have time to look for my friends. After all, my friends weren't rich people...they were simple people."

"Would you like another tea, my friend?" Sardar quietly asked. He waved to the young man who was working for the boss to bring another tea.

"Yes, please," he said. He took out his cigarettes and offered one to Sardar, then he lit one for himself. Then he reached into his pocket and took out his prayer beads, took another puff and looked at Sardar.

Sardar froze. His mouth fell open and he couldn't speak. He was looking directly into the man's hand, which held the prayer beads. The beads were a dark ocean green, and there was a Buddha figure on each one.

Sardar couldn't believe what he was seeing. He touched the prayer beads, "They are very beautiful." he already had tears in his eyes. Suddenly, he turned his face and burst into tears, and then he turned again and grabbed the young man in an embrace. "How are you, my son, Arras?"

The young man was quite surprised. He tried to push the old man away. But something stopped him and let Sardar continue to hug him. "How do you know my name, uncle?" he asked.

Sardar broke away, wiped his eyes, and looked at Arras. "You have grown to be a fine man, my son." Arras continued to look at him with wonder.

Sardar finally chuckled. "Do you remember who gave you these prayer beads?"

"My teacher! Are you...Uncle...?"

"Yes! It's me," Sardar said, grabbing him again and kissing him. "It has been long time, my son! The last time I saw you, you were a little boy, and now look at you! But tell me what are you doing here?"

A man came in Sardar greeted him and welcomed him. He turned back to Arras, ready to listen.

"Well, after you and Kameran left, I went to another city to finish my studies," Arras said. "Then, as you already know, there was war again. Somehow, I managed to finish my secondary, and after the war I was able to get in the education institute, where I became a teacher just like you. Later, I asked to be transferred here, so I could teach the children of this city that has been up against so many atrocities."

"What happened to you mother and sister?" Sardar asked.

He looked at Sardar, and he was quiet for a while. He had tears in his eyes. Sardar recognized those tears; they were tears of sorrows and grief. He put his hand on Arras's shoulder.

"Well," Arras said. "My sister…he swallowed, was married. She had three beautiful children. She moved to another village where her husband's family lived. My mother moved there too." he paused. "After the chemical bombing, they were all..." again he paused, trying to control his tears. "They were all dead except for my brother-in-law. He is still missing, like hundreds of thousands of other Kurds. There is never any news, and no one knows anything. No one knows whether they are alive or dead. The Kurdish leaders have no interest in pursuing their case. They are too busy filling their pockets. I still wait to hear something, and meanwhile I'm haunted by the terrible death of my mother, my sister with her three children."

"I know your pain and your tormented soul, my son," Sardar said. "I have gone through the same thing. I too lost all my family and friends and their families. I watched those I loved most vanish in front of my eyes. Yet I'm still here, my son. My family and I sacrificed everything, yet nothing has changed. Kurdistan is destroyed, and the sadistic leaders are only getting fatter."

Another man came toward Sardar and put some money on the table to pay for his tea. Sardar took it and gave him back some change. He thanked the man and the man left.

"There is nothing we can do." he said. "They have the people's consent, and our people are still applauding then. We all are ignorant. We need time to learn."

Arras was just as heartbroken as Sardar was, but he was happy to find his first teacher. This was the man who gave him the inspiration to become teacher, a man who showed him fatherly love, a man who was sitting in a teahouse without any history.

"I have to go, Uncle Sardar," Arras told him. "But I'll be back soon."

He left the teahouse and Sardar sank into a deep dream. He had been living his quiet life, thinking no one would ever recognize him, but now he had found someone to tell his story to. He was aware that his death was approaching. He wasn't that sick; in fact, his health was pretty good for someone in his age. But he knew it was time to join his family and his lifelong love.

He invited Arras to live with him. Arras accepted the offer with great joy. Sardar was in hurry to tell everything to the man who was once his student and was now his friend.

The Final Farwell

Sardar and Arras had many long nights talk. Sardar was in hurry to tell him everything that had happened to him and his family. From the day, he and Kameran had left Mawat. They laughed together and they shed many tears for their beloved one they had lost and would never see again.

One snowy night, Sardar came home and found Arras waiting for him in the kitchen. He had cooked food. They ate with much appetite, they had few cups of tea and smoked many cigarettes. While Arras was busy washing the dishes, Sardar went to his room and came back with his old safe box and some papers. He put down the box and held the papers in his hand. "Are you finished, son? He asked Arras. "Come and sit with me."

Arras finished washing the dishes, dried his hand and sat facing Sardar on the kitchen table. Sardar looked at him and said, "Son, I want you to listen to me, and listen carefully." he lit a cigarette. "You know I always considered you as my own son." Arras looked at him and nodded, yet he his worries increased. Sardar pushed the papers closer to him, "these are the papers for this house. I have already done all paperwork, I registered it in your name. I don't know how long I'm going to live." he said. "It's a big house, more than enough for you. It has four rooms, big kitchen and bathroom, plus the big garden as you know."

Arras was worried, "Why you are doing this, Uncle?" he said already moist appeared in his eyes.

Sardar pushed the box in front of him and said, "Here! Look at this. There is money in there, it's my nephew's Shwan, he had wanted to marry before he was killed. And I kept it didn't have the heart to touch it." he turned away and wipe his eyes. "Now it is yours, try to find a good girl here in Halabja, and get married." he chuckled. "I already talked to the boss, he is a good and kind man. He will help you to find a good girl."

Tears were already running down Arras's cheeks, he looked at Sardar and opened the box. He stared at Sardar without saying a word, he closed the box.

"Son, try to live life, have a family and few kids." Sardar quietly said. "Don't seek revenge, because the criminals are too many and too powerful, instead live life. Revenge is like a darkness, it will cover your life and it will blind you. You will never have peace if you looking for revenge."

Arras wiped his tear with his hands and said, "You are my father, and I'll do everything to honor you and your family and all those you have lost. I promise you, Uncle."

"And one more thing, son," he said. "If you wake up one day and wouldn't find me, please don't search for me." he left the papers and the box on the table, stroked Arras' head and went to his room.

Next day the boss came in the teahouse and sat next Sardar, "You are in a good mood, my friend! What is going on?" he asked Sardar.

"Nothing, boss. I'm just happy," Sardar replied. "I really don't know, but if you have a little time, I would like to tell you something, boss."

"Okay, tell me. What is on your mind?" he said.

"Well, boss, I have known you from long time," Sardar smiled, "but I have the feeling that I'll not be around for much longer. it's my time to leave. I think it would be tonight or the night after."

"What are you talking about, old man?" the boss said angrily. "You are well and you will live long, don't leave me alone, please!" he hid his face.

"It's not in my hands, boss. When the time is here, no one can change it," Sardar replied. "What I'm trying to say is that if you one day you come in and I'm not here, don't go and search for me. I'll be long gone. That is all I want from you, boss. You have been my last friend and protector. I'll never forget what you have done for me. We have gone through a lot together and there is nothing to regret," Sardar wiped the tears from his eyes.

"You're just trying to make me angry," the boss said. He went to the back of the shop. He was afraid he would never see Sardar again.

Few days before, he arranged with a driver to reserve a seat for him to take him to Slaymany. The entire time he had lived in Halabja, the city of Slaymany had never left his mind. The only thing he wanted to do was to go back to the city where he was born, the city where he found his first love. He wanted to see for the last time, the city where he got married. He wanted to see the city where he taught its children, the city he fought for. He was going to see the city he loved from the first moment he had walked on its soil. He wanted very badly to do that. He didn't want to waste any more time, because he knew he didn't have long to live.

Around eleven o'clock at night, the same day he had spoken to the boss, he sat in the middle of the semi-darkness of the teahouse, smoked a cigarette. He found a piece of paper and started writing, 'boss,' the note said, "you placed your key and your trust in my hands, and now I'm returning them to you, so you can pass them along to someone else. As I talked to you about Arras, help him to find a good girl and get married."

He put the envelope on the desk and put his coat on. He grabbed his crutches and took one last look at the teahouse. Then he locked and left.

The next day, very early in the morning, he woke up, and without waking Arras, he put a piece of paper next to the door of Arras's bedroom door. The note said, "From the very first day I met you, I thought of you as my son. Now after all this time, I have found you healthy and well. I'll not be here for your wedding, but you will always be with me. I love you, son."

He took out a suit, although it was a little big for his thin body, it would be good for the job he wanted to do. He had a nice blue shirt and a pair of black shoes...although he needed only one shoe. He also had a little money, enough for two weeks or so. He put his belongings into a small bag. He stood and took a last look at the house and then quietly walked out. He headed to the place where he could catch a ride to Slaymany. He found the car that was about to depart, he stepped up into the car that would take him to his final destination.

He arrived in Slaymany in late December, 2004. when he got there, all he had was a little money tucked in his pocket, his crutches, a small bag and a broken heart. He took a deep breath and looked around. The city he had left many years ago wasn't the same now. Or maybe it wasn't the city that had changed; maybe he was the one who had changed. But that didn't matter to him. What was important that he was back in the city where he, his father, his grandfather and other before them had been born.

It was a very cold day, but that didn't matter either. He found a little hotel. He took a room, put his small bag in the room and went out.

The first thing he wanted to do was find a hammam, a Turkish bath. He found one just close to the hotel and went in, and for a while he felt he was living again. He stayed for many long hours, enjoying it very much and leaving the place feeling clean and refreshed. Now he was hungry, so he found a restaurant where he could enjoy a perfect Slaymany meal. He ate with gusto and followed his meal with a cup of tea and few cigarettes.

He walked out of the restaurant and buttoned his old coat. It was windy, and the cold air blew through his thick white hair and long beard. He pulled his hood up over his head, bent his frail body over his crutches and started walking.

He took the road that went to his old home from the school where he had studied and later taught. It was the road he had taken for many years. He walked slowly, taking small steps and pushing himself against the wind. It was so cold it seemed anyone would have to be crazy to come out in such weather, but for him it wasn't crazy. He was doing something that made sense only to him.

He went through all the narrow streets and passed the old same houses and the small store where he had bought sweets and other things when he was a boy. His heart was beating faster and his breath becoming heavier. When he entered the neighborhood...his neighborhood, he saw the street lights and the electric poles. Salih's home was first if you came this way, from downtown.

Three houses down from Salih's were Sardar's and Kameran's houses. He stopped and looked at his old house for a long time. Several people passed by him and looked at him as if they felt sorry for him. They thought he was nobody but a homeless beggar. He just stood there and looked, no one came out or went into his old house, as if there were no one living there. He remembered a time when he was a boy and his home was crowded with family and friends all the time.

He turned to Kameran's house, and the door was half open. He peeked inside and saw two boys playing in the hallway, the same hallway where he, Kameran and Sirwan had spent many hours playing. He remembered being scolded by Kameran's mother, until finally they would be kicked out of the house. Sardar giggled remembering the good times. Suddenly someone gently tapped on his shoulders. "May I help you, uncle?" a young man asked.

Sardar jumped and clutched at his crutches, "No, my son, no, I was just tired and was resting for a while," he replied and positioning his crutches and walking away.

Sardar felt sad again, but deep inside he really wasn't. He felt strange, and he couldn't explain how, he was rich, he thought. It was true he was alone and had no one, but most people didn't half the memories he had of his family.

He started walking back toward downtown, but before he did, he stopped and looked at Salma's home. There up on the roof top was the place he had started his love story, the place from which he had thrown dozens of matchboxes with love letters inside them to Salma. And then the next day she would throw him the answers to his letters in the same way.

He was the happiest boy in the entire world then. He had a girl who loved him very much, and nothing else was important.

He was very happy to have had Salma as his wife. He had kept a warm place for her in his heart. Now he smiled and walked slowly along. He stopped and looked back at his neighborhood. He would come back tomorrow for one last look.

He went back to downtown. Many people were outside despite the cold weather. He went to the teahouse where he and his friends had met to drink tea and play domino. He entered the teahouse and didn't recognize anyone who was working there, neither the owner nor the workers. He sat in a corner and ordered a cup of tea. He stayed until it was dark. Then he went back to his hotel. But he could sleep the whole night. He knew he was dying, but that it wouldn't happen this night.

The next day he woke up very late. He didn't feel very well. Probably he was getting sick, but that wasn't important anymore. He dressed, grabbed his crutches and went down to hotel's lobby to have something to eat. He stayed there for long time and then he went back to his room. He slept for a while longer, and this time when he woke up, it was already dark outside. He sat on his bed for a while, then dressed, put his coat and went out.

First, he went to the same restaurant as the day

before. He had another meal, some tea and a few cigarettes. And around seven or eight o'clock, he went out to his final destination. He pulled his woolen hat onto his head and slowly walked along, using the streets he knew best. It was snowing heavily, but that wasn't going to stop him from completing his mission. He made it back to the street that led to his childhood neighborhood, and he slowly entered the street. Again, he was flooded with memories. He remembered the dusty road he and his friends had taken to their school, chased girls where they were young. Now the street had been paved. The neighborhood looked like it had been abandoned. Even though it was winter, he wondered where the crowd were...the kids playing, the women sitting in front their houses, chatting and gossiping.

He had noticed that many new houses had been built. The neighborhood felt like the old place, and yet it didn't. As he approached the home where he was born, where he played, grew up and got married, his heart start beating faster.

The house his mother and his wife Salma lived, he began shaking, not because he was cold or even because he was sad. No, he was finally happy. He smiled as he approached Salma's house, his house.

There was no one around, and the neighborhood was suffused with silence. There was nothing but the snow. He sat at the doorstep of the house. He bent down and kissed the doorstep, and his tears fell through his white beard. Each tear told the story of his love that didn't die.

His life's story came back to him, and it was almost as if he were watching a show in a theater. His hope, the light of his existence, his wife and all his children, were gone, and with them had gone his restless soul and his joy. If his life was show in a theater, now the curtain was being pulled down. The lights were switching off one by one, and the audience had vanished forever. The old actor was alone on the empty stage.

The snow was piling up on his half-frozen body, yet he chuckled from time to time, remembering some jokes he had told Salma. He reached into his pocket and found his last cigarette. His white beard was already covered with snow. He felt cold, but he didn't move; he couldn't feel his leg anymore. He knew this was it. He sighed. Sixty-five years of pain, and now he felt in peace.

The silent neighborhood and the sky itself seemed to know the old man was gone. Snow fell out of the sky onto his lifeless body. He made no sound and uttered no cry. Sardar had died where he wanted to die.

THE END

www.ingramcontent.com/pod-product-compliance
Lightning Source LLC
Chambersburg PA
CBHW062007170626
46813CB00001B/66

9781775045908